Praise for the writing of Zena Wynn

True Mates

"*True Mates* grabs your attention in the opening scene and doesn't let go."

– Amy Wynn, *eCataromance*

"*True Mates* was a scorcher."

– Reviewer Name, *Review Site*

"Zena Wynn's *True Mates* is a wonderful story. From the first page to the last, the book is fortified with humor, passion and drama."

– *Literary Nymphs*

Nikolai's Wolf

"Ms. Wynn certainly keeps her readers on edge until the final page wondering if the star-crossed lovers will have a future together."

– Mickey, *You Gotta Read Reviews*

"I love the way Zena Wynn has made the story come alive for me. I could barely pull myself away…"

– Dianna, *Night Owl Reviews*

"With insightfulness and well written ability, author Zena Wynn has made a truly good shifter series for everyone to enjoy."

– Margo Arthur, *The Romance Studio*

LooSeId®

ISBN 13: 978-1-60737-406-0
TRUE MATES

Cover Art by Croco Designs
Cover Layout by April Martinez

Printed in the U.S.A. by
Lightning Source, Inc.
1246 Heil Quaker Blvd
La Vergne TN 37086
www.lightningsource.com

Contents

TRUE MATES

Dedication

To my friends ReRe and Bern, who pushed and encouraged me to get this story written and submitted. To my kids, who put up with my countless hours in front of the computer, and my sister, who turned out to be my biggest fan. A special thanks to my editor, Jana, who challenged me and pulled stuff out of me even I didn't realize was in there. None of this would have been possible without all of you.

Chapter One

She hung, hands tied together over her head, her toes barely touching the ground. She wore a loose, flowing nightshirt, which barely covered her shaved mound. The brilliant light of the full moon shone like a spotlight, magnifying the surrounding shadows. A breeze stirred, playing with the hem of her garment. Her nipples tightened painfully in response to the cool air.

"I'm going to kill him," she said to herself. "He's dead, just as soon as I get down from here." She didn't know how in the freaking hell he'd done it, but somehow, in some way, he was responsible.

Kiesha pulled and tugged her wrists this way and that, trying to loosen them from the ropes binding her. When the bonds refused to relax, she tried twisting her body, hoping that if she put enough pressure on the rope, it would come undone from the tree limb. Every time she rotated in one direction, momentum carried her back to the same position in which she began. She panted and grunted, then escalated to cursing, venting her frustration as her efforts remained fruitless.

Over her mutterings, she heard a noise. Pausing in her struggles, she listened closely. Loudly, she called out, "Conor, I'm going to kick your butt when I get down from here. You are so dead! If this has anything to do with your harebrained ideas about werewolves and all that other bull you're always talking about..."

Ever since she had known Conor, he was always spouting off about werewolves. Going on and on about what was true and what was myth. He'd said he was training her because one day she would need to know. Yeah, right. As if she believed that crap! But she listened to him anyway, because her momma had taught her to be nice to people, even if she thought they were crazy. Humor them, she'd said. What could it hurt? We wouldn't want to hurt their feelings now, would we?

Thanks to *The World According to Conor*, she now knew the proper way to greet a werewolf, the hierarchy in werewolf packs, and a bunch of stuff she considered useless. *This is what I get for humoring the man*, she thought. *I'm hanging from a tree, half-naked in the middle of the woods on the night of a full moon.*

She heard another sound; it sounded closer than before. "Conor! Get me down from here!" As she waited for him to respond, the hair on the back of her nape stood on end. Something—or *someone*—was watching her. She'd assumed it was Conor, but now it occurred to her that maybe it wasn't. Suddenly, every horror flick she'd ever seen flashed through her mind. Her mother had always warned watching that stuff would come back to bite her.

Kiesha breathed slowly and deliberately, trying to calm the panic seeking to take hold of her mind. She looked around the clearing, straining to see into the shadows. She thought she saw a pair of yellow eyes staring back at her. Lots of pairs. *Oh, this was* so *not good.* As she watched, creatures materialized from the dark thicket into the shadows at the edge of the clearing.

Wolves. Big ones. Five of them.

Frantically, she tried to remember everything she'd ever learned about wolves. *Don't stare them in the eyes. No, wait. That was dogs. Show no fear. Well, forget that!* She was already so scared, she was surprised she hadn't pissed on herself. Why, oh, why, hadn't she watched *Animal Planet* while she'd had the chance? Then maybe she'd know what to do.

Did wolves eat humans? God, she hoped not.

She chanted "Oh, God. Oh, God. Oh, God" under her breath until it became a mantra. Her mind blanked by fear, she could think of nothing else to say.

At the sound of her chanting, the wolves paused and looked at each other. Some form of communication seemed to pass among them. One by one, they stepped forward into the clearing. Staying totally still, she waited to see what they were going to do. *Conor, if I die tonight, I will haunt you forever*, she thought to herself.

One of the wolves stepped ahead of the others and into the moonlight. It was large and gray with a white muzzle. Along his back, the black-tipped fur formed a pattern. It was hard to tell, but his eyes appeared to glow. No, must be a trick of the moonlight. He eased forward slowly, almost creeping, his ears to his head. If she didn't know better, she'd say it was trying not to scare her. As if! Who wouldn't be afraid of a wolf the size of a pony?

It crept toward her, sniffing the air. Maybe it was just curious. She really didn't know and didn't care, as long as it didn't eat her. As it got closer, she looked directly into its golden eyes, too afraid to move. It came within inches then sat back on its haunches. The wolf stared at her, tongue hanging out of its mouth, head tilted to the side. She swore the thing was laughing at her.

"Find me funny, do you?" she asked. Its ears tilted forward as though it—he, if the size of that thing between its legs was any indication—was listening. "You try waking up tied to a tree in the middle of the woods surrounded by predators and see how you feel." A strange light entered its eyes, and she somehow knew he was laughing at her. *Great! He thinks I'm a comedian. Glad someone's being entertained.*

While her attention was focused on the gray wolf, the others had quietly eased closer and now sat near him in a semi-circle facing her. As she glanced from wolf to wolf and nothing happened, fear subsided and curiosity took its place. One by one, her muscles relaxed as the tension left her body. She'd never been this close to a live wolf before. If she survived, she might never be again.

Taking advantage of the opportunity, she studied the rest of them. The wolf next to the gray one was just as large, but built on a leaner scale. His black fur was frosted with white. The third wolf was all white with the exception of his nose and muzzle, which were black, drawing attention to those killer fangs of his. The fourth wolf was all black, except for one white sock on the front paw. It might have been comical if he hadn't looked so vicious. The last one was blond. She wondered if wolves had dumb blond jokes like humans did.

Some sort of signal seemed to pass between them once again, and she tensed. *What now?* One by one, they leaned forward and began to sniff her, starting at her feet and ending at her crotch. One came so close that she felt the moist air from his nostrils on her mound.

"Hey! Cut that out. I'm not some bitch in heat for you to be sniffing at!" One of the wolves made a snuffling sound that reminded her of laughter.

Then the gray wolf moved closer. Beginning at her feet, he slowly ran his nose up her legs, leaving a trail of cool dampness in its wake. With a quick swipe of his tongue, he licked her clit. She gasped as she clamped her thighs together and tried to move away. His growl was low and mean.

He licked her clit again as she swung back into position. Then he tried to shove his nose into her crotch. "Back off, you mangy mutt," she said, and kicked at his head with her foot. He danced gracefully out of the way. Again, she heard that snuffling sound, this time from the rest of the group.

As she dragged her toes to stop from swinging back and forth, the gray wolf looked at the others and nodded. She blinked. *He couldn't have just nodded his head.* She must be imagining things. No, better yet, she was dreaming. This was a nightmare from which she couldn't wait to awaken.

The wolves threw back their muzzles and howled at the moon, a sound of joyful celebration. It startled her and she jerked, accidentally biting down on her tongue. The pain assured her that this was no dream.

As she sucked on her tongue, trying to ease the pain, the gray wolf stepped forward again. One minute, a wolf stood before her; the next, a man.

A naked, aroused man.

Conor wasn't crazy. Werewolves were *real*. "Oh, man, I am so screwed." Then everything went black.

Chapter Two

Alex Wolfe grinned as he lunged forward to catch his sagging mate. The grin became a full-blown laugh as he thought of how pissed she was going to be when she came to.

He supported her waist, her mound pressing against his bare stomach. The laughter faded as heat took its place. He remembered the taste of her. Salty-sweet flavor had exploded in his mouth, even in wolf form. He'd had only one thought: more. Then, she'd kicked at him. Instinct made him jump out of the way, even as his mouth watered for another sample. She was everything Conor had promised and then some.

He looked down at the woman in his arms. Kiesha Morgan, his true mate. God, he'd all but given up hope of ever finding her. He'd been praying and waiting for her for over twenty years. There were women he could have chosen to mate with, of course. As alpha, he'd had his pick of women from his pack and others. But he'd wanted, *needed*, a true mate bond. Nothing else would do. He'd pretty much given up hope when he'd received the summons from Conor.

Conor was legendary among shape-shifters. He had the ability to sniff out potential mates among humans. Alex didn't know what Conor was or how he did it. What Alex did know was that he was extremely powerful, and could do for shifters what they were unable to do for themselves.

The human nature of a male shape-shifter allowed him to mate and reproduce with any female of his species. Humans were a little trickier. You could mate with a human; you could not reproduce with them unless they were your true mate. Only with a true mate could both sides of his nature bond—human and animal. Humans called them soul mates.

Focusing once more on the woman in his arms, Alex studied her features. She was beautiful. With his keen eyesight, he could see her as though it were high noon instead of midnight. Her creamy complexion was the color of honey. If those high cheekbones were any indication, she had some Native American somewhere in her family tree. Her face was a classic oval, and that hair…he loved her hair. It was a thick mass of brown corkscrew curls, hanging below her shoulders.

Alex leaned forward and buried his nose against her neck, inhaling deeply to get her scent into his being. His cock throbbed insistently. He was desperate to bury himself balls deep in her warm, moist sheath. *Mine*, he thought. *All mine.*

Her generous breasts begged to be sucked. He wanted them bare. His gaze traveled past her nipples, puckering in the cool night air, and over the slight swell of her stomach and womanly thighs. She was a nice handful. No twigs for him. A man wanted something to hold on to, someone he could fuck without fearing she would break. Alex gave into the need to cup her ass. Oh, yeah. Bootylicious, as the kids would say.

He stroked downward until he could grip the back of her thighs, then parted her limbs so her pussy was openly displayed. She would wake soon, but before she did, he wanted one more taste. Alex dropped to his knees, then draped her legs over his shoulders. He leaned forward and buried his noise against her nether lips, once more inhaling the delicious aroma of her womanly scent. In the background, he heard the other wolves as they left the clearing, but his focus was on the woman in his arms. He reached out and parted her nether lips, giving him an excellent view of her pussy. Then, he slowly tongued her from her cunt to her clit, his eyes closed, savoring the taste of her juices as they flowed into his mouth. Over and over he licked, alternately spiking his tongue deep into her pussy for more of her salty-sweet flavor.

His grip tight on her hips, he held her still as she moaned and arched into his mouth. He fingered her clit while plunging in and out of her pussy with his tongue, just as his cock longed to do. Faster and faster he went as he felt her orgasm approaching. Finally, her thighs tightened around his head, her back arched sharply, and climax swept over her.

Alex pried Kiesha's thighs open from the viselike grip they had on his head. Swiftly rising from the ground, he left her dangling as he circled around behind her. He bent and hooked his right arm under her knee, lifted her leg, and opened her body to him. Aligning his cock with her still spasming pussy, he embedded himself deep inside. Shit, she was tight, wet, and oh so hot. He wasn't going to be able to last long. Fortunately, he had all night.

With his left arm around her waist, he thrust, slowly at first, then with greater speed. Her sexy moans and whimpers drove him crazy. Tilting her pelvis back, he changed his angle and plunged even deeper, each thrust hitting that sweet bundle of nerves located deep inside of her. The tips of his fingers stroked her clit. She screamed as she came.

Alex lunged forward, locking his teeth onto the tendon where her neck and shoulder met as he climaxed. Biting down, he marked Kiesha as his mate for all eternity, even as he spurted cum into her waiting, hungry womb. Her internal muscles continued to clamp down, squeezing and releasing, draining him dry. Spent, Alex licked his mate's shoulder, healing the wound he'd made while marking her, then leaned against her back, struggling to regain his strength. She was finally his. He'd marked her, claimed her, and now he'd never let her go.

Chapter Three

Kiesha came to slowly, her mind struggling to comprehend what had happened. As she tried to move, her memory returned in a series of images. The moonlit clearing. The wolves. A gray wolf one minute, man the next.

She gradually became aware of hard, masculine hands holding her legs and a delicious heat centered at her core, causing her womb to clench in response.

Oh, God, he was licking her slit.

His tongue stroked between her thighs, setting her pussy on fire, but not where she needed it most. As she struggled to get closer, to force his tongue to her clit, he clamped down hard on her hips, inhibiting her movements.

She whimpered. She was so close. Something inside of her was building, growing with every stroke of his tongue. Her body strained, *reached*... She only knew what she needed most was being denied.

Then she felt it.

A light, feathery touch, right on the perfect spot. Again, she tried to get closer. Again, she was denied. *Harder*, she wanted to say. *Stroke it harder*. All that came out of her mouth was a soft moan. Somehow, he must have known what she was trying to convey because the touch on her clit became harder as his tongue plunged deeper and faster. Every muscle in her body tightened right before she exploded.

Aftershocks rippled through her. The warmth of his body moved to her back. He gripped her thigh and used it to lift her right leg as his cock rubbed against her now exposed opening. *Yes*, she thought. *I want that inside me*. She caught her breath as he thrust sharply into her, her folds parting like butter to a sharp blade. Then he began to move.

All she could do was feel.

The slide of his cock as he worked in and out of her pussy. The cool air on her breasts as they hung bouncing in the soft breeze from the force of his thrusts. One arm was hooked under her knee, opening her body to his plundering; the other, locked around her waist, held her tight. With her hands tied together above her head, she accepted his mastery over her body.

He pulled her hips back. This new position caused shock waves to ripple from head-to-toe as the head of his cock hit nerve endings she'd never known she had. The fingers against her clit provided just the right amount of external stimulation.

Oh, my God, I can't take any more.

She opened her mouth to plead with him to stop and instead screamed as a climax rushed over her. She barely felt him bite down on her shoulder, so lost was she in the sensations racking her body.

Her head fell forward as she struggled to catch her breath. Now *that* was an orgasm. It made all the orgasms she'd experienced in the past pale in comparison. The pressure on her arms eased as she was freed from the tree. Cradling her against his hard body, he lowered her to the ground. He loosed the rope tying her hands together, and then massaged her wrists to help the blood circulate. She lay boneless on the cool, moist ground, looking up at the moon.

Kiesha struggled to make sense of what had just happened. Never had she felt such bliss. Hadn't known it was possible, to be completely honest. Now that she knew what all the fuss was about, part of her was scared shitless. The sheer intensity of the orgasms he'd given her was addictive. What would she be willing to do—to give—to experience it again and again? How much of her valued control would she be willing to relinquish?

As her thoughts ran round and round in her head, he unbuttoned her nightshirt, exposing her breasts to the chilly night air. His mouth latched onto her breast, suckling hungrily.

I'm lying on the ground in the middle of the woods with a man I don't know who's just given me the most amazing orgasm in my life.

She should have been upset, freaked out. Under normal circumstances, she would be. However, nothing about tonight was normal, and right now, she couldn't seem to work up enough energy to care. She'd worry about it later. Besides, what he was doing with his mouth was nothing short of amazing. She'd never known her breasts were so intimately connected to her womb. Every suctioning tug produced an answering one deep inside.

Her hands rose to his hair. She arched her back, driving her left breast deeper into his mouth. "What's your name?" she asked.

"Do you really care?"

"Not really, not so long as you keep doing this."

He lifted his head to look at her. His teeth gleamed in the moonlight as he smiled. "My name is Alex."

"Alex?"

"Yes, Alex. That's the name you'll scream when I make you come again."

"Yes, yes, whatever you say. Just don't stop." She pushed his head back down to her needy breast.

He laughed as his mouth resumed its teasing. He suckled on one nipple as he plucked the other, alternating back and forth between the two. Alex kneed her legs apart, then settled between them, rubbing his erection against her swollen clit. With each tug of her breast, she felt an answering pull low in her belly. Arching her hips, she rubbed against his cock, seeking relief from the fire building between her legs.

"Do you want me?"

"Yes." She moaned.

"What do you want me to do to you?" She arched against him in reply. "Uh, uh, uh. Answer me," he demanded, moving his cock away from her. She tried to lift her hips, but the weight of his body pinned her down. Frustrated, she yanked his hair.

Laughing, he teased her entrance with his cock, barely entering before withdrawing to rub it back and forth over her clit. "Tell me what you want."

"I want *you*, Alex." She arched against him, trying to entice him with her body.

"You want me to what?"

"Alex, please," she protested, giving his hair another hard yank. "Quit toying with me."

"Please? Please what?"

"You know what I want."

"You have to say the words," he calmly demanded, all the while never stopping that persistent rubbing against her clit.

Frustrated, she shouted, "Fuck me! Please! Please fuck…OH!" Before all the words could completely leave her mouth, he slammed home. He was so deep inside of her she swore she felt him at the back of her throat. Already on the edge, she fell straight over the cliff.

He grabbed underneath her knees and lifted her up higher, giving his cock better access. Propping her calves on his shoulders, he took her deeper and harder than she'd ever been taken before. The look on his face was feral. He was growling and straining, his face partially shifted, as he grew impossibly larger and longer inside of her. Instead of scaring her, his loss of control excited her.

Her fingers dug into the moist ground, trying to gain purchase. She thrust back, digging her heels into his back to gain the leverage she needed. She felt it approaching, coming up from her toes. Tightening her legs, she arched her back, balancing on her shoulders and arms. "Alex!" she screamed as her climax roared through her.

His whole body stiffening, Alex thrust deep, instinctively seeking her womb. Once, twice, then a final time. Fire streaked down his spine to his balls. With his head thrown back, his neck corded, he howled his release to the heavens.

Drained, he collapsed on top of her, only shifting his weight to the side when she protested.

"Mine," he growled. He tucked her close, wrapped himself protectively around his mate, before drifting off to sleep.

Chapter Four

The sound of running water woke her. Alex had carried her from the woods to his house. Kiesha lay there, disoriented, staring blankly at the ceiling, taking inventory of her aching body.

Her shoulders and arms screamed from bearing the brunt of her weight for so long. Her wrists were chafed and sore from struggling against the rope used to bind her. Deep between her legs, muscles complained against their recent handling. It had been a long time since they'd been used like that. Who was she kidding? They'd *never* been used like that. That man—werewolf, whatever he called himself, was hung, well, like a wolf, she guessed. And what was that expansion thing he'd done inside of her? As if he wasn't large enough already.

She hadn't had enough sleep. It was difficult to think straight. She needed a bath in the worst way. She didn't want to imagine what sort of creepy crawlies lurked in her hair.

The bed dipped and a face moved into her field of vision. The werewolf—Alex—smiled at her while his hungry gaze wandered possessively over her body in a manner she recognized from previous lovers. *Damn, here we go again.*

Give a man a little bit of action and he thought he owned you.

"Good, you're already awake. I filled the whirlpool and turned on the jets. It's ready whenever you are."

Annoyance forgotten, Kiesha grinned in delight at the thought of a bath. She struggled to get up and groaned instead, flopping back down in pained defeat. She was too sore to move.

His smile disappeared. "Are you hurt?" His gaze roamed over her, presumably looking for injuries. "Damn, I was too rough with you. I hurt you, didn't I? I'm sorry, baby. I lost control."

Blushing, she thought about his lack of restraint. She remembered how his eyes had shifted, his face becoming something other than human. The addictive sensation of his body hammering into hers. Her nipples tightened in response. Her pussy moistened. "No, you didn't hurt me," she said, her throat dry.

At the hoarseness in her voice, he looked into her face sharply and took a deep breath. She wondered if he could scent her arousal.

Alex still looked concerned, but a lot less worried. "Poor baby. Let me see if I can help you." He removed her nightshirt, then gently rolled her over onto her stomach and massaged her shoulders.

At first, she tensed, expecting it to hurt. Gradually, she relaxed as he worked the kinks and soreness out of her shoulders and all the way down to her feet. She lay in a sensual haze, not quite asleep, but close to it. His hands felt *so good.* She'd had massages before, but this was the best ever. Better than any spa she'd ever been to. All too soon, he finished. He placed a kiss on her spine and then rolled her onto her back.

Alex scooped her into his arms and carried her into the bathroom, lowering her into the waiting tub. Kiesha moaned with pleasure when the warmth of the water penetrated her battered muscles. She closed her eyes and relaxed her head against the rim, letting the jet-propelled water massage her body. Removing his jeans, Alex joined her in the tub.

She watched, eyes barely open, as he relaxed against the opposite side of the tub. Now that she was no longer in the grip of mind-numbing lust, it was time to take control and get some answers. "You're a werewolf," she stated lazily.

"We prefer the term shape-shifter."

Lifting her eyebrow, she remarked, "I prefer to be a size six, not a sixteen, but it doesn't change what I am."

His heated gaze swept over her body, beginning with her face, sliding over her breasts, then down to the portions submerged beneath the churning water. "I prefer you the way you are." She blushed and glanced away. No man had ever looked at her the way he did. He stared at her as if he was hungry and she was a beautifully prepared steak made just for him.

Time to get back to the subject, she thought. "I *saw* you change from a wolf into a man. That, by definition, makes you a werewolf."

"Werewolf has such a negative connotation, don't you think?" He playfully wagged his eyebrows at her.

"Lord, help us. You're a freaking *werewolf.* Deal with it," she exclaimed as he burst out laughing.

Her mind frantically cast around for another topic, something to take her mind off being naked in a tub with a man she barely knew when she remembered Conor. "What was the purpose of tying me up and hanging me out in the woods like a side of beef? Why would anyone do that to me? It *was* Conor, wasn't it? And I was so nice to him. How could he betray my friendship like this?"

Viewing her blank expression, along with the hurt in her eyes that she was trying to hide, he felt a wave of compassion wash over him. It had to be difficult for her, being thrust into his world the way she'd been. Reaching across the tub, he took her by the waist and pulled her forward until she sat cradled on his lap. Cupping her face with his hands, he looked her in the eye. "It wasn't done to hurt you."

She snatched her face away, anger evident in the way she held her body. "I'm not hurt. I just want to know what's going on."

Closing his eyes, he leaned his head back against the wall, and wondered where to begin. How could he explain things in a manner that would make this all acceptable to her? "It's a long story."

"I think I have time."

With a sigh, he settled his arms around her waist and began. "Once, a long time ago, we took humans as mates. Then, we were hunted, causing the elders to forbid the practice in an effort to hide our existence. How can you live with someone without being able to reveal who you truly are? What the elders couldn't have foreseen is that generations of inbreeding would result in a lower birthrate. Between the alphas killing each other and being hunted by humans, we've almost become extinct. A male shape-shifter can only breed with a female of the same species. The ratio of male to female is high and getting higher every generation, making it harder for males to find mates." Despite his effort to keep his voice impassive, some of the frustration and worry he felt for his species leaked into his voice.

"What does this have to do with me and why Conor left me in the woods?"

"A shape-shifting male can also breed with a human female, if she is his one true mate."

"Still not connecting the dots here. Sorry."

Alex arched an eyebrow at her tone of voice. "A potential true mate is a human with DNA compatible to shifters. Because they occur so rarely, they are highly prized." He looked pointedly at her.

Visibly frustrated and confused, Kiesha opened her mouth to demand that he get to the part of the story related to her. He quieted her by placing his finger against her lips. "I told you it was a long story."

He watched as she hesitated for a moment before deciding to let him continue. "Because shape-shifters are both human and beast, we need mates who appeal to both of our natures. That's why we call them true mates. They can speak to both sides of our nature. It's only with them that true bonding can occur. Like our wolf counterpart, once mated, we mate for life. During the bonding process, we give our mates a piece of our soul and gain a piece of theirs in return. It's a bond that grows stronger as time progresses."

Lifting her by the waist, he turned her so she faced him. Picking up the soap, he rubbed it until his hands were completely lathered. "Conor has the ability to sniff out true mates among humans. When he finds one, he summons the shifters." He urged her to her knees as he began to bathe her body.

"A true mate is only identifiable by smell and by taste. It's the scent of our mate that first attracts us. Later, it is the taste of them that confirms their identity to us." Scooping up water with his hands, Alex rinsed the soap from her body. "Lean back, so I can wash your hair."

He supported Kiesha by the waist as she leaned back in the tub until her hair was totally saturated. "The other wolves in the clearing, they were like you?" He nodded before he took the shampoo and lathered her hair. "Well, that explains all of the sniffing," she muttered.

Kiesha paused, obviously gathering her thoughts. "What do you mean—'summoned?'"

Using the tips of his fingers, he massaged her scalp. Kiesha purred in pleasure as her eyes fell to half-mast. "The summoning is a little harder to explain." She leaned her head deeper into his massage. "What? You got an e-mail? A phone call?"

He stopped massaging her scalp and looked at her. "No, nothing as simple as that."

"Okay..."

She nudged his hand for him to continue massaging her scalp. “It was more like a compulsion,” Alex continued. “A mental file transfer, if you like. I just knew where and when to meet.” He knew a lot more than that, but he didn’t want to scare her. He urged her to lean back again to rinse the shampoo from her hair.

With her back arched at a sharp angle and eyes closed, Kiesha swished her hair around in the water. “So, on the basis of this mystical voodoo crap, you left your home in the middle of the night just to get a sniff of me?” Straightening, she caught him ogling her breasts. She leaned to the side and gathered her hair together, squeezing the excess water from it while she waited for his answer.

“Put like that, I guess it does sound strange.” From a human standpoint, he could understand her skepticism. But he was more wolf than man and knew there were a lot of things in this world that defied reason. That didn’t make it any less real. Backing her up out of the way, he stood in preparation of exiting the tub.

Her eyes on his cock, now at the perfect level to suck on, she asked, “Don’t you want me to return the favor?” His cock jerked in anticipation, until she motioned, indicating the soap. He thought for a moment, then sat down on the edge of the tub and leaned back, giving her complete access to his body.

When she couldn’t find a washcloth, she decided to do without. Situated between his thighs, she lathered her hands and began washing his broad, muscular chest as she continued her questioning. “You think that I’m your mate?”

Not wanting to provoke him, she strove to keep her tone neutral, but her disbelief leaked in anyway.

"I *know* you're my mate."

"Why? Because of the way I smell? My taste? That doesn't make any sense."

He captured her hands and waited until he had her full attention. "No, there's more to it than that. My soul recognizes your soul. My wolf recognized you as its mate and the man in me agrees. I'm not sure how to make you understand. If you were a shape-shifter, this would be so much easier."

"But I'm not a shape-shifter and I don't understand." She continued to rub the soap onto his chest, her hands doing more caressing than actual washing, while inside, a debate waged. Alex obviously thought she was his soul mate, which her softer side thought was romantic as hell. *He's full of crap. Don't believe a word he says*, her inner bitch argued. She told both sides to shut up and simply reveled in the freedom of being able to explore his hard, muscular body as she willed.

He really was a handsome man, with a strong face, full of character. His eyes were a rich shade of chocolate so deep she thought she could drown in them. There was a hint of gold in the iris. His black hair was cut military short and had a hint of gray at the temples.

Her breasts rubbed the smattering of hair on his chest as she reached around to wash his back. It felt so good; she leaned closer, giving Alex a full frontal body rub while her hands explored the hollows and ridges of his back. His chest hairs abraded her nipples, sending tingles down her spine. It became more and more difficult to focus on what she was saying as she lost herself in the euphoria of being the ying to his yang, female softness to his male hardness. Her body screamed at her, urgent in its demand to experience another one of the astounding orgasms only he could give.

Why he thought she was his mate would have to wait. They'd done enough talking.

While she wasn't interested in being anyone's mate, she'd gladly become this man's lover. She focused her attention on his cock, which was long and thick. It had filled her almost to the point of pain, stroking every nerve ending inside her vagina. All thoughts of washing forgotten, she cupped his balls with one hand, then rubbed the sensitive area of his perineum with the fingers of the other.

"Baby, be sure you can handle what you're starting. I don't know if I'll be able to control myself much longer."

Kiesha disregarded his concern and continued her rolling massage. She moved her other hand to the base of his cock and stroked slowly upward.

With eyes closed and his head leaning back against the wall, he arched his hips with each upward stoke of her hand. "Harder."

Kiesha could tell his control was beginning to slip. Using both hands now, she tightened her grip. As one hand slid up his shaft to the head of his cock, the other one settled on the base in preparation of making the same journey. Over and over she stroked, squeezing harder each time until his hips left the edge of the tub. He growled, drawing her attention to his face, and his eyes began to shift. She thought she caught a glimpse of fangs as he gritted his teeth. His hands gripped the edge of the tub; his knuckles were white. Hmmm, could she make him lose that fierce control?

Curious, she performed a maneuver she'd read about in a magazine while waiting in the doctor's office. With one hand at the top of his shaft enclosing the head, and the other at the bottom, she squeezed gently and rotated her hands in opposing directions. *That* got a reaction.

With a roar, he shot to his feet. Before she could react, he flipped her over the side of the tub and impaled her from behind. Water sloshed over the sides and onto the floor. His claws dug into her skin while he hammered into her, totally out of control. In a matter of seconds, he was pumping his seed into her.

Kiesha held onto the side of the tub, frustrated. She was so close. She whimpered in distress when he stood, withdrawing from her body.

"Don't worry, baby. We're not even close to being finished." In an economy of motion, he cut off the jets and released the water. Once out of the tub, he bent down and flipped her over his shoulder. "Let me get you somewhere a little more comfortable."

In the room, he dropped her onto the bed, pinning her beneath him. "Now, where were we?" His cock still hard, he nudged her thighs apart and slid home. "Oh, yeah. Right about here." Raised on his forearms above her, he began a driving rhythm.

"Oh, God! Yes!" Arching her back to take him deeper, she wrapped her legs high around his waist.

"You're mine. Tell me you're mine."

"I'm yours," she cried, out of her mind with pleasure.

"You're my mate. Say it!"

Her breath caught on a sob as she agreed with him. "Yes, I'm your mate." At that point, she would have agreed with anything he said. With a growl of satisfaction, he gave his hips an extra little twist that pushed her right over the edge. His second climax followed quickly.

Kiesha lay beneath him, utterly sated. She tightened her grip when he tried to roll away.

"Let me pull the covers down."

Satisfied that he wasn't trying to leave, she let him loose. Personally, she didn't have the energy to move. Soon he was back, lifting her body and rearranging her on the bed. Climbing in beside her, he pulled her into the curve of his body.

Already starting to feel a chill, Kiesha snagged the sheet and pulled until it covered them. Her body in the state of relaxation only sexual fulfillment can produce, she closed her eyes. There were still issues to be dealt with, but tomorrow was another day. She could fight with him later about his crazy belief that she was his mate. The events of the evening catching up with her, she drifted off to sleep.

She wouldn't have lain there so peacefully if she'd seen the determination in his expression. Despite the confession he'd forced out of her tonight, he knew he still had a battle on his hands. Things said in the heat of passion often had no validity in the light of cold reason. No matter, she was his and he kept what belonged to him. He'd try to be patient and give her time to adjust to the changes in her life, but the bottom line was she was his mate. By his side is where she belonged. He had every intention of keeping her with him until she accepted the fact that she was his and they belonged together.

Pulling his mate even closer to him, he wrapped his body protectively around her. Inhaling deeply of her scent, both wolf and man were at peace as he drifted off to sleep, one last thought drifting through his mind. *Mine!*

* * *

By the strength of the sun shining into the room, she could tell morning had passed and afternoon was here. Giving a languid stretch, she was acutely aware of Alex's arm around her waist.

Her hips were curved into his, cradling his erection. *Umm*, she thought, *there's nothing like waking sex.* Arching her back, she sleepily rubbed against him.

His hand that had been resting against her stomach leisurely fondled her breast. Not fully awake, he nuzzled his face against the back of her neck until his lips found the place where he'd bit her earlier. Alex licked and suckled the wound, causing lower things to tighten.

She pressed back against him, trying to get his erection to where it could do the most good. She grew slick with her own juices as her arousal built. Slowly, patiently, he teased at her entrance, sliding back and forth over her opening. His hand glided down to play with her clit, and then slid up to tug on her nipples. Over and over he continued, while the fire of her arousal built to an inferno. “More,” she said. “I need more.”

“I’ll give you more when you’re ready for it.” His hands and cock continued their slow torture.

“I’m ready *now.*” She struggled to get closer, lift her leg to open to him more. His leg locked down on hers, holding her in position. On and on he went until she was pleading with him, begging for the fulfillment only he could give her.

Exerting tremendous control, he entered her, inch by inch. Advancing and retreating, he slowly gave her a little more of his length with each stroke. She arched her hips to force him deeper, but Alex stopped her. “No,” he said, withdrawing from her completely. “Be still.”

He wouldn’t move until she complied. Then he pushed into her again, bit by bit, inch by inch. “Deeper.”

“No. Wait for it.” Another stroke in and out.

“I can’t stand it.”

“You *will* stand it. All of it.” His tone was firm and commanding.

She shuddered, on the edge of orgasm. Alex forced her to reach a peak, stopped, then pushed her to climb even higher to the next peak. Her nerves were so sensitized she swore she felt each individual hair as it stood up on her arms. Tears rolled down her face while she struggled to endure.

He was determined to give her all the pleasure her body could handle. He would not lose control this time, as he had in the past. The wolf was firmly leashed. He removed his hand from the breast he was playing with and moved it to tease her clit, prolonging the motion. She was begging in earnest now, nerves stretched to the limit, tears streaming from her eyes. "Now!" he said, as he pressed hard against her clit. At the same time, he thrust deep and began a driving rhythm. She exploded. One orgasm turned quickly into another, then another one still until, unable to handle any more, she blacked out.

Clamping down hard on her shoulder with his teeth, he pumped streams of cum into her as his control shattered and he reached his own release. Slumping down on the bed, sated, he gathered his unconscious mate into his arms. The wolf in him howled in triumph. The caveman in him swelled with pride at the knowledge that he'd overwhelmed his mate with pleasure.

Alex held her as she regained consciousness. He kissed her tenderly on the lips as her eyes opened, then licked the tears drying on her cheeks. "How do you feel? Any soreness?" Once again, he'd lost control and been too rough with her. She was human, not lupine. He'd have to try harder to be more careful with her.

"Fine, just fine."

"Are you sure? I forgot my own strength there at the end. I could have seriously hurt you."

She scowled at him. "Haven't you ever heard of afterglow? You're killing my buzz. Did I complain? Was I screaming in pain?"

Heat entered his eyes as his cock lengthened against her. "You screamed, but it wasn't in pain. I believe I heard my name."

She blushed endearingly and he laughed. “If you’re really all right, go take your shower while I make some coffee and get breakfast started.” Getting off of the bed, he walked over to the dresser and pulled out a shirt and a clean pair of jeans.

“A domesticated werewolf?”

Growling and baring his teeth at her playfully, he left the room.

Chapter Five

As Alex left the bedroom, he heard Kiesha enter the master bathroom. He showered in the guest bathroom and dressed quickly before proceeding to the kitchen. The clock on the stove said it was almost eleven, closer to lunch than breakfast. Now was the perfect time to make some phone calls while his mate showered.

Grabbing the phone, he speed-dialed Carol Johnson, his beta in the pack. "Good afternoon to you, Alex. Congratulations on finding your true mate."

Leaning his back against the counter, he rolled his eyes. "The way information spreads in this town never ceases to amaze me."

"Hey, what can I say? Good news travels fast. Besides, Sam was there last night too. You know what that means." Oh, man, did he ever. Sam was known for his inability to keep his mouth shut. "So, what's up?"

"I need you to handle the pack for a few days." He turned around and pulled a frying pan down from off the hook over the center island, then placed it on the stove. Spreading bacon out in the pan, he waited for it to begin to fry.

"No problem. I'm already on it. Sam said that your mate was human. How's she handling it?"

Pretty good, he thought to himself, *all things considered.* She didn't believe a word he'd said, but she hadn't gone running and screaming into the night. That had to count for something.

"You can imagine." Alex knew that if anyone would know the challenge he faced, it would be his beta. She'd met her true mate in college. He'd also been human and unaware that shape-shifters existed. Their relationship had been very rocky in the beginning. Now, however, they were expecting their first child.

"She'll come around. Mark did. Let me know if we can help in any way."

"That brings me to the second reason I called. She's going to need clothes. She has nothing with her."

"Oh, poor thing. I'll check around in the pack and see what I can come up with. What size does she wear?"

No expert on women's sizes, Alex remembered her sarcastic comment in the tub. "According to Kiesha, a size sixteen. Oh, and she'll need shoes too. I don't know what size." He wasn't going to even try to guess.

"Okay, I'll get a couple of different sizes of shoes and bring them with me when I come. The pack will want to meet her soon, you know. She is their new alpha-fem."

"Yes, I know, but she's not ready for that yet. She's still adjusting to the idea of what I am, and what she is to me. I'm not sure how she'll handle being surrounded by a group of us." She might run so fast in the other direction that even his shifter abilities wouldn't enable him to catch her.

"True. It took Mark some time to adjust. He still gets a little leery sometimes. Just be patient with her. It'll happen. I'll come around this evening with the clothes and things."

"Thanks, Carol. I appreciate it."

"My pleasure. You just concentrate on that mate of yours. Enjoy the honeymoon," she said as she disconnected the call.

He took out another pan to cook the sausage, his mind on other things. He loved being alpha but there was no denying that it kept him busy. Temporarily turning control of the pack over to Carol and her mate would give him the time he needed to focus on his reluctant mate. He didn't need any interruptions. Kiesha was now his number one priority. She was far more important than the pack and his business.

Now, to handle the other time-consumer in his life—his veterinarian practice. He dialed the next number on his list. "Hello?"

"Pete? It's Alex."

"Boss man, how's it hanging, dude?" Despite how he sounded, Pete was a top-notch student and would soon be a first-rate veterinarian. Right now, he was interning with Alex as a part of his degree program. Alex had already offered him a position after graduation. If business continued to pick up, he might consider offering him a partnership instead. It was a major decision to make, but between pack-related business and now a family of his own, he would need the extra help.

"I found my one." Getting out a bowl, he began cracking eggs into it. He wasn't sure how much his mate would eat, but his appetite was always healthy. He decided to add three more eggs to the four he usually ate.

"Awesome, dude. You need me to do anything for you? Let me know. I'm your *hombre*."

"That's why I'm calling. I need you to handle the practice for a while until things settle down here."

"Say no more. I'm totally on it."

"Call the rest of the staff and let them know you're in charge."

"Roger that, and may I say congrats to you and the new missus?"

"Thanks, Pete. I'll check in with you later."

Hearing the shower cut off, he poured the eggs into the frying pan. The bacon and sausage were close to being ready, and biscuits were in the oven.

Looking around, he decided they would eat at the table in the breakfast nook. It would be nicer than eating at the bar. The table sat near a window with a view overlooking the valley below. He set the table and began dishing out the food as he heard Kiesha coming down the steps.

"Food's ready."

Placing the plates on the table, he checked to see if he'd overlooked anything. *Coffee!* He grabbed the coffee and some cups, and, at the last minute, placed juice on the table as well. Alex turned around just as she entered the room wearing one of his shirts and a pair of his shorts.

* * *

Sitting down in the chair Alex offered, Kiesha looked at the massive amounts of food set before her. “Are you expecting company?” There was a platter filled with bacon and sausage, another platter of biscuits, and a bowl full of scrambled eggs.

He frowned. “No, why?”

“You fixed all this food for *two* people?”

“Shifters eat a lot. We have high metabolisms so we are constantly burning calories.”

“You eat like this every day? At every meal?” *Must be nice not having to worry about your weight.*

“Is that a problem?”

“Since I don’t have to pay for your groceries, it’s not.”

Alex laughed. “Don’t worry about it. I can afford to keep us fed.”

Ignoring the reference to their implied future together, she poured herself a cup of coffee. As she fixed her plate, Kiesha couldn’t help but notice the contrast in the amounts of food on their plates. She’d always considered herself as having a healthy appetite, but compared to the amount of food on Alex’s plate, her portion sizes were downright meager.

As they settled down to the business of eating, a companionable silence fell over them. She glanced around the room as she ate, taking in all the details. It really was a lovely home. The kitchen was a chef’s dream, and the massive living room was perfect for cozy get-togethers or just laying around on a lazy afternoon. It had such a warm feel to it. She could easily picture herself living here.

Too bad she wouldn't be staying long.

Monday morning she would be back at work, this weekend nothing more than a lovely memory. If it wasn't for his insistence that she was his mate, she would suggest they see each other occasionally and scratch their mutual itches. She doubted Alex would be content with them being "friends with benefits." Too bad. Men sure knew how to mess up a good thing.

Gazing out the window, she noticed the breakfast nook faced the back of the house. There was a porch out there, one that ran the entire length of the house. She loved porches. Upon closer inspection, it was a deck, like the kind you found on lake or beach houses. Looking through the rails beyond the porch, she noticed the view for the first time.

The view overlooked a valley, not the water she expected to see. Putting down her fork, she stood to see better. Yep, definitely a valley down there. Where there were valleys, there were mountains. She'd thought they were on the coast. There weren't any freaking mountains where she lived.

She stepped away from the table and opened the French doors that led onto the deck. Alex voice came from behind her. "That view is what made me pick this spot to build. I spend a lot of time out there in the evenings relaxing."

Ignoring him, she walked onto the porch and crossed over to the rail, her mind unable to comprehend what she was seeing. "Alex?" she called. "Where am I?"

She saw him stiffen slightly out of the corner of her eye at the tone of her voice. She could hear the hesitation in his voice when he answered. "Sweetie, you're at my house. Well, our house now."

She pointedly overlooked his reference to their mated status. She had more important things on her mind right now, like where the hell was she? "No, *where* am I?" She waved her hand at the view. "*This* is a mountain. There are no mountains where I live." She spoke slowly and distinctly. "So, I'll ask you again. Where am I?"

"You're in North Carolina, baby, near Refuge. Where did you think you were?"

Her eyes bulged and her mouth dropped open. *Don't panic. Remember, control is your middle name.* She would not give into the panic she felt building. In total disbelief, she said, "In Florida, where I belong."

"As my mate, you belong with me."

"You don't understand. I need to get home." Kiesha was pacing back and forth agitated, her mind filled with questions. Forget about how she got here. Her mind just couldn't deal with that right now. Focus on the important issue—how to get home. She had money in the bank, but no way to access it. She could rent a car or catch a plane, if she could remember her debit card number. She could reserve it on-line. Shit! She didn't have her driver's license with her. That left out rental cars. With no identification, she couldn't even catch a plane, providing she remembered her number and could find her way to the nearest airport. Not only that, she would probably have to show her card when she got there. She couldn't call someone to come and get her. How would she explain her current predicament?

She was stuck. Trapped. Alex wouldn't take her anywhere and he wouldn't voluntarily help her to get home. He wanted her here, with him, and here she would stay unless she could find someone to help her. This was his town and his people. Who here was going to help her? Panic tightened her chest, making breathing difficult as she thought of and then discarded one solution after another.

"Kiesha, calm down before you hyperventilate."

"Calm down? You're telling me to calm down?" She exploded. "I have no money, no transportation, nothing. I don't even have clothes of my own. Hell, I can't even get any money to get those things, because I have no ID!"

"Kiesha, it will be okay. Whatever you need, I'll provide it for you." His tone and facial expression told her he didn't see what the big deal was.

She struggled to get hold of herself. Panicking never did any good. Control. She had to stay in control. "I have things I need to get back to. I can't stay here. I have a life, a business, people who depend upon me."

Dodging her gesturing hands, he caught her as she stalked by and pulled her close. He enfolded her in his arms, tightening his hold when she struggled, trying to get loose. "I will take care of you. It's what mates do."

Slowly relaxing in his arms, she let out a deep breath and leaned into his body, giving in to his determination to hold her. "Alex, I know you think I'm your mate, but I'm used to taking care of myself. I'm not comfortable with the idea of anyone trying to take care of me, especially some man I barely know." In her mind, it would be too much like payment for services rendered.

Stroking her back, he rocked her. "I don't think you're my mate. I *know* you are. Let me take care of you. I've already handled the clothing situation. Carol, my beta, is coming later with some things for you to wear until you can get your own."

She rolled her eyes and then thumped her head against his chest in exasperation. "Exactly how am I supposed to get my own clothing when I have no money?" He just didn't seem to get the seriousness of her situation.

Alex pulled her by the hand through the kitchen, into the den, and over to the computer where he reached down to turn it on. "Sit." While it was booting up, he reached into his back pocket and pulled out his wallet. He rifled through the contents until he found his VISA Gold card. He plopped it down in front of her on the desk. "Go on line and buy whatever you need. Charge it to this account. Clothes, shoes, lingerie, whatever. Don't worry about the cost. Use express delivery."

Deeply touched, she picked up the card. "I'll pay you back for this. I promise."

Angrily, he looked her in the eyes. "No, you will not. You are my mate. My job is to take care of you. Let me do my job. Please."

"Okay," she softly agreed, though she fully intended to pay him back, no matter what he said. After kissing her softly on the forehead, he left the room.

Watching him as he walked off, she looked at the VISA, then the computer. No one had taken care of her since her mother died. She was the provider. She was the one to whom friends and family turned. It was the reason that none of the few relationships she'd had lasted. The men she dated all wanted a woman to take care of them. She wanted a man, not a momma's boy. It was why she was alone. *You don't have to be alone anymore*, her consciousness said. *You can have Alex as a mate.* A mate who was more than capable of providing for her, if this VISA Gold was anything to go by. All she had to do was accept the terms of the relationship he was offering.

She looked at the credit card in her hand. This was the nicest thing anyone had done for her in a long time. With it, she could do any number of things; he'd just given it to her and walked off, no strings attached. He was putting a lot of trust and faith in someone he barely knew.

With one simple act, he had restored a measure of control over her circumstances to her. Heart overflowing with gratitude, she jumped up from the computer and rushed out to find him. He was in the kitchen cleaning up. She ran up to him, threw her arms around him, and kissed him. Staggering back a step, he quickly found his balance and took control of the kiss.

Alex grabbed the back of her head and shoved his tongue into her mouth, causing her to moan deep in her throat. Heat flared rapidly out of control between them as passion took over. Lifting her by the waist, he set her on the counter, bringing her level with his height. He gave her shirt a hard yank, popping the buttons and exposed her breasts to his view. His mouth left hers, latched onto a breast, and suckled deeply. Moaning, she pulled him closer. Alex lifted her by the waist with one arm and stripped his shorts off of her legs. Then, he unsnapped his jeans and pushed them down, freeing his cock. He pulled her body to the edge of the countertop and plunged inside. He took her fast and furiously. She'd barely climaxed when he exploded deep inside of her pulsing sheath.

Still hard inside of her, he stepped out of his jeans, which had sagged down around his ankles. "Wrap your legs around me." Kiesha did as he asked and locked her heels into the small of his back. As he lifted her off of the countertop, she wrapped her arms around his neck, nuzzling and licking his ear. Cursing, he swiftly carried her up the stairs to the bedroom, still embedded deeply inside of her. There he proceeded to spend the rest of the afternoon loving her.

Chapter Six

It was the sound of the doorbell that woke him. One glance at the clock told him who was at the door. He shook Kiesha. "Company's here. Time to get up."

With a long, drawn out groan, she flipped the covers over her head and said, "Tell whoever it is to go away."

Chuckling, he snatched the covers off of the bed and smacked her on the bottom. "Get up. That's Carol with the clothes for you. You can get up on your own or I can wrap you up in the covers and she can meet you like this."

"You're just plain evil. You are so going to pay for this," she said as she climbed out of bed and went into the bathroom.

"Looking forward to it, babe." He put on his jeans and went downstairs to open the door.

* * *

A soft knock sounded at the bedroom door. Kiesha opened it to find a very pregnant, attractive African-American woman, her arms loaded down with bags. Kiesha quickly reached out to grab some. "Here, let me help you with those."

"Thanks," she said, entering the room and closing the door behind her. "I'm Carol Johnson. I don't mean to intrude, but I brought some things I thought you might need. I hope I got the sizes right. This should be enough to get you started until you can buy some more. I couldn't imagine not having anything to wear. Lingerie is in that bag there." She pointed to the bag to which she was referring.

Carol was so friendly that Kiesha couldn't help but feel relaxed with her. "Thank you. It will be nice to have some real clothes to put on. Something that fits." Dumping the bags onto the bed, she began to go through them, pulling out things and seeing what was there. Remembering the lessons that Conor had taught her, she asked, "You're Alex's beta? Does that mean he's the alpha?"

Settling herself on the bed, she looked at Kiesha and arched her eyebrow. "He hasn't told you much about himself, has he?"

Thinking of all they'd done instead of talking, she blushed. "We've been busy." She hoped Carol wouldn't ask.

Carol laughed like she knew exactly what they'd been busy doing. "I can imagine. I remember how it was when I was first mated. Alex won't like it, but you can ask me anything, and I'll see if I have an answer for you."

Making more space on the bed for Carol, she urged her to rest her back against the pillows. Kiesha looked around at all the stuff Carol had brought with her as she thought about where to begin. She had no idea. There was so much she didn't know. "Are your females really expected to just give up their whole lives simply because some male claims he's her mate?"

Carol looked at her sympathetically. "Yes and no. It's a bit more complex than that. First of all, mates are a matter of instinct. Both parties recognize the other, so the female is not left taking the male at his word. There's always a period of adjustment for any couple, a period of courtship if you will. What makes it difficult is the mating fever."

Kiesha looked up from one of the bags she'd been looking in. "What's a mating fever? That sounds interesting."

Propping extra pillows behind her back, Carol made herself a little more comfortable. "We call it a fever, but it's more like a frenzy. To make sure the mating bond is established, each party is hormonally driven into a sexual frenzy that causes them to copulate as frequently as possible."

"Is that why Alex and I…I mean, is that why things have been so…"

"Intense?"

Kiesha nodded. Intense was a good word. Yes, that would certainly explain it. "Yes, intense. Is it always like this?"

"Well, things do calm down a bit once the bond is established, or else we'd never be able to get anything done. We'd spend all of our time in the sack."

She could imagine, given the way she and Alex had been going at it. "So, you're saying once this bond thing is achieved, it won't be this intense?" She wasn't sure if she liked the sound of that. What was she thinking? She wasn't Alex's mate. It shouldn't matter to her if the sex remained intense after bonding.

"Oh, you'll still have a strong desire for each other. Shape-shifters are a pretty passionate lot. The bond is particularly intense between you and Alex right now because you are human. Even now, as big as I am, my mate and I have a difficult time keeping our hands off of each other."

"What does my being human have to do with anything?" God, it felt so strange referring to herself as human, as though it was she who was unnatural.

"Alex is going to kill me for telling you this, but I think you have a right to know. Alex explained to you about true mates, right?"

Kiesha sat down on the bed and gave Carol her full attention. "He explained how my DNA was compatible to his, making it possible for us to have children. I got the impression there might have been a shifter somewhere in my family tree."

"That is entirely possible, but what he didn't tell you is that your DNA is just the building block. With each exchange of body fluids, your DNA becomes more like his, thus allowing you to procreate. The mating mark is what started the process, and the bonding ceremony will finish it."

That son of a bitch. "Are you telling me that each time we kiss, make love, or, well, you know..." Trailing off uncomfortably, she waited for Carol to get the hint.

"Do the horizontal mambo?" she asked with a smile.

"Yes, each time we do that, I'm becoming a werewolf?"

"We prefer the term shape-shifter."

"I don't care what you call yourselves. Don't I have a say in any of this?" Kiesha jumped up off of the bed and began to pace, too unsettled by what she was hearing to sit still. Knowing Alex was a shape-shifter was one thing. Becoming one as well was not in her future plans.

"You could say no, and keep your hands off of Alex. While you're at it, you'll have to find a way to keep his off of you too."

Yeah, that was likely to happen, Kiesha thought to herself.

"Other than that, I'm afraid you don't," Carol continued. "The Creator has his way of doing things, and this is the method he's chosen to keep our species from dying out."

Lovely, just lovely. What was she supposed to do now? She still didn't believe she was the man's mate. She definitely didn't want to grow fangs and turn furry.

"I know it's a lot to adjust to, but is it really so bad? That man down there would kill for you. He's everything most women say they are looking for in a man—your perfect match. Why don't you relax for a few days, and just give the relationship a chance?" she suggested.

Relax! She can't be serious, Kiesha thought. Taking a good look at Carol, Kiesha realized she was dead serious.

"I'll go and let you get dressed now. The guys are downstairs cooking dinner. Come down when you are ready." Carol worked her way off of the bed and left the room.

Picking out a pair of jeans and a top from the pile, she changed out of the shirt she was wearing. As Kiesha put the rest of the things away, she thought about her conversation with Carol. What did she have to lose by giving Alex a chance? Nothing, besides losing a bit of her humanity. *I'll still be me.*

But what about her business? Who would run things while she played lovey-dovey with the shape-shifter? Her friends would wonder what happened to her. Could she really afford to stay here on the chance that she might be Alex's mate? What would gain if she did? Possibly a whole lot. Would she regret it if she didn't give things a chance? After thinking about it for a minute, she decided that, yes, she probably would. How often did a really good man come along? She would be a fool to give up this opportunity, despite the risk involved.

She didn't have to commit to anything permanent. Besides, she hadn't taken a vacation since she'd started her business two and a half years ago. She could afford to take a week off, sit back, and see what develops.

Mind at peace, she left the room and went to join the others.

* * *

In the kitchen, Alex turned to Mark. "What do you think they're discussing up there?" He reached into the fridge and pulled out the steaks he'd left to marinate.

"Knowing my mate like I do, I'd say they were talking about you." Mark was at the sink washing his hands to assist Alex with the cooking.

"That's what I was afraid of." Deliberately avoiding thinking of all the things Carol could be telling his mate right now, he handed the steaks to Mark and started washing the potatoes. Drying them, he wrapped each one in foil with butter and seasonings, and placed them in the heated oven.

"Don't worry. Carol will know how to handle it. She just wants to see you happy. We all do." Turning on the grill, Mark adjusted it to the proper temperature.

"Thanks, I appreciate that. It's a lot for Kiesha to adjust to, and I haven't even told her everything." Reaching up in the cabinet, Alex hunted for a bowl large enough for salad.

"She'll come around. I did. I won't say it was easy, but compared to a life without my mate, it was the best choice I could've made." Just then, Carol walked into the kitchen. Mark crossed over to her side, escorted her to the bar, and helped her settle on a stool. Rubbing her stomach in an affectionate greeting to his son, he went back to grilling.

"Alex, you didn't tell her anything," Carol complained.

"I tried to," he began. "I kept getting sidetracked." Actually, he'd only thought about telling her. He still wasn't sure how she felt about him being a shape-shifter. He hadn't been willing to chance her reaction to finding out she was becoming one as well.

"I'll bet," Mark said with a deep laugh.

"She wasn't very happy with the information I gave her. You should have told her she was changing. It's a major deal." Alex could tell Carol was worried about the way he was handling things.

"Carol, don't be so hard on the man. I don't remember you being real forthcoming with me about what was going on either."

"That's why I'm so concerned. I don't want him making the same mistake that I did. I almost lost you. I couldn't stand to see him go through the same thing that we did, not if I can help it."

Ignoring their byplay, Alex focused on what was most important to him. "How'd she take it?" He was more concerned about the present, meaning his own relationship, rather than their ancient history.

"About like you'd expect. I talked to her and, hopefully, gave her a few things to think about." Alex hoped she was right. He couldn't stand the thought of losing his mate now that he'd found her. All he could do was hope for the best.

Chapter Seven

They all looked up as Kiesha walked into the kitchen. Alex crossed over to her and kissed her. "I'm sorry I didn't tell you."

She leaned into his body and wrapped her arms around him. "It's probably best that you hadn't."

Alex placed his arm around her waist and guided her over to the bar into a seat next to Carol. After lifting her up onto the stool, he went back to preparing dinner. Kiesha watched the proceedings for a while before asking, "Is there anything that I can do?"

He shook his head. "No, you just sit there and relax. Everything's under control."

In no time at all, dinner was ready. They settled at the same table where she and Alex had eaten breakfast. Since it was dark outside, they couldn't enjoy the view.

Dinner was very relaxing. Carol and Mark told a little bit about themselves and their courtship. She learned that in addition to being the beta, Carol was also one of the town's three nurses. Mark was the town's only pharmacist.

Together, they made an attractive couple. Carol was tall and slender, her complexion the color of roasted peanuts. She wore her cinnamon-colored hair in a short afro that suited her narrow face. Mark was the same height as his wife, a bit short for a man, Kiesha thought. He shaved his head bald. It looked good on him. His complexion was a bit darker, more the color of milk chocolate. They were clearly in love and totally into each other. It was very heartwarming to see.

She also learned that Alex was a veterinarian by trade. He was responsible for the health and welfare of the town's animals, as well as most of the shifters in the area. Many shifters would not go to see a human doctor for fear of discovery.

They lingered over the meal. When they could eat no more, everyone assisted with clearing the table. It was too early for the evening to end, so they carried their drinks into the living room. As Alex lit a fire in the fireplace, Carol and Mark settled on the couch, cuddling close together. Kiesha sat on one of the loveseats facing them, a little envious of the affection they displayed.

When Alex was finished, he pulled Kiesha up off of the love seat and sat down. Once he was settled, he pulled her down to sit on his lap and began playing with her hair.

"Kiesha mentioned earlier that she owned her own business."

"Really? What kind of business are you in?" Mark asked lazily, his arms around his mate, supporting her as he rubbed her belly.

"I own a chain of consignment stores," Kiesha replied, trying to ignore the growing erection under her hip and the responding wetness she felt between her legs.

"Consignment stores? I've heard of those. It's where people bring in clothes for you to sell for them, isn't it?" Carol asked.

"That's one type. Actually, almost anything can be sold on consignment. I sell furniture, clothing, tools, machinery, and various other odds and ends. I study the resale market to see which items really sell, and make my decisions on the basis of it. I have three stores now, in addition to the items we sell online." Monday she would have to get in touch with her managers and let them know how to contact her. She had a very competent staff, so her stores could run without her, but she'd never been out of reach for so long before.

"Sounds great. I wonder how well one would go over here?"

"You should consider opening a store here," Alex said. "We're kind of isolated and Refuge is a small town. You could probably do good business with the folks who don't feel like driving down the mountain to shop."

"I'll keep it in mind." At this point, she wasn't willing to commit to any permanent course of action. She wanted see how things worked out between her and Alex before making any decisions concerning her business.

"You wouldn't even have to close your stores in Florida," Mark said. "You could use the stock there to supply your business here and vice versa, giving you just that much more variety. If you decide to pursue it, I believe I have the perfect location for your store."

"She said she'd think about it, and I'm sure she will." Carol smiled at her sympathetically.

"Yes, dear." Mark rolled his eyes, obviously used to being chastised by his wife.

Kiesha smiled at Carol in gratitude. She didn't need any more pressure. She was already dealing with enough from Alex. Underneath her, Alex stiffened and growled low in his throat. *What's his problem?* Kiesha thought. *If anyone should be growling in aggravation, it should be* me. Before she could question him, Alex picked her up and set her to the side of him. Then he stood and commanded in a hard voice, "Stay here."

Kiesha looked at Carol to see what she thought about Alex's tone of voice, only to realize both Carol and Mark's demeanor had changed as well. "What's wrong?" Obviously, they knew something she didn't.

"Blood." Carol said. "A lot of it." Mark got to his feet, giving his wife a "stay put" look. Both Alex and Mark headed for the door. Alex was visibly bristling, power radiating outward from him like an aura. Before they could reach it, a hard knock sounded at the door, causing it to vibrate. "Alex, it's Nikolai. Open up."

When Alex opened the door, Kiesha saw the man she presumed was Nikolai, holding a wounded animal in his arms. It was a bloody mess with parts of its body ripped and shredded. The teeth and claw marks were visible from where she was seated, half a room away.

"Please enter, Nikolai." Alex pushed the door open wider. Nikolai strode past him carrying what appeared to be a large, bloody dog. That must have been one hell of a fight. It was a wonder the thing was still breathing.

"I found her down by the ridge. She must have been attacked. She's lost a lot of blood." He strode further into the living room, clearly looking for a place to lay her down.

"Place her over here. Carol, go get my supplies while I take a look at her." Alex swept the throw off the back of the couch and laid it on the floor in front of the fireplace. Carol rushed as fast as her advanced stage of pregnancy would allow.

"You say you found her out by the ridge?" Mark asked.

"Yes. You won't find any sign of her attackers there now. I checked before bringing her to you. From what I could see, she must have dragged herself quite a distance before her strength gave out." Nikolai's gaze never left the wolf being examined on the floor.

Carol came back with the needed supplies. As Alex moved to clean her wounds, Nikolai gave warning. "Be careful. I had to place her under compulsion before I could get close enough to her to help. She was very defensive and half crazed with pain."

Her wounds cleaned, Alex was able to determine the extent of her injuries. While many of the wounds were severe and needed stitching, none were life threatening. She was already beginning to heal.

"Do you recognize her?" Mark asked Alex. "She doesn't smell like pack."

"Yes, I know who she is. She's not one of ours. Her name is Shannon. She belongs to the Sparrowhawk pack. Her brother's the alpha," Alex finished grimly.

"Are you going to contact him? Tell him what's happened?" Carol asked.

Alex shook his head. "We don't know what happened, but until I do, this stays between us. We'll keep an eye on her and protect her while she's healing. She would heal faster if she could shift, but she's lost too much blood."

Then everything clicked in Kiesha's mind. She realized what she'd initially thought was a big dog was actually a female shifter in wolf form. She watched as Alex stitched up the worst injuries and poured some kind of liquid on them. What really caught her attention was the protective way Nikolai watched the whole procedure. She had the impression that if Alex made one wrong move, he'd snatch up the wolf and take her out of there.

While he worked, Alex quietly spoke. "We have got to keep word of this from getting out. The pack wouldn't normally be a problem, but this is a small area and news travels fast. We can't take a chance on word getting back to the wrong ears." Finally finished, he removed his bloody gloves as Carol quietly began to clean up. "She needs to be watched for a few hours."

Carol responded as she put what was left of the supplies back in the bag. "She can come home with us. She'll need clothes and stuff. If we're keeping her presence a secret, we won't be able to send someone to her home to pick up her things. If necessary, I'll tell the pack I need some more items for Kiesha. Let them believe you got her size wrong."

"Do whatever you think best." Alex turned to Nikolai. "Is there any way that she could be tracked here?"

"No, but I'll backtrack and make sure."

"Thank you. You have the gratitude of the Raven pack for bringing her to us," Alex said with a solemn nod of his head.

Nikolai took one more lingering look at the wolf he'd rescued before striding out of the door.

The minute the door closed behind him, Carol turned to Alex. "Did you see that?"

Alex must have understood her reference. "Yeah, I noticed." He glanced at his patient who was resting quietly under the influence of the painkillers and antibiotics he'd administered to her.

"That might be a problem," Carol warned.

"Only one problem at a time. We'll worry about the rest if and when it presents itself," Alex said in response to her warning.

Totally lost, Kiesha waited to see if they were going to say anything else that would explain those cryptic remarks. No one did. She'd have to question Alex about it later when they were alone. With the evening well and truly over, Carol and Mark said their good-byes, loaded their unconscious patient into the car, then headed home.

Now that they were alone, Kiesha felt free to indulge her curiosity. "What just happened here? Who is Nikolai, and what problem were you referring to?" She might not have understood everything that happened but she was intuitive enough to sense that she'd barely scratched the surface in her understanding of the events of tonight.

"Nikolai is a vampire. He usually keeps to himself. Shannon, the wolf he found, is sister to Rory McFelan, the alpha of a neighboring pack. We have an uneasy alliance with them. It's more of a truce, really. They believe in the old ways—dominance fights, survival of the fittest. The majority of the packs today have evolved beyond that. Dominance fights that end in death are very rare these days, although they've never been officially outlawed. Most of us believe that there should be more involved in being a pack's alpha than the ability to kill your way to the top. To survive in this world, we've had to become more than our beasts."

Kiesha's mind was still stuck on Nikolai being a vampire. If vampires were real, what else was real? Santa Claus? The Tooth Fairy? God, her head hurt.

"Shannon being found hurt in our territory could be used as a ploy by her brother to start a war. To keep the peace, we would be forced to negotiate terms. Like their namesake, they like to prey on smaller packs, but because of our size, the Sparrowhawks usually leave us alone. Their alpha usually only starts things with packs he knows he can dominate. Our territory borders theirs, and Rory would love an opportunity to gain more territory for his pack. I wouldn't put it past the bastard to be the one behind this."

"What problem was Carol referring to? You didn't say."

"She was referring to the way Nikolai was watching Shannon." Alex had a serious frown on his face, as though he was contemplating something unpleasant.

"What was wrong with the way Nikolai was watching Shannon? Why would it be a problem?"

"Nikolai is a vampire. Shannon is a shape-shifter. The two don't mix. We can't afford to offend Nikolai. The last thing the pack needs is trouble with a powerful vampire."

Considering the way Nikolai had watched Shannon, she wondered if Nikolai was aware that shape-shifters and vampires didn't mix. She didn't think so, and if he did, he didn't appear to care.

Suddenly exhausted from all the drama, Kiesha sagged into the couch, longing for bed. Alex noticed and encouraged her to go on up to bed. "I'll be up as soon as I finish closing up down here."

Wearily, she trudged up the stairs and into the bedroom. As much as she wanted to flop down on the bed, she knew she'd sleep better if she showered first. Her clothes left a trail on the floor behind her as she entered the bathroom. Adjusting the water to the perfect temperature, she secured her hair out of the way before stepping in. She so did not want to get her hair wet tonight. She didn't have the energy to fool with it.

She stood there, head down letting the heated water beat against her back and relax her muscles. It had been a long and trying day. Her mind reeled from all the shocks it had been dealt. Today, she'd discovered she'd been mysteriously teleported across three—or was it four?—states, vampires were real, and oh, yeah, let's not forget, she was becoming a werewolf.

She'd had her quota of weird for the day.

She stood under the shower massager, deliberately thinking of nothing until she was almost in a self-induced trance. Feeling a draft, she roused herself as the shower door opened.

Alex eased into the shower with her and picked up the soap. Motioning for her to turn around, he adjusted the spray and began washing her back. As he worked his way down her body, he lightly massaged her tight muscles. Once he was finished, he turned her around.

Alex took his time, giving special attention to her breasts and the area between her legs, enjoying the feel of them and the desire gathering in her eyes. Deciding she was sufficiently aroused, he switched their positions and arranged her body until she stood bent over, with her hands braced against the rear wall, exposing her sex to his view.

Alex snuggled up behind her, spread her legs wider apart, and eased his cock slowly inside of her. He slid in and out, reaching around to stroke and pull on her nipples while he kissed and suckled her neck and shoulders, allowing the pleasure to build slowly. As he felt her climax nearing, he held to the same slow and steady pace, forcing it to come gently. Alex felt Kiesha shake when the climax hit, and he shuddered with her as her sheath gently contracted around him, milking him of his seed and leaving goose bumps in its wake.

In the cooling water, he washed quickly before turning off the water and exiting the shower. Alex dried them both before hauling Kiesha to bed. It had been a long, eventful day. They were both tired. Ever since he'd climbed out of bed, he'd thought of nothing but the next time he'd be able to bury his cock inside his mate. Now that his physical needs were taken care off, he could allow her to rest, and they'd both be able to get some sleep.

Chapter Eight

As he left the house, Nikolai breathed in deeply of the night air. Opening his senses, he gathered information from the wind. The night was quiet, the animals of the forest still as if they recognized the predator in their midst. Other than himself and the people in the house, the woods were empty.

He shape-shifted into a large raven as he stepped off of the porch and flew back to the spot by the ridge where he'd found the she-wolf. Circling the area, he assured himself that he was alone before landing and shifting back to his natural form. It wouldn't do to startle some unsuspecting human.

With his sense of smell and keen eyesight, he followed the trail of blood back until he found the spot where the attack had occurred. His years of experience as a hunter, along with his excellent night vision allowed him to be able to read the signs in the earth and know exactly what had occurred.

They'd chased her to this spot. Two—no, three of them, in wolf form. Cornered, she'd turned and fought. From the looks of the tracks on the ground, they took turns attacking her. There was blood spilt here. From its scent, he knew it wasn't hers. She'd wounded one of her attackers, taking him out of the fight. She'd taken on another one here, while the third one sat back and watched. Tired from the chase and the fight, she'd been wounded, but still she'd fought on, defeating the second attacker.

The third one had engaged her. There was something different about the way this wolf fought. Nikolai sensed that this wolf had been stronger than the other two. Weakened as she was, it could have easily killed her. Instead, he'd gone for a crippling blow, almost as if he were punishing her. Once she'd been down, he'd backed away and left her alone.

She'd managed to run away from the area of the attack before she'd collapsed. The third wolf had followed, tracking her every move. Once she'd collapsed from exhaustion, he'd sat at a distance and watched, before turning back in the direction he'd come, taking the others with him, and leaving her there.

Nikolai studied the tracks on the ground. He could see tracks in the earth where he'd found her. Here, where the scent of their blood combined, is where she'd attacked him when he'd gotten too close. In her fragile state of mind, she didn't realize he was trying to help her. Going for his throat, she'd gotten his arm instead when he'd thrown it up reflexively. She'd bitten deep enough to draw blood. It was only after she'd ingested some of it that he'd been able to link with her mentally and calm her down.

He saw where his footprints deepened in the earth as he'd lifted her in his arms. This was the spot where they disappeared as he'd flown off to get medical attention from someone he trusted. Unlike others of his kind, he hadn't been blessed with the ability to manipulate the weather, but he did have one ability at his disposal.

Nikolai stood in the middle of the clearing, spread out his arms and levitated a few inches above the ground. Then he began spinning around so fast that he became a blur. Working his way around the clearing, he erased all signs of their presence from the area. He spun so fast, the blood his shirt had absorbed while carrying the she-wolf flew out and splattered the surrounding area in an arc. Good. Now any shifter attempting to track her would be confused, for her scent scattered in many different directions before tapering off to nothing.

Her safety assured, he assumed the shape of a hawk. Using their mental link as a guide, he followed her to the home where she was resting. Masking his presence from the shifters inside, he turned into mist and entered the home, reforming himself at her bedside.

Something about her spoke to him. That was how he'd discovered her. The scent of her blood had called out to him; he'd been unable to resist. It had been many years since he roused himself enough to care about anything.

Nikolai gazed at the she-wolf who'd managed to spark his interest and found himself curious as to what she looked like in human form. Not one to deny himself anything he truly desired, he connected to her mentally and commanded her to shift. He watched as she flowed seamlessly from a wolf to a beautiful redhead. He studied her naked form, surprised to realize that he was hard. It had been so long since he'd felt real physical desire it took him a moment to recognize the feeling.

While he luxuriated in the forgotten pleasure of arousal running through his veins, he tried to figure out what it was about her that called to him so. He'd seen beautiful women before, ones with better figures. She was a bit on the small side for his taste. He liked his women to be model tall to complement his own six-four stature. He'd be lucky if this one came to his chest. She had to be five-two, maybe five-three if she stretched herself.

The word pixie came to mind.

His eyes followed the slight curve of her stomach to the apex of her thighs below. The sight of the red curls there caused his cock to jerk in his pants. How interesting!

As he stared at those curls, he imagined himself parting them with his tongue and tasting her essence. Lost in his fantasy, it took a while for him to notice her breathing had sped up. Nikolai glanced at her face. Seeing that she was still asleep, he let his eyes wander again. Her breasts caught his attention. Where before they'd been lax in her drug-induced sleep, now her nipples were pointed little beads, proclaiming her arousal. He could smell her desire. It amazed him that she was so attuned to him.

Nikolai closed his mental link with her, stepped away from the bed and backed himself into a corner of the room. He wanted to determine if it was his thoughts or his presence to which she was responding. He looked away from her and willed his body to cool down. He thought of the mundane and kept his eyes off of the bed until he was in control again.

As his arousal subsided, he looked once more at the woman. Her nipples were still peaked and the curls between her legs glistened as the juice of her arousal dampened them. The beast within him rose and he lost a good deal of the control he'd just attained.

Unable to resist the temptation, he crossed back to the bed and reached out to dip his finger in her honey-dampened curls, being careful not to touch the flesh below. Once his finger was coated in her juice, he brought it to his mouth and tasted her essence. The taste of her caused his fangs to explode in his mouth as his beast jerked on its leash. In this instance, retreat was the better part of valor.

Nikolai quickly streamed out of the house and headed home, tightening the leash on his beast as he left. His sense of fair play wouldn't allow him to jump an unconscious woman. Had he stayed any longer, he'd have given in to the demands of his beast and taken her, right or wrong. It didn't help knowing that on some level of her consciousness, she'd been aware of his presence and her body had responded, welcoming his. He needed time to research what this meant.

* * *

Once home, Carol and Mark got their patient settled then turned in for the night. "What did you think of Kiesha?"

Mark undressed and watched his mate go through her nightly ritual. "I think she's a good match for him. Strong. Look at all the challenges she's handled so far. She's one gutsy lady. I think she'll be good for the pack."

"That's what I think too. You should have seen her when I told her about the effects of the mating bond. She was angry, but not hysterical, like many women would have been. She was able to reason, even through her anger. I was seriously impressed with her composure."

"Babe, you really should have let Alex be the one to tell her about the mate bond. It was his responsibility. You could have done some major damage by interfering." Mark scolded, even as he gently helped her undress and climb into bed.

"I know. It's just that I remember how difficult it was to tell you about it and how it was affecting you. I was afraid it would drive you away, just when I was doing everything I could to hold on to you. I only wanted to help. I didn't want Alex to have to go through all of the pain and heartache that we went through."

Mark kissed her lightly to show he wasn't really upset with her meddling, then turned and sat at the end of the bed on the side where she was laying. He picked her feet up and placed them in his lap as he thought back to the early days in their relationship when the mating fever was at its strongest.

It had been rough learning that the woman he loved was a shape-shifter. He'd never forget the first time he'd seen her turn into a wolf. She had tried to tell him, but he hadn't actually believed her until she had shifted in front of him. That had been a shock. Then he'd learned about the true mate bond and how it was affecting him physically. It had been more than he could handle. He'd tried walking away and stopping the process. No way was he becoming some creature out of a horror movie, but it had been too late. His heart had already become attached to his mate's.

Nothing could be worse than going through the pain he'd suffered at their separation. He'd discovered he'd do anything, be anything, to be with his love. Now he was happier than he'd ever been. He'd made his mate his wife, and they had a child on the way. So what if he turned into an animal once a month? Life didn't get any better than this. "I know, and better still, Alex knows. He may have even been relieved that you did it for him, although he'll never admit it to you."

"Mmm, that feels good," she said as he massaged her feet. "You give the best foot rubs."

Mark hit a spot that caused her to gasp. He smiled in recognition of what that sound meant. "Right there?" He did it again, smiling, as he smelled her arousal scenting the air.

"Yes, right there. Man, who'd have ever thought that my feet were an erogenous zone? Oh, that's making me wet."

"*I* make you wet." He kissed her big toe and then licked the arch of her foot.

"Yes, you do," she said with a smile. "You always have, right from the very beginning."

"Can you handle me tonight, babe? I feel the need to sink this big cock into your warm pussy." He stroked his cock for emphasis, enjoying the feel of his hand on his arousal as he rubbed it.

"Bring it on. I'm more than ready for you. Been anticipating this moment all day."

"You sure? I don't want to hurt you or the baby." Carol was within weeks of her delivery date. He didn't want to cause problems for her or the baby because he was horny.

"I'm sure. Let's do it the same way we did last time. That was comfortable for me."

Mark knelt on the floor, pulled her body down to the end of the bed and arranged her hips at the very edge. He spread her thighs and draped her knees over his forearms, opening her wide. "Comfortable?"

"Yes." Carol reached down and linked their hands together while he dragged his cock back and forth across her slit, testing her readiness. He could feel how wet she was, and eased his cock inside, giving her plenty of time to adjust to the feel of him. Mark checked her face for any signs of discomfort as he pressed steadily forward until he was fully embedded.

Circling his hips, he began a gliding motion. At the end of each forward thrust, he rotated his cock before slowly withdrawing, hitting all of her hot spots.

"Damn, baby, that feels good." Carol's fingers clenched, digging her nails into the back of his hand.

"You like that, do you?" Mark groaned as her pussy tightened around him.

"You have no idea."

"Everything still okay?"

"Junior and I are fine. Please don't stop what you are doing."

"Yes, ma'am. My goal is to please. Your wish is my command." Mark's attention was completely focused on his mate's pleasure.

"Oh, I'm coming."

"Let go, baby. I got you."

As she came, he drove into her a little faster and let go of a little of his control, allowing himself to come. Mark rested for a moment, gathering his strength. He couldn't believe he'd almost given this up. What an idiot he'd been. A love like this only comes once in a lifetime.

He gently kissed her stomach before withdrawing from her and getting to his feet. He went into the bathroom and wet a washcloth. Bringing it to the bed, he cleaned their combined juices from between her legs. "Don't want you being all sticky while you are trying to sleep. My sweetheart needs her rest."

She gave a sigh of appreciation. "I love how good you are to me."

He kissed her lightly on the forehead. "I love you, and I'll always be good to you." He helped her maneuver back to the top of the bed, where she flopped against the pillows. As she got comfortable, he cut off the light and climbed in beside her before gathering her close, his arm protectively cradling their child. Once again, he gave thanks to God for blessing him with his mate and unborn child before drifting off to sleep.

Chapter Nine

For the second morning in a row, Alex woke with a raging hard-on. Kiesha slept peacefully at his side. He glanced ruefully at his erection. "Behave yourself." He rolled out of bed. As much as he would enjoy burying himself inside her warm sheath, he knew she'd been through a lot and needed her rest. Not wanting to disturb her, he moved quietly as he went about the business of preparing for the day.

It was Sunday; his practice was closed except for emergencies. He headed downstairs to prepare breakfast. While his mate slept, he took the opportunity to take care of some business he'd put on hold. He checked in with his staff at the clinic and gave instructions for the coming week. Carol was handling the pack, so that was one less thing on his plate. If she needed him for anything, she would call. He wanted an update on Shannon, but that could wait until later in the day.

Business taken care of and food done, he prepared a tray and carried it upstairs to surprise his mate with breakfast in bed. The movies always made it out to be so romantic when the hero did it for his ladylove. Maybe it would earn him some brownie points.

His mate was going to relax today. He would make sure of it. He had planned to take her around and show her the town, but decided today was for kicking back and taking it easy. No worries, no problems. It would be just the two of them, spending a relaxing day together, getting to know one another.

Alex set the tray on the dresser, then crossed to the bed and kissed Kiesha awake. Their kiss became heated, tempting him to forget breakfast and crawl back into bed. *Romance*, his head whispered. *Remember to romance her. Forget the romance and just fuck her*, his other head said. *We'll all be happier.*

He pulled back, called on his restraint, and whispered hoarsely, "Breakfast. I brought you breakfast." Backing quickly off of the bed, he crossed over to the dresser and grabbed the tray, presenting it to her. When she had herself situated, he placed the tray on her lap, picked up his plate, and settled a safe distance away from the temptation she presented.

"This is so sweet. Thank you."

"I know the last few days have been stressful for you. I thought we could spend the day relaxing, talking, and getting to know each other. Ask me anything you want, and I'll try to answer it for you." He was willing to lay his heart bare if that was what it took to keep her in Refuge.

"I need to take care of some business first, but other than that, relaxing sounds great. If you don't mind me using your computer, I need to e-mail my managers to let them know where I am and how long I'll be gone. I also need to see about getting some ID here. That's priority."

"Is there anyone you can contact to send your things to you? A relative or a friend?" As much as he enjoyed having her here completely at his mercy, he understood that she wouldn't be able to enjoy herself until she had some measure of control over her circumstances.

"I have a cousin I'm close to. I can call, have her go by my place, and mail my wallet to me."

"My home is your home. Feel free to use anything I have, whenever you'd like. And don't worry about long distance charges. Make as many calls as you need. I'll give you my contact information, and you can distribute it as necessary." He wasn't trying to isolate her from the people in her life. He just wanted her to give him—give them—a chance.

"Thank you. Calling my cousin will take the longest because she'll be full of questions."

"Take all the time you need. I won't be going anywhere. It's been a long time since I've allowed myself a lazy Sunday. While you're on the computer, why don't you go ahead and order your things? We got a bit distracted yesterday, and you didn't get the opportunity to do so. Have them sent express delivery. We can pick up your clothes when we go to town tomorrow to pick up your wallet." Done with breakfast, he gathered up the dirty dishes and placed them back on the tray. Kissing her lightly on the cheek, he said, "I'll take this downstairs while you get dressed. If you need me, I'll be in the kitchen."

* * *

Entering the den, Kiesha turned on the computer and logged on to her e-mail account. As promised, Alex had left his contact information on the desk for her use. The e-mail to her store managers took only a minute. Giving herself a little more time, she went to some of her favorite clothing Web sites and ordered whatever caught her fancy. She didn't worry about how much money she spent, since she would reimburse Alex as soon as she had access to her accounts. Now came the hard part—her cousin Shayla.

Shay was the closest thing she had to a sister. Because of that, Shay felt free to ask questions others would shy away from. Damn, she was not looking forward to this. Picking up the phone, she dialed Shay's number.

"Shayla, it's Kee. Pick up the phone. I know you're there. Shay, pick up." Shayla was one of those people who screened her calls. An unfamiliar number—a long distance one at that—guaranteed that she wouldn't be answering until she knew who was calling.

"Kee, where you callin' from, girl? This is a long distance number." Trust Shay to state the obvious.

"I know, Shay. Look, I need you to do me a huge favor, and you can't ask any questions, okay?" *Mainly because I haven't thought up any answers you would believe*, Kiesha thought.

"Does this have to do with why you're callin' me long distance? Where are you?" Once Shayla got something on her mind, she was like a dog digging for a bone.

"No questions, remember? I need your help." If Shay didn't come through for her, there was no one else she could call.

"You in trouble, girl? Why didn't you say so? You just tell me where you are. I'll round up my posse, and we'll come handle business."

"You don't *have* a posse. Now, hush and listen. I need you to go to my place and get my purse for me. When you get there, give me a call at this number, and I'll tell you what to do next. You still have a key, right?" She'd given her one a while back for emergencies. This certainly qualified.

There was silence on the other end. Shayla silent was never a good thing. "You want me to go to your place and get your purse? How the heck did you leave your purse at home? Where are you, and how did you get there?"

Oh, God, this was going to be bad. She knew it. Desperate times called for desperate measures. Time to beg. "Shay, please! Please, just do as I ask, and call me back as soon as you get there."

"All right, I'm going. I wouldn't do this for just anyone."

"I know, Shay. I really do appreciate it. I know it's a lot to ask." Thank God, she was going to let it go.

"When I call back, you'd better be prepared to answer some questions." Oops, relaxed too soon.

"I'll answer your questions when you call back." *Maybe by then, I'll have thought up a convincing lie.* No way was Shay believing the truth. Disconnecting the call, Kiesha joined Alex in the kitchen.

"That was fast. Everything go all right with your cousin?" She sat at the bar as she watched him slice meat into cubes and place it in a slow cooker. It looked like some type of steak.

"We'll see. She's on her way to my place now. I told her to call when she got there, and I'd give her the rest of the instructions then. Now I need to think of something convincing to tell her." He sure was cutting up a lot of meat. She wondered what he was making. Not that she was complaining. Every meal he'd prepared so far had been delicious. "I'm not sure what I'll do if she doesn't come through." She'd just have to find another way. She would get home, even if she had to walk.

"Easy. If she won't send your things to you, we'll gas up the SUV and go and get them." She gaped at him with her mouth open. "Kiesha, I'll do everything within my power to convince you to stay here with me, but I want it to be because you choose to do so, not because you have no other choice."

Stunned, she couldn't think of a reply. Most men would have taken advantage of her until they had gotten what they wanted from her. Not Alex. He was taking a big risk here.

The phone rang. It was much too early for Shayla to call. Alex rinsed and dried his hands before answering. "You must be Shayla. Hold on a moment. Kiesha's right here."

"Shay?" She must have broken some serious speed records going to the condo.

"Who is that hunk with the yummy voice?"

"How do you know he's a hunk? You haven't seen him."

"Girl, did yo mamma teach you nothing? The ugly ones don't come with voices like that. It's against the laws of nature or something. I want *all* the dirt. Is Mr. Yummy the reason you're away from home without your purse and, from what I can tell, any of your clothes?"

"Are you going through my things?" Damn, she should have realized Shayla would snoop. She wasn't really nosy, but when she wanted answers, she was really determined.

"Yes! Now, tell me what's going on. Oh, my God," she said excitedly. "You got laid! I knew it. It's about damned time too. Any longer and your stuff would have dried up. Was he any good? Never mind. Don't answer that. Obviously, the man's doing something right if he messed your head up enough to make you leave home empty-handed. He take you off on some kind of romantic retreat?"

Kiesha wanted to crawl under the bar and slink out of the room. Alex could hear every word being said, judging by the big grin on his face. "I'm spending the week at his home in the mountains. He surprised me. I've been here since Friday and just realized my purse was at home, not in his vehicle like I'd originally thought. That's why I need you to mail it to me." Not a bad lie for the spur of the moment.

"Homeboy must be really good if you went two whole days before you realized you left your purse at home. Loaded, too, if you haven't had to spend any money. Not like those losers who expected you to pay for everything." Oh, God, would the torture never end?

"Shayla, please."

"Okay, okay. I'll stop teasing you now. It's not like he can hear what I'm saying. Give me that address, and I'll overnight your wallet and cell phone, which you also left. You still have that account with UPS?"

"Yes, I'll give you the account number and the address where I am. I'll also e-mail you Alex's phone number and address so you can contact me if anything comes up."

"Everything will be fine. Don't worry about home. You just take time and enjoy yourself. You deserve it."

After giving Shayla the information she needed, Kiesha disconnected the call, looking everywhere but at Alex. She knew her face was red. Shay could be so embarrassing sometimes, though she wouldn't have been quite so forthcoming had she known Alex could hear every word she said. Damn wolf hearing. Thank God Alex had decided not to tease.

"I hope you like beef stew." Putting the last of the ingredients in the slow cooker, he moved it closer to the outlet and turned the pot on.

"I like anything I don't have to cook." She watched as he cleaned up behind himself. He was very handy in the kitchen.

"You don't like to cook?"

"Not really." Boy, was that an understatement. "It's never been one of my favorite things to do. Since I live alone, I eat a lot of takeout or buy frozen dinners." Sounded like a reasonable excuse, but the truth was, she hated cooking.

"Fortunately for you, I love to cook. I'm always trying new recipes." The man was too good to be true. He cooked *and* cleaned. "Why don't we take a walk? I can show you around the property. You haven't been outside since you got here."

Sounded like a good idea to her. She was beginning to feel a little cooped up. Putting on jackets and shoes, they walked outside. Walking through the woods, he showed her where his property ended and his neighbor's began. Alex lived near the top of a mountain in an area known as Raven's

Peak. There was only one person who lived higher than he, the vampire Nikolai. The town of Refuge was further down the mountain and in the valley below was a Cherokee Indian reservation.

They talked as they walked. At first, Kiesha was a little reticent, but as she saw his genuine interest, she couldn't help but be more open. Alex was a really good listener. He asked intelligent questions and knew how to draw a person out. So they talked and walked, before hunger and the cold drove them back inside.

After filling up on a hearty lunch of beef stew and French bread, they strolled into the living room. Alex lit a fire; they relaxed on the couch in front of it. She kept waiting for him to make a move. Although he was very affectionate, he kept things under control. While she felt his arousal pressing against her, he did nothing to act on it. She couldn't help but be touched and impressed by that, even as she cursed it.

As daylight turned to twilight and twilight to evening, she learned that they had a lot in common. They shared similar taste in movies and music. Politically, they belonged to the same party and believed in the same things. Getting hungry again, they headed back into the kitchen for more stew. Once they were finished eating and the kitchen was cleaned, Alex suggested they watch a movie.

They found a comedy neither one of them had seen. After laughing their way through the movie, which turned out to be funnier than she had expected, they shut everything off and headed off to bed.

As Kiesha lay in bed waiting for sleep to claim her, she reflected back over the day. It had been the most relaxing Sunday she had ever spent, bar none. Alex was the most intriguing man she'd ever met. Not only was he an expert lover, but also a good guy all around. One she would happily call friend. That's something she'd never experienced before, a lover who was also a friend. *Something to consider*, she thought as sleep claimed her.

Chapter Ten

She was back in the woods. The full moon lit the area around her. Kiesha recognized this as the clearing where she'd first met Alex. Remembering what happened the last time, she waited for Alex to appear.

A noise broke the silence of the night, and a big black bird flew into the clearing. A raven. It circled the overhead before gliding lightly to the ground. As it neared the earth, it shape-shifted into the form of a man. A tall, strikingly handsome man that was very familiar to her. Conor. Boy, did he have a lot nerve, showing up like this, and a lot to answer for. "What are you doing to me? Why did you bring me here?"

"To give you that which you most desire."

"And who made you the authority on it?"

"Is it not what most of us truly desire? To love and be loved in return?"

His being right didn't make her any happier with him. "Conor, I'm not saying you're wrong, but even so, why me? I don't know if I can give him what he wants, or be what he needs. He thinks I'm his mate and wants me to stay here with him."

"What if you are his mate? What has he asked that is so difficult for you to do? Has he asked you to change who you are?"

"No."

"Has he asked you to give up your business? Turn away from your family or friends?"

"No."

Alex had done the opposite. He'd encouraged her to expand her business by opening a store in Refuge. It had been his suggestion that she give her family and business associates the information they needed to contact her.

"So what is it he desires that is so difficult for you?"

"He wants me to be in love with him. To be his soul mate." She wasn't even sure she believed in soul mates.

"Can you tell me that love for him is not already stirring in your heart?"

That was the problem.

Love wasn't supposed to happen this quickly. It took time, lots of time. How did she know if what she felt was real, if it would last? Could she walk away from her stable life into the uncertainty of a future with Alex? What guarantee did she have that this feeling would last?

As though he'd read her mind, Conor responded. "Ah, you trouble yourself much over nothing. Love is not as complicated as you make it out to be. True love is based upon commitment to the well-being of another person. It's this commitment that will sustain you through good days and bad. Romantic love comes and goes, but commitment, she stays forever. That wolf, he is committed to you. He would *follow you to the grave and beyond. Living is about taking chances and giving it all you've got. That's what makes life worthwhile. What do you have in your safe, little world that can compare? I urge you to think about it."*

Kiesha woke with a start. She must have made some sound of distress because Alex made a comforting sound in his sleep and pulled her closer to the heat of his body. Though she was unable to see the clock, she could tell dawn was a long way off. She had truths to face and decisions to make. It was going to be a long night.

* * *

Sometime during the night, she must have fallen back to sleep. When she woke again, she found herself face-to-face with a sleeping Alex. Her thoughts went back to the conversation with Conor she'd had during the night. Did she love Alex? Possibly. She could admit, if only to herself, that she had strong feelings for him. The real question was, if she loved him enough to take a chance on what they had lasting? She didn't know. But as Conor had said, all she could do was give it her best.

"Hey, you." Sometime during her introspection, Alex had woken up.

As she focused on him, she tried to let go of the fear of tomorrow and embraced the feelings she had for this man. She grabbed a hold of her courage, and took a leap of faith. "I love you."

He blinked. "What did you say?"

"I love you." *At least, I think I do*, she thought to herself, waiting expectantly for his reaction.

He sat up in the bed and propped the pillows behind his back, his gaze never once losing contact with hers. "What's this all about?" he asked after lifting her onto his lap.

As Kiesha adjusted her legs to a more comfortable position, she thought that this was so not the reaction she expected. Singing the *Hallelujah Chorus* might have been over the top, but the least he could have done was show some excitement. Didn't he know the struggle she'd gone through to get those words out of her mouth? "Do you question every woman who tells you she loves you?"

"Only when the woman saying the words is you. Don't get me wrong, baby. I would love nothing more than hear you say those words and mean them, but I'm sensing a little uncertainty here. So I ask again, what's going on in that head of yours?"

Alex looked as if he was willing to sit there until hell froze over or he got an answer; she figured she'd crack long before people below started complaining of frostbite. "I had a dream last night. Well, I think it was a dream. With Conor, who knows? It might have been real."

"Conor?"

"Yes. I was back in the clearing where you found me and he was there. I confronted him. Asked why he was messing with me, with us?" She fell silent, still perturbed by Conor's response.

"What did he say?" Alex prompted her to continue.

"To give me what I desired most—love. I argued with him, but what if he's right? What if you are the love of my life, my soul mate? How can I just walk away, but then, how can I stay? This is all happening too fast. I don't know what to think anymore. I'm afraid to move forward, but more afraid of not moving at all. I like my life. It's comfortable and safe and suits me. I'm not sure I want to give it up just to be with you, but if I don't, I'm scared I'll regret it for the rest of my life. God, I'm so confused."

"First of all," he began. "I'm not going anywhere. I waited a long time for you. I'm not going to rush it. Yes, I want you here with me. I love waking up with you in the morning and going to sleep with you curled up beside me at night. I know this is all happening fast. Because I understand, I'm willing to give you all the time that you need to adjust. That means no pressure, no ultimatums. *We* will happen, all in the Creator's timing. So I need for you to stop worrying about what may or may not happen and just enjoy us being together now. Let's take it one day at a time, okay? Can you do that for me?"

The weight and pressure she'd been feeling rolled off of her shoulders as she agreed.

"Good, now I have someone dying to get reacquainted with you." He lifted her up and brought her back down, impaling her on his erection. "Damn, you feel good. Keeping myself from this hot little pussy just about killed me yesterday."

"Well, hello, stranger." She clenched her inner walls, gripping him tightly.

"Ride me."

"It would be my pleasure, sir." She placed her hands on his shoulders and lifted off of him until only the tip of his head was within her, then slowly sank all the way back down. Up and down she went, savoring the sensation of his cock inside. Then he took control.

Alex held her by the waist and began to thrust upward as he slammed her body down, creating a delicious friction. Head thrown back, nails digging in his shoulders, she threw herself into the rhythm. Kiesha made circular motions on her downward thrust that ground her clit against his pubic bone. Senses on overload, her climax radiated outward from the center of her body until it took control of every muscle and every nerve ending.

When her body stiffened, Alex flipped her onto her back, never once missing a stroke, and pounded his way into a howling orgasm.

Not wanting to crush her, he rolled over and pulled her on top of him until she was draped across his body. He silently ran his hands down her back until they cupped her ass. Damn, it was fine! He played with it while he thought about the things she'd revealed earlier. Though he and Carol had told her a lot about the mating bond, they hadn't told her everything. There was much she still didn't know about it, things that could have potentially alleviated much of her fear. On the other hand, it could very well have added to it. Her emotional confusion was evidence that the bond was working.

He toyed with the idea of explaining in more detail about the bonding process, but decided against it. It wasn't that he didn't want her to know. It was that the process was different for each couple. There were some elements to it that were similar and those had been explained to her. The rest was anyone's guess. Cradling her as she slept, he pondered the mysteries of the mating process and prayed that Kiesha stuck around long enough for the process to be completed.

* * *

Shannon woke in unfamiliar surroundings. Hearing her name, she turned in the direction of the voice. There was a very attractive, very pregnant black lady standing in the doorway. Yeah, she knew the politically correct term was African-American, just like she was supposedly Irish-American, but who gave a crap? *We are what we are.* She tried to focus her attention on what the woman said.

"Oh, I'm glad you're awake. How do you feel? I'm Carol, beta of the Raven pack. You're in my home, since I'm also a nurse. I need to take a look at you and see how you're healing. Do you want to eat first and be examined later, or be examined now and eat later?"

She must have looked confused, because Carol brought the tray over to a table by the bed. "Here, maybe you should eat first. I'm sorry. You must still be groggy from the medication Alex gave you. Alex is the Raven pack's alpha, as well as its physician. He stitched you up after you were found and brought to us. You've been out of it for almost twenty-four hours. There's water by the bedside. The bathroom's over there through that door. I'm sure your bladder's about to burst."

After the second barrage of information, Shannon realized three things. Her head felt like it was full of cotton, probably from the meds she'd been given. Her bladder was indeed making itself known, and she was hungry enough to eat a horse. She decided that her bladder was the most urgent of her needs. She moved to get out of the bed. Carol stepped forward to help her. At first hesitant, she reluctantly accepted the assistance, only to be glad she did when the room spun as she stood on her feet.

"Don't worry. It will wear off. You were in wolf form when Alex worked on you. The pain reliever he gave you was strong enough to put down a grizzly. Once you get some food in your stomach, your strength will come back and you'll be good as new. Can you handle it from here, or do you need me to come in with you?"

Shannon shook her head and grabbed hold of the sink for support, shutting the bathroom door behind her. Nurse or not, there was no way someone was watching her pee. Once finished, she washed her hands at the sink as she studied her reflection in the mirror. She looked as groggy as she felt.

She opened the door to find Carol waiting for her. Once she was back in bed, Carol propped the pillows behind her back and smoothed the covers over her before setting the tray on her lap. "Here you go. Eat first. We can talk later. Alex will be by sometime tomorrow. He'll want to know what happened to you. In the meantime, relax. You're under the protection of the Raven pack. No one but the alphas and my mate know that you're here." Carol smiled and left the room.

Shannon looked at the food on her plate and dug in. There was a big, juicy steak, grilled to perfection. Shifters needed protein, especially when they'd expended a lot of energy doing something like healing. Apparently, she'd been fairly bad off. She remembered the attack. She'd taken on and defeated two of the strongest males in her pack before facing off with her brother. Usually, they were fairly evenly matched. This time, however, she'd been in two major fights after being chased for miles, was exhausted, and wounded. Her brother could have taken her out, but that wasn't his goal. He'd intended to teach her a lesson, and force her to bow to his demands. Like hell! The day she gave in to his demands would be the day the world came to an end.

Eating and drinking her fill, she set the tray to the side as exhaustion caught up with her. Reclining again, she searched her memory for the events that happened after the fight. The medication was still strong in her system, making recollection difficult. The last thing she remembered as she drifted off to sleep was a compelling pair of deep brown eyes.

* * *

The phone rang, breaking the silence. Kiesha wanted to scream. What did a person have to do to get some uninterrupted sleep in this house? She was so tired, and her muscles were still sore from Friday and the excessive sexual activity she'd been getting lately. Home was looking good, if only so that she could rest.

Her pillow shifted beneath her and she felt the vibration of Alex's voice as he answered the phone. Only then did she realize that she was sprawled on top of him like he was a mattress, her head being cushioned by his chest. "She's asleep right now. Can I take a message?"

She held out a hand for the phone.

"Hello?"

"You're still in bed at this time of morning? You slut! I'm so jealous."

Don't be, she thought. Kiesha sat up in bed and propped the pillows behind her back. She needed all of her faculties to deal with Shay. "What time is it, and did you call for any purpose other than to harass me?"

"It's a little after ten, and I called to tell you that your stuff will be available for pickup after three."

"Thanks, Shay. I really appreciate this." She heard the shower come on in the bathroom. For a moment, even though she was tired, she wished she could be in there with Alex instead of on the phone.

"Kiesha, I know I was giving you a hard time yesterday, but seriously, is everything all right? You're not in any trouble, are you?" That's one thing Kiesha loved about her cousin. She may talk like a flake, but she had a good heart and that foolishness she spouted hid a really sharp brain.

"He wants me to marry him. To pack up, move here, and live with him. You know, the whole happily-ever-after thing?" She felt safe talking. Alex was in the shower and couldn't hear her. Besides, Shay was the one person she'd always been able to count on.

"You're there with no money so he must be reasonably well off, and I know you wouldn't be there if he was abusive. So what's the problem?"

How could she say this without sounding stupid? "I haven't known him that long. I don't know if I'm ready to make that kind of change in my life."

"Kee, this is me you're talking to. You are not now, nor have you ever been afraid to take chances, so what's really going on? It's not your business. You can run that from anywhere. And I know it's not me you're afraid to leave. I'm not going to let you go somewhere and lose contact." There was a pause, and then she said, "I know. You're in love with him, aren't you?"

"I think so. Maybe. I'm not really sure." This wasn't something she wanted to get into right now. Sometimes Shay was too perceptive.

"Listen to me. This is about your fear of letting people close. You're afraid of being hurt."

"Shay, what are you talking about? I've been in love before."

"No, ma'am. Not really. You don't let people get close enough to you to risk being hurt, and I'm not just talking about men. You haven't really let anyone close to you since Auntie Miriam died."

At the mention of her mother, Kiesha felt a hole in her heart open up. It had been two years since she died, and it felt like yesterday. "That's not true. I've been in relationships. I'm close to you!"

"Because I won't let you push me away. And it is too true. When Aunt Miri died, the family tried to reach out. You pushed every one of us away. And don't get me started on your so-called relationships. You deliberately choose men you knew you'd never become attached to. That's why it never really bothered you when the relationships didn't last. You never expected them to. That's what has you so freaked about Alex. He got in under your guard."

"So what, I'm some big, emotional coward? Is that how you see me? You know how hard it is for a successful black woman to find a decent man. The ones on my economic level want someone white. Those that aren't think I'm some sort of sugar momma."

Kiesha couldn't believe she was defending her previous relationships to Shay, of all people. They had the same philosophy when it came to men, or so she'd believed. "So what if I play the game? It doesn't mean I'm emotionally frigid." *I'm crying. I* never *cry. Damn.* She took a deep breath to calm down.

"Oh, no, sweetie, that's not what I'm saying. You feel things very deeply. That's why it hit you so hard when Aunt Miri died. But ever since then, it's like something inside you died, too. Now it's time to let it go, Kee. I don't want to see you grow old and alone because you were too afraid of being hurt to let someone in."

Kiesha wiped the tears running down her face. "I promise I'll think about what you said. I didn't realize I was pushing everyone away."

"We know, sweetie. No one's mad at you. We gave you the space you needed. That's what families do. Now you go love on that big man of yours. Don't be afraid to admit to yourself how you really feel and remember, I'm just a phone call away."

She heard the shower cut off. "Bye, Shay. And thanks." They disconnected the call as Alex came out the bathroom.

"Is everything all right?"

Kiesha looked at him, seeing him in light of everything Shayla had said to her. This was a man worth holding on to. "Maybe not right now, but it will be." She determined right then and there that she would not let fear of being hurt keep her from living. Even after only knowing him for such a short period of time, she knew losing Alex would hurt. Whether it happened now or five years down the road, she planned on grabbing all the happiness she could with him. Tomorrow would take care of itself.

Chapter Eleven

Alex took in the sight of his mate smiling at him while tears ran down her face. That must have been one hell of a conversation with her cousin. The tears scared him; the smile confused him. She'd never smiled at him quite like that before.

"What's on the agenda for today?" she asked.

Alex knew she wanted to change the subject. Hesitating briefly, he decided to let her get away with it. If she needed to talk, he hoped she knew that he would listen. "I thought we could go into town and I could show you around. We need to stop by the office, since that's where your things will be delivered. I also need to go by Carol's house and check on my patient."

"Great," she said, jumping out of the bed. "Shay said my stuff would be ready after three. By the time we're finished running around, it should be here. Let me grab a quick shower, so we can get going."

He was amazed at her sudden change of mood. A minute ago she was in tears. Now, she was bouncing around, full of energy, and happy as a lark. "You want to eat here or grab something in town?"

"In town," Kiesha replied, pausing at the bathroom door. "You're an amazing cook, but I'm ready to get out of this house and see some more of my surroundings."

"In town it is, then." He watched until she'd closed the door behind her, locking herself in the bathroom. Something was going on. He didn't know what it was, but she seemed more at peace now than she had earlier this morning. Whatever had happened, he was grateful.

He dressed quickly and casually in a pair of jeans and a black pullover. Then he headed downstairs and picked up the phone. He walked to the door and checked the temperature outside while he dialed Carol's number.

"Good morning, Alex. How's Kiesha?"

"She's fine, Carol. How's my patient doing?" he said, jumping straight to the reason for his call.

"She's doing well, amazingly well considering the condition she was in. She's almost totally healed, having just a few shiny pink scars to mark where the injuries are. Even those are in the process of fading. I don't know what to make of it. She's healing way faster than she should be."

"How's her appetite? Has she eaten anything?" The weather felt a little brisk. He closed the back door and pulled a jacket out of the closet. He grabbed one for Kiesha, as well.

"I took her a tray last night, and she ate just fine. She was still groggy from the medication so I didn't get a chance to question her. When I checked on her this morning she was still sleeping. She's going to need some clothes to wear until we figure out what to do with her. She's a tiny little thing. I'm not sure that anything I have will fit."

"I'm bringing Kiesha into town. We'll stop first and grab a bite to eat, then we'll be over. Once I find out what her story is, I'll have a better idea of how to proceed. Has anyone asked about her yet?" The shower cut off. Kiesha would be down soon.

"Not that I know of. Of course, yesterday was Sunday, so she probably won't be missed until later today. For now, no one but us knows where she is."

"Well, until we know what's going on, let's keep it that way." He didn't want the wrong person knowing Shannon's whereabouts until he knew for sure there was nothing to worry about.

"Okay, she can wear something of mine until then. If I go back to the pack asking for more clothes, it will only cause speculation that we don't need. What about her rapid healing?"

"I'll let you know once I see her. She may be a naturally fast healer, or there may be something else going on. Only time will tell." He looked up as Kiesha started down the stairs. She had on a tight pair of black jeans, a white T-shirt, and tennis shoes. As she walked down the steps, she fastened the buttons of one of his shirts over her T-shirt. From the looks of things, she wasn't wearing a bra. Just like that, he was hard.

"I'll see you when you get here," Carol said and disconnected the call. Alex barely noticed. He wondered how to get Kiesha out of the clothes she'd just put on.

The way those jeans cupped her mound was criminal. The sight of her nipples puckered against the T-shirt made him want to rip it off of her. She looked up and noticed. "No.

Food now. Play later. If you get me naked, we won't make it into town today."

Alex knew she was right, but he wasn't happy about it. He handed her a jacket, slid his wallet into his back pocket, and grabbed his keys.

* * *

Kiesha thought about what Shayla had said as she and Alex rode down the mountain toward town. It had hurt. It had also been a real eye opener. She hadn't realized she'd been so wrapped up in herself and her grief.

Her mom had been her world, her best friend, and her refuge. She knew many of her friends had thought the relationship they'd shared was unnatural; maybe they'd been a bit envious of it. It had always been the two of them against the world.

Growing up had been difficult for her. Her white friends considered her to be black while her black friends thought of her as white. They'd wanted her to choose—to be one or the other—and she hadn't been willing to deny either of her heritages. So, she'd been alone a lot, spending time at home with her parents.

Shay had been right about so many things. While she'd gone through the motions of living, she hadn't really been alive. Yes, she'd taken her mother's life insurance money and opened her businesses. She'd sold the house and bought a condo, further isolating herself from her family.

Everything in her life was about control, *her* control. The men in her life were there for one purpose only, and it had little to do with love. She ran the relationship and when they outlived their usefulness or became too attached, she ended it and moved on.

Looking at the past two years, she knew her mother would be ashamed of her. Her mom had been the most alive person she knew. Every day was an adventure. She'd lived every day to the fullest. She'd taught Kiesha to do the same.

Shayla was right. The fear of moving was just a convenient excuse to hide behind. Her real fear, the one she'd hidden even from herself, was of opening her heart and living again. Unknowingly, she'd been trying to bury herself with her mom. Kiesha was ashamed of herself.

She looked at Alex as he drove. This was a man she could respect. She already trusted him. Those were two major components of love. She knew he loved her. Oh, he hadn't said the words, but his every touch and action said it for him. It was in the care he gave, and the attentive way he listened to her. He wanted to know her, not just her body, but her mind. She would be a fool to give this man up, and her momma hadn't raised no fool.

While they were in town, she would look for a good location to open another store. She really could run her business from anywhere. Another location would be the icing on the cake and give her something to do, as well as make her feel like a part of the community.

She wouldn't tell Alex just yet. She'd made such a mess of things this morning he wasn't likely to believe her. This was one situation where actions needed to speak louder than words. She'd have to show that not only was she committed to him, but also to his world and all that entailed. Something inside of her clicked. This felt right.

Alex reached out and touched her hand. "Penny for your thoughts."

She laced her fingers with his. "Oh, they're worth more than a penny. Inflation, ya' know?"

He laughed. "Tell me the price. I think I can afford them."

She thought about the conclusion she'd come to and smiled secretively. "Not right now, but soon."

Gesturing ahead, he told her the town would be coming into view as they rounded the next curve. She realized they'd been traveling down the mountain for quite a bit. The road was long and curvy, surrounded by woods with small lanes branching off here and there descending into nothing. She'd known Alex's property was near the top of the mountain, but she'd not known how close to the top they actually were. Its name of Raven's Peak seemed very appropriate. No wonder the man drove an SUV with four-wheel drive.

As they rounded the curve, the town of Refuge lay before them. At this distance, it looked like land that time had left behind. There was an enduring quality about the place. Like most small towns, the majority of the businesses lay on the main drag. She saw roads shooting off from it. Some went up the mountain, but most angled downward before disappearing into the forest. Through the trees she caught sporadic glimpses of houses.

"This place obviously doesn't get a lot of tourists."

"No, we don't. You have to know where you're going when you come to Refuge. It's not on the beaten path. It's also very easy to get lost. The heavily forested area is a turnoff to skiers, unless you are into cross-country skiing, and even they stay closer to the more populated trails."

She looked around and guessed that if she were going to be a shape-shifter, she'd want to live in a town where she could avoid detection and possible exposure too. Somewhere like this, a place out of the way.

Alex continued to tell her about the town and its origins. It had been founded by Native American Indians running from the government, which was trying to force them onto reservations out west. Over time, other vagabonds and misfits had found there way here as well, thus giving the town its original name of Misfit. It was a place to which you came to get lost from the world. Television reception was iffy unless you had a satellite. Cell phone reception was even trickier. A lot of the modern world had passed them by and they liked it just fine. It was the kind of town kids couldn't wait to move away from, but found themselves returning to when it came time to raise their own children.

As he talked, he drove down Main Street. They parked in front of a small diner with a sign out front that read, EAT AT MOE'S.

"Shouldn't that be 'Eat at Joe's'?" she asked, referring to the famous restaurant chain.

"Naw. Hugh saw the sign somewhere and thought it was funny. He couldn't name his restaurant Joe's, so he named it the next best thing."

Kiesha shook her head at the idiosyncrasies of the small town mind. She waited while he got out of the truck and came around to open her door for her. As she turned toward him in preparation of getting out, he stopped her by stepping between her legs. “I’ve been wanting to do this since before we left the house.” Not touching her other than with his lips, he gave her a kiss that almost made her cream her panties. When Kiesha reached out to take a hold of him, he stepped out of reach. “If I touch you, I’m going to strip you naked and be in you, public street or not.”

She ran the tip of her tongue around her lips, savoring that last little taste of him. She watched as his eyes followed the motion of her tongue and laughed when he groaned. “Baby, you’re killing me.” He reached down and adjusted the fit of his cock in his jeans. Stepping back, he allowed her to exit the vehicle and clicked the locks into place behind her.

Alex gestured toward the door and motioned for her to go ahead of him. It was a little early for the lunch crowd so there weren’t that many people around, either on the street or in the diner. As they walked to the door, Alex found himself distracted by the swaying of her ass in those jeans. He loved the way the denim hugged her ass. The way she had his shirt tied around her waist actually drew attention to her generous curves rather than drawing the eye away, which, he was sure, was what she intended.

He reached past her and opened the door, catching a whiff of her scent as her body brushed against his before entering the doorway. He bumped into her when she stopped abruptly. Doing an about-face, she pushed past him and rushed back outside. She rushed to the truck and leaned her back against its side with her head down around her knees, dragging in great gulps of air.

Alex hurried behind her, wondering at her strange behavior. At her side, he crouched down so that he could see her face. "What's wrong?"

She shook her head. He placed his hand against her forehead. Her skin felt clammy and her face was flushed. He was very surprised because she was fine a minute ago. He waited impatiently while she composed herself.

Finally, she seemed to get herself under control. She stood up and swayed on her feet. The blood drained from her face, leaving her pale. Alex caught her by the waist. "Whoa, easy there." He managed to get the passenger side of the vehicle open and eased her inside. "What's wrong? What happened to you? You were fine a minute ago." He rapidly fired questions at her. He was unwilling to wait another moment for answers, not when her health and safety was at stake.

"The smell," she said, keeping a strong grip on his shirt as she eased her head back against the seat.

"What?" Of all the things he'd expected her to say, that was not on the list.

"The smell! The grease, food, perfume and sweat. Hell, even the trash. All of it hit my nose, and my stomach reacted. My God, how could you not smell it?"

That's when Alex realized what was going on. Her sense of smell increased. A shape-shifter's sense of smell was much stronger than that of regular humans. Until a person learned how to control it, the difference was overwhelming. This was the first sign he'd had that their mating was changing her DNA, adapting her cells to his. He hadn't expected it to happen this soon or he would have tried to prepare her. "Ah, baby, I'm sorry. I didn't think this would happen this soon."

"What do you mean 'this soon'?"

"I mean, this is some of your shape-shifter senses kicking in. Did you know that a wolf's sense of smell is almost a hundred times keener than humans?"

"No, I didn't know. How can you live like this? The smells, the combinations…they are so overpowering."

"They can be at first. You learn to control it so that it doesn't overwhelm you."

"How do I do that?"

"You focus until one scent becomes stronger than all the others."

"I'm not sure I understand."

"All right. Close your eyes." He waited while she did as he said. "Okay, now tell me what you smell."

She took a deep breath. "I smell you. Your scent is all around me."

Okay, again not exactly what he was expecting. Although once he thought about it, it was understandable that his scent would be the strongest. "What else can you smell?"

"I smell leather. I smell leaves and dirt, flowers and old oil on the asphalt. I smell other stuff, but I can't identify what."

"Good. Now out of the list that you gave me, pick one scent." He waited minute. "Have you picked one?"

She nodded. “Okay. Now what?”

“I want you to focus and concentrate on that one scent until the others all fade into the background. You can’t totally get rid of the other smells, but you can trick your brain into reducing your awareness of them.”

She inhaled, moving closer to him and burying her nose against his neck. “Mmm, you smell delicious. I could eat you up.”

His dick throbbing, he resisted the temptation to lay her down in the truck and fuck her blind. “Do you see what I mean?”

“Yes.” Then she stuck her tongue out and licked him on the neck.

With a low rumble, he snatched her out of the truck. “Lesson’s over.” Pulling away from her, he closed the truck and adjusted his stance to give his aching balls some room. They’d drawn up tight against his body. If she made one more move like that, he’d shoot a load in his pants. “You ready to eat now?”

Kiesha loved the effect she had on his body and winked at him. “Sure.” They walked back toward the door of the diner, with Kiesha in the lead. This time, knowing what to expect, she was able to brace herself and find her focus scent before all of the other smells overwhelm her. She smiled at Alex, pleased with her success. She walked on into the diner and found a booth for them to sit at.

They slid into the booth, Alex on one side and she on the other. A blonde Barbie doll of a waitress bounced over to the table to take their order. Her nametag read Cyndi. She leaned against the bench where Alex was sitting. She looked at him and asked suggestively, "See anything you like?"

Kiesha hated her on sight. With her bleached hair and obviously fake boobs displayed in her low-cut waitress uniform, Kiesha took one look and immediately thought bimbo. "We haven't decided yet," she said coldly.

Ignoring her, Cyndi leaned over Alex and gave him an up close view of her cleavage, then opened the menu on the table. "Let me show you our specials for today." She proceeded to elaborate on each special, her finger pointing to the items on the menu, her face so close to Alex's that if he turned his head, they'd have kissed.

Kiesha heard a low-pitched growl. Cutting Cyndi off, Alex asked her to bring him a sweet tea. "Baby, what do you want to drink?"

"Tea." Kiesha eyed Cyndi like she was considering eating her for lunch.

"Cyndi, please bring us two sweet teas while we look over the menu and decide what we want to eat." As soon as Cyndi walked off, Alex took hold of her hand. He brought it to his mouth and placed a kiss into the center of her palm. Then he closed her fingers over her palm one by one, and licked each one until he reached her index finger. The look in his eyes was heat personified. She forgot her jealousy as her nipples puckered against her T-shirt, a reminder of her bra-less state. She squirmed in her seat as her pussy grew damp. At this rate her panties would be soaked. Alex smiled wickedly at her.

Cyndi returned to the table and plopped their drinks down with a *thunk*, causing some of the tea to slosh over the sides. "You ready to order yet?"

Ignoring Cyndi's obvious displeasure, he turned to Kiesha. "Burger and fries okay with you?" At her nod, he turned to back to Cyndi. "Bring us two burgers, fully loaded, and two orders of curly fries." Cyndi wrote their order and stalked off.

Business began to pick up as the lunch crowd wandered in. Many customers approached their table to speak to Alex, their curiosity about her evident. She caught more than one of them sniffing the air around her, causing her to look at Alex with raised eyebrows. Others were bolder, asking leading questions in hopes of learning gossip. Kiesha took it all in stride, having been raised in a small town. She fielded questions with the expertise of a career politician, disappointing many a busybody at their failure to draw anything meaningful out of her.

They were finally able to be alone when food began to flow out of the kitchen. Knowing how scarce work in small towns could be, Kiesha wondered about some of the people in the diner. Who did they work for, and how were they earning their keep? She decided she'd have plenty of time to learn the ins and outs of Refuge's economics.

Chapter Twelve

After lunch, Alex took her on a tour of Refuge, which included a trip to his office. The facility was very impressive. It was easy to see why he was highly respected by his staff. Alex actually had two waiting rooms, one for his human patients and another for the animals. Both were full. It was obvious that his practice was very lucrative.

"How are you able to treat both humans and animals? Aren't you afraid of malpractice suits? Or are all the humans shifters, like you?"

"Yes, they're shifters, though I'm licensed to practice both. I completed a double major in college and did my residency in Charlotte. Since Dad was the town's previous veterinarian, I grew up helping out. When he was ready for retirement, I bought the practice from him and expanded it."

"What kind of hours do you work? I'm sure that being the only vet means long hours, but you're also a doctor. And you're the pack's alpha. Are you sure you have time for a relationship?" Kiesha wasn't a needy person, but she did want to spend some time with her mate.

"I've already considered it. Pete's almost finished with his degree. I've discussed bringing him on as a partner, and he's interested. I'm also toying with the idea of creating some type of internship program for high school students that are interested in becoming veterinarians. Not only would it give us more help, but it would offer some deserving students a much needed hand up."

Kiesha was very impressed and made a mental note to consider an internship for her business. Opening a store in Refuge would not only keep her busy, it would provide another source of employment for residents.

She'd found the perfect location during their tour: an empty building located almost in the center of town. Alex said it had once been the hardware store. After the owner died, with no one to take over, the business folded. She wondered if this was the location Mark had been referring to that night at the house.

The building was available for lease or sale. If she were going to open a business, she would be interested in purchasing, but only if the price was right. She was sure she could negotiate them down to a reasonable price, maybe even below market value, because of its remote location. The fact that it had been sitting empty for so long was a point in her favor.

Operation Alex had begun. Her goal was to convince Alex of her love and commitment to him through her actions, since she'd totally screwed up with words. She'd always believed actions spoke louder than words. Now, it was time to put her money where her mouth was, so to speak.

There was enough equity in her other three stores to easily finance this purchase. She might even decide to operate her Internet store out of this location. There was a lot for her to consider.

When they arrived at Carol and Mark's, Kiesha was surprised to find Mark at home. It was still well within normal business hours. She got the greetings out of the way before turning to Mark. "I'm surprised to see you here. I thought you'd be working."

He laughed. "That's a reasonable assumption. Since I run the only pharmacy in town, I'm usually closed on Sundays and Mondays. Those are typically my slowest business days. My customers know how to reach me if there is an emergency."

One of the advantages of working in a small town, she thought. You weren't expected to keep big city hours. "It's really good you can do that. Keeps you from getting burned out and allows you to spend time with your family."

"Why don't you come into the kitchen with me and keep me company while Carol and Alex go check on their patient? You can tell me how you like our little town." He led the way into the kitchen.

There were pots simmering on the stove and something that smelled divine bubbling in a skillet. Kiesha stood at the island and watched as he stirred the contents of one pot. "Is cooking a requirement for the men around here?" True, she hadn't met all of the men in town, but Alex and Mark both cooked, and the town's only diner was run by a man. She sensed a theme.

"I can't answer for all the men in town, but my momma made sure I knew how to cook. She insisted I learn how to cook, clean, and do some basic sewing. Said a woman wanted a man who could take care of himself. So here I am, and I'm grateful to her too. The skills she taught me have really come in handy, especially now with the baby on the way." Both Carol and Mark had demanding careers. Kiesha imagined that Mark's handiness around the house was a big plus.

"I know Carol has already explained some things to you, but I wanted you to know you could feel free to ask me any questions you might have. I know what you're going through because I've been there myself. It's not easy. I just wanted you to know you had a friend if you needed one."

Kiesha was touched by the offer. If anyone could understand what she was going through, it would be Mark. "This whole thing has been crazy. One minute, I'm at home asleep in my bed. The next, I'm hanging from a tree in the woods, hundreds of miles from home. Then I discover that shape-shifters are real. I meet Alex and the sex...well, I'm sure you know what I mean. But it's okay. I tell myself that I deserve a vacation, and what's better than a mountain retreat complete with a hot guy? Then I have *the dream*."

"What dream?"

"The dream in which Conor confronted me and my decision to return home at the end of the week. He made me see Alex wasn't asking anything of me that I wasn't capable of giving, if I really wanted to. Then, while I was still dealing with that, my cousin Shayla called and issued her own set of truths. She made me see that my reluctance to commit stemmed from a fear of being hurt. Now, I can accept my feelings for Alex and admit to them. I would tell him how I feel, but I tried before and made a mess of it. I'll have to show him or he'll never believe me." She then went on to explain "Operation Alex."

Mark laughed at some of the things she shared, but for the most part was very supportive. "If you need any help, or just want a man's point of view, I'm here for you. Personally, I think you should forget about the operation and just tell Alex everything that you've told me. You might just discover that Operation Alex is unnecessary."

Before she could pursue that line of thought, Alex and Carol came into the kitchen.

"How'd it go with Shannon? Did you find out what you wanted to know?" Mark asked.

Carol gave a huff of disgust. "Not very well at all. Physically, she's all healed, but we weren't able to get any information out of her about what happened. She was about as open as a clam."

"She clearly knows what happened to her, but she's not sharing that information with us. She also seemed to be very uncomfortable around me," Alex grumbled. "I need to know what happened so that I know how to proceed. As alpha, I'm responsible for the safety of my people. I can't protect them if I don't know what or where the threat is coming from."

Listening to them, Kiesha thought, *Ya think?* Alex was a big man. He was intimidating without even trying to be. If Shannon was attacked, and her attackers were men, no wonder she'd clammed up. That's what *she* would do. "Can I try?" They all turned to her in surprise. Even Alex looked doubtful. "You said I'm you're mate, right?"

"You are," he confirmed.

"That means I'm an alpha, too, right? At least, that's according to what Conor told me when he was explaining all of this shape-shifter business to me."

"That's correct. You lead by my side."

"Okay. So let me go talk to her and see if she'll open up to me." Kiesha was reasonably confident that Shannon would.

"But we already tried," Carol began. "What makes you think she'll talk to you when she wouldn't talk to us? I'm not trying to be rude, but if Shannon wouldn't tell us anything, what makes you think you'll succeed where we failed? You're the alpha-fem, but you're still human and new to our way of doing things."

"One, I'm not a big, intimidating male. No offense, honey, but you are a very large man. You can be quite intimidating when you go into alpha mode. Two, because I *am* new. That means I have no personal agenda and no ulterior motives. I could care less about pack politics. There's no reason for her not to confide in me."

Carol still looked doubtful but Kiesha wasn't concerned about her. Since he was the alpha, Alex had the final say. She waited patiently, projecting confidence until he gave her the go ahead.

"All right, Kiesha. Give it a try."

Kiesha followed Carol to the room where Shannon was resting. She waited until Carol had walked off before knocking on the door. She heard a voice inside invite her to come in. She stuck her head around the door. "Hi, I'm Kiesha. You must be Shannon." She entered the room and closed the door behind her. As she came closer to the bed, she said, "Wow, you're really pretty. Boy, I'd never have guessed. Last night, you were a big, bloody mess. Who'd have guessed that such a large wolf could turn into such a tiny woman? You look really good compared to the other night."

When Shannon just sat there with her mouth hanging open, Kiesha blushed. "Oh, I'm so sorry. That was rude, wasn't it? I'm always doing that—just blurting out whatever I think. You'd think I'd learn by now to control my mouth. I'm new to this whole shape-shifter business, and still learning what's proper and what's not. I didn't even know you guys were real until a few nights ago."

"It's all right. No offense taken. I can see how this would all be strange to you. Can I ask you a question?"

"Sure." She couldn't imagine what kind of information Shannon would want from her, but she was game.

"Why do you smell of Alex?"

"What do you mean 'smell of him'?" Kiesha discreetly sniffed herself.

"You carry his scent on your body, as if you were his mate."

"Oh, that," Kiesha said, still not sure about the smelling like Alex bit. Was that a good thing or bad? "Well, according to him, I *am* his mate. Got the bite mark to prove it."

"If that is truly the case, why isn't he mated?"

"I just told you, *I* am his mate."

"Among shape-shifters, each mate wears a mating mark as a notice to other shifters that they are taken. You are marked. Alex is not. Why hasn't he been marked?"

"You mean to tell me that I'm mated and he's not? Nobody told me I had to mark the man, not even Alex. You'd think they would have mentioned something important like that. They tell me everything else about this true mate business, but let something like this slip under the radar. Somebody has some serious explaining to do. What until I get my hands on that mate of mine..."

"Wait! You are true mates?"

Kiesha paced around the room. She wanted to go confront Alex, but she needed to get this out of the way first. "So I'm told. Being human, I'm kinda dependent upon whatever information they chose to give me." After this latest bombshell, she was beginning to question just how open they were really being with her. There seemed to be a lot of information conveniently left out of these heart-to-heart chats she'd been having. "Why? Does it make a difference?"

"Yes, actually it does. True mates are very rare. Most men, especially alphas, won't wait for one. They go for the quick and easy mating, rather than taking a chance on not finding their true mate, and they force the women in their pack to do the same."

"Yeah, Alex mentioned that. He said he preferred to wait, instead of just settling for just anyone. He wanted the real deal." With everything else that had been going on, Kiesha had forgotten that bit of the conversation until Shannon made her think of it.

"What about the women in the pack? Does he force them to take mates?"

"You have to realize that I've only been here a few days, but since the beta is also mated to her true mate, I'd have to say no. Is that important?"

"My brother is one of those alphas that insist that all females of childbearing age be mated, especially the strong ones. It's been a source of contention between us. Kiesha, I don't mean to cut this short, but could you call Alex back into the room? There's been a misunderstanding. I'm willing to speak with him now."

"Sure, no problem. I'll go and get him. You need anything, you just let me know." Kiesha left the room, her mind occupied with the thought of Alex not being mated. When she entered the kitchen, Alex, Carol, and Mark were waiting for her. "Alex, she wants to see you." He seemed startled, but quickly left the room to answer the summons.

"Did she tell you anything?" Mark had asked the question, though Kiesha could tell Carol was equally interested in the answer.

"Yes. She told me I was mated to Alex, but apparently he isn't mated to me." She still wasn't happy about it.

"Don't worry about it," Carol said. *Easy for you to say*, Kiesha thought. "Alex is mated to you, even though he hasn't yet been marked by you. The marking will happen when you're ready, as part of the bonding process."

"So this isn't some attempt to bind me to him but leave him footloose and fancy free?" She didn't want to believe that. She was still freaked out about discovering Alex wasn't mated to her, especially now that she had made the decision to stay with him.

"Lord, no. Wherever did you get an idea like that?"

"I don't know. I guess my imagination is running rampant. Why is this the first that I'm hearing of this?" It would have been nice to know this information sooner, instead of being blindsided by it.

"Probably because it never occurred to any of us to mention it. We all believe Alex is your mate. There was never any question of that. The marking would have happened naturally once *you* accepted *him*."

Once Kiesha felt reassured, the conversation moved on to other things. She told Carol about her visit to town and the impressions she'd gained. She mentioned Alex's idea of an intern program at the high school for budding veterinarians. Mark thought it was a great idea and wondered how he could integrate the idea into his business.

While they were discussing it, Alex came back into the kitchen with Shannon trailing behind him. "Shannon is now under the protection of the Raven pack and has pledged her allegiance to me. I won't go into the details of what happened. Carol, organize an escort for Shannon to return home and pack her things. She'll be living in my parent's house until she can find accommodations of her own. She's also going to need a job, since most of the work she did was for her pack. Check among the pack and see who's hiring."

"What type of work do you do?" Kiesha was curious as to what sort of work packs needed doing that paid a salary.

"I'm a CPA, a certified public accountant. I use to handle the business accounts for my former pack and its members."

"Are you serious? Consider yourself hired. I've been keeping the books for my business, but it's getting to be too much. If you're willing and available, you can do it."

"I'm interested. What kind of business do you have?"

"I own three consignment stores back in Florida. I also conduct a lot of business via my Internet store. My managers handle the day-to-day accounts, though I check to make sure everything is correct. It's starting to take up more time than I've been willing to devote to it. If you handled the accounts for me, it would be a tremendous load off of my shoulders."

"Yes, I'll take the job. We can discuss fees and services later."

"I'm done here. Are you ready to go home?" Alex asked Kiesha.

"You're welcome to stay for dinner. There's more than enough," Mark offered.

"Maybe another time. We've been gone all day. I'm ready to head home."

Kiesha pulled Shannon to the side. "I'll get with you tomorrow with more information about the job." Then she followed Alex out the door.

Chapter Thirteen

Once home, Kiesha kissed Alex briefly and excused herself to the office. He made a note to himself to purchase another computer. He didn't think one was going to be enough to meet both of their needs.

He carried her packages up to their room and laid them on the bed. Curiosity got the better of him; he opened several to see what purchases she had made. He recognized the name of a chain known nationally for their sexy lingerie, and laid all the rest aside to focus his attention on that one. Man, oh, man, lingerie. He found bras, flimsy excuses for panties—thongs, he thought they were called—and more. Lot of lace, satin, and sheer stuff that made his cock stand at attention. He put one he liked best on the bed, and stored the rest of her things before going downstairs to prepare dinner. He hoped she would take the hint. He really couldn't wait to see her body in that shimmering bit of nothing.

Kiesha contacted the realtor about the property she'd discovered. She had them e-mail her the necessary information and expressed an interest in purchasing the building. Looking around, she made a note to talk to Alex about adding a fax machine to his home office. It would make conducting business from home so much easier.

Next, she phoned her loan officer at the credit union. She had planned to contact them tomorrow, but decided there was no reason to wait. She e-mailed her business proposal, along with the statistics on the building she wanted to purchase. She had enough available capital to purchase the building outright, but she preferred to use the bank's money and keep hers in reserve.

Once she got the ball rolling on the purchase of the property, she e-mailed her store managers about her intent to open a new store location in Refuge, asking them to keep an eye out for merchandise that could be used to stock the new location. She had some idea of things that would sell well, but she wouldn't know for certain until the business was up and running.

She'd accomplished enough for one day. She left the den to find Alex in the kitchen fixing dinner. "We need a fax machine. I could get a lot of work done at home if we had one." She stuck a finger out and dipped it into the sauce he was making, bringing it to her mouth for a taste.

He slapped her hand. "Hands out of the pot." She laughed as she moved away and sat on what she was beginning to think of as "her seat" at the bar to watch him cook.

"What did you say to Shannon to cause her to open up like that?"

"Nothing really. I was more stunned at the things she was saying to me to question her about what had happened the night she was attacked." Boy, that was an understatement. She hadn't even asked the first question. At least not any question pertaining to Shannon's injuries, which had been her intention when she'd gone into the room.

"Why? What did she say to you?"

"She wanted to know why I was mated but you weren't. When I asked her to explain, she said that you'd marked me, but I hadn't marked you, and wanted to know why. Since no one told me about the mating mark, or that it was something I was supposed to do, I was understandably confused."

After wiping his hands on a towel, he came around the bar and spun her around to face him on the stool. He cupped her face, looked her in the eye, and said in a serious tone, "I am your mate. I'm just as mated to you as you are to me, mark or no mark. I couldn't even conceive of being with anyone else now that I've had a taste of you." He sealed his words with a kiss. It wasn't a bonfire of a kiss, the kind they usually shared. This was more of a slow burn, a promise of things to come. "Don't worry about the mark. It will happen in time. In the meantime, I hope you like spaghetti, 'cause that's what's on the menu for tonight."

Unable to help herself, Kiesha began telling him her plans. "I wasn't going to tell you this—I wanted it to be a surprise—but I contacted my bank. Soon, I'll own the old hardware building in Refuge. I think it will make a great location for one of my stores. It's certainly large enough and it's in great condition, considering how long it's been sitting empty. My managers are already keeping an eye out for merchandise for this location. I even know who I'm going to ask to manage it for me. My best friend, Mary Elizabeth, works for me as one of my assistant managers. I'm going to see if I can talk her into relocating."

Once Kiesha started talking, she couldn't stop. It all came out. Her plans for remodeling the building and the employment opportunities it would bring to the residents of Refuge. She spoke all through dinner. He asked no questions other than a few for clarification. Soon, dinner was over and they worked together to put up the food and clean the kitchen.

When the kitchen was clean, Alex asked, "You want to watch another movie tonight before turning in? I'll let you choose this time."

Smiling seductively at him, she shook her head. "I have a better idea." Holding his gaze with her own, she began unbuttoning the shirt of his that she was wearing. It parted to reveal her nipples, already peaked in anticipation of the pleasures to come. "Why don't we relax in the tub? Afterward, I'll model some of the more interesting things I purchased with you in mind. Or, if you prefer, after our bath I could give you a massage." She wanted to rub her hands all over his body. The thought of it made her wet.

He snagged her by the hips, pulling her against his body while rubbing his arousal against her suggestively. "Whatever you want to do, I'm game. Lead the way."

She backed away from his body and shrugged his shirt off of her shoulders. Then she reached down, grasped the hem of her T-shirt, and pulled it over her head before letting it drop to the floor on top of his shirt. Underneath his avid gaze, she ran her hands down her body, cupping and fondling her breast before trailing her hands down to unsnap the button on her jeans. She slowly lowered the zipper, revealing the skin beneath one inch at a time.

By the time she finished, Alex was audibly panting. Shimmying her hips, she eased the jeans down until they sagged around her ankles before toeing off her shoes and kicking the jeans off of her feet. The only item of clothing remaining on her body was an itsy, bitsy, sheer thong, which barely covered anything at all. Alex reached out to bring her to him, but she jumped agilely out of the way. "Uh, uh, uh." She shook her finger at him. "Tonight, I'm in control."

Ales reined in his beast, which was jerking at its leash, and allowed his mate to take the lead. The scent of her arousal was making him crazy. Kiesha turned her back toward him, spread her legs and shook her butt from side to side to a beat only she could hear. Seductively, she bent from the waist and picked up the clothes off of the floor. Her action gave him an enticing view of her damp, cloth-covered pussy. She was as turned on as he was. The proof of her arousal caused his dick to jump in his pants. He didn't know if he was going to survive this night with his sanity intact.

He followed her out of the kitchen, enjoying the sway of her almost bare ass. As he entered the bedroom behind her, he began to take off his clothing when she stopped him. "Allow me." He immediately prayed for strength.

She slid her hands inside the front of his jeans, her fingers lightly grazing his cock, and tugged him into the bathroom. He got another glimpse of her ass as she stepped away from him for a moment to fill the tub. When she turned back, she slid her hands up his chest, taking his shirt and easing it over his head. Once the shirt was off, she pressed kisses all over his chest, nibbling and licking at his nipples, causing him to groan. "I love your chest."

Kissing her way down the center of his chest, she opened the button on his jeans and pulled down the zipper with her teeth. Alex inhaled sharply and made a low-pitched growling sound. She was so sexy.

Kiesha stepped back and admired the effect of his jeans framing his long, hard cock. He wasn't wearing underwear and his jeans had sagged just enough to form a "V," drawing attention to his erection. "Mmm, that looks good. Maybe I should see if you taste as good as you look." Slowly, she bent over and rubbed her face against his erection before licking the tip delicately. She made sure he had a good view of her butt, knowing he had a thing for it. She allowed her breath to caress him as she eased his jeans down his legs. When they were around his feet, she tapped his leg, signaling him to lift up so she could remove the jeans from his body. Once they were completely off, she tossed them to the side.

A single glance showed that the tub was full. She leaned over and turned the water off. She felt Alex's hands as they glided over her behind. Smiling at him as she turned around, she motioned to her thong. "Will you help me with this?"

"You want me to use my mouth or my hands?"

"Your hands will do." She couldn't handle his mouth near her right now. She was too turned on. Alex slid his hand inside the lacy fabric and cupped her mound. Then, he teased her lightly before ripping the panties off of her body.

Not exactly what she had in mind, but the primal urge behind the action made her shiver with arousal.

He helped her into the tub before sliding in beside her. She immediately turned to him and rubbed her body against his, purring like a cat because it felt so good. She had poured some bath oils into the tub, and the oily water caused their bodies to glide sensuously together. She'd wanted to prolong the anticipation and drive Alex crazy with need, but tables turned on her. In her attempt to make him lose control, *she* was losing control. She needed relief. Now.

She pulled on his neck until his mouth met hers. She moved his hand from her waist and guided his fingers between her legs. She rubbed against his hand, showing him what she wanted him to do. "I thought I could wait, but I can't. I need to come now. Please, make me come."

Alex took control of the kiss as he gave her what she needed. He thrust his fingers inside of her wet sheath, beginning with two and then adding another, all the while grinding the palm of his hand against her clit. She rode his fingers, her motions frantic as she sought relief from the pressure building inside of her. In seconds, she exploded, her hands fisting in his hair as she rode out the wave of the orgasm.

Kiesha collapsed against Alex's chest, trying to get herself together while he stroked her back. "Thank you," she whispered against his neck.

"My pleasure."

Now that she'd gained some relief, she could get back on track with her program, which was simply to drive him crazy. A simple, but hopefully effective plan. She bathed him with her hands, paying particular attention to those spots that caused him to moan, committing them to memory as she explored his body. As many times as they'd made love, this was the first time she'd been in control. She allowed him to bathe her in return, his efforts bringing a second release.

Kiesha drained the tub and motioned for Alex to get out as she followed. She quickly dried them both off before leading him out of the bathroom. At the bed, she spread a towel over the covers and had Alex lay on it. When she noticed the nightgown he had laid out, she smiled wickedly and put it on.

In the bathroom, she found the oil and set it by the bed where it could be easily reached, then lit the candles Alex had scattered throughout the room. After turning off the overhead light, she put on a bluesy jazz CD she'd found earlier to help set the mood.

Alex lay on his back, hands beneath his head, watching her every move. His erection stood upright, long and proud, the tip damp with a bit of precum. "You look great in that outfit."

She bowed in a mock curtsey. "Why, thank you, kind sir." She'd have to be sure to buy a few more like this. He'd chosen a low-cut, red, sheer chemise held together at the top and on the sides with strings. She wore it without the matching thong, her body both covered and on display at the same time.

Kiesha twirled a finger, motioning for Alex to roll over onto his stomach. Then, she picked up the self-warming oil and trickled some on his body. Smearing the oil on his back, she liberally coated her hands and massaged his feet. She took her time. It gave her pleasure to be able to please him.

His muscles flexed and relaxed as she worked out the knots. When she reached his lower back, she straddled his body. Each stroke caused the lips of her pussy to lightly rub against him, sending a tingling sensation up her spine.

As she stretched to reach his neck, the angle caused the friction on her pussy to increase. Though she'd climaxed twice already, she could felt another building. She fought against the need. She was determined that he be deep inside of her when she came again.

Kiesha lifted until she crouched above him. "Turn over." Once in position, she dropped back on to her knees, her pussy directly over his cock. She had intended to massage both sides of his body, but that was going to have to wait.

"Leave it on," he commanded, when she began to remove the chemise.

"Okay." She slid her slit up and down his erection, the movement building the pressure in her womb. Kiesha fisted his cock, angling him for penetration. Alex held her, helping her to balance as she slid her body down on top of his thick shaft. With her hands braced against chest, she began a slow circular motion, grinding her clit against his pubic bone. The cords on his neck stood out as he held himself in check, allowing her to take her pleasure with his body.

"Sit up," she said, and Alex shifted forward. Kiesha gripped the headboard and leaned forward to kiss him. As she pulled away, she rode him, slowly at first, then faster as she gained more confidence. Taking her hands off of the headboard, she thrust her hands in her hair, arching her back.

Alex played with her breasts, twisting and tugging on her nipples in the manner that she liked best. The added sensation caused a growl to rise up and roll out of her throat. She felt something stirring, deep down inside of her.

When she growled, Alex's eyes narrowed. Kiesha knew he had been holding back, allowing her to set the pace. She literally felt his control slipping as he braced his hands on the bed and began to thrust upward. His movements upset her balance. She grabbed his shoulders to steady herself. Once in sync with his rhythm, she met each of Alex's strokes with one of her own. Something powerful broke loose inside of her. On its heels came her release. It roared through her, mightier than she'd ever felt before. Unable to handle it, she reared forward and locked her teeth on his neck, biting down hard until blood welled up in her mouth.

Feeling her marking him as her mate, Alex's beast broke loose. He flipped Kiesha onto her back, his body still power driving into hers. He licked and ate at her mouth until all traces of blood were gone. He lifted his face until they were nose to nose and noticed that her pupils were different. The gold-colored eyes of a she-wolf stared back at him.

He rose to his knees, lifted her up, and flipped her over in one simultaneous motion. Alex grabbed her hips, then pulled her toward him. Once she was on her hands and knees, he began to fuck her the way his wolf demanded. Her upper body was pressed to the bed, her legs spread as wide as they could go, ass up in the air, submitting herself to his domination. He growled in approval before locking his teeth down on her shoulder.

Alex wrapped an arm around her waist and held her tight as he hammered into her body, not allowing her to move. She whimpered with each thrust, heating his blood and driving him crazy. With his teeth locked onto her shoulder, he moaned. He felt her pussy clamp down in a viselike grip, then Kiesha threw her head back against his shoulder and howled her release to the world.

Locked tight in her body, her release brought about his. He pressed deep inside of her. Her body contracted around his, milking the seed from his body until he was totally drained.

He rolled onto his back, his arm still pinned beneath her, and gasped for breath. Shit, he'd never felt anything like that before. Glancing to the right, he noticed Kiesha hadn't moved. "You all right?" She mumbled something. "S'okay, long as you're all right." Damn, now he was slurring his words.

His wolf was content. He had his mate, and from the smell of her, there would soon be a cub running around the house. He had no idea if his mate even wanted kids. "Babe, how do you feel about children?"

She was totally clueless as to what he was hinting at. She was still blown away by the experience she'd just had. She'd bit him…hard. She reached up to feel her teeth. She was too far gone to notice, but they'd felt a little different, sharper maybe. She thought she'd felt her canines lengthening right before she'd locked down on his shoulder.

"How do you feel about us having children?"

"I hadn't really thought about it." Her teeth felt normal enough now. Maybe she'd imagined the whole thing.

"Honey, maybe you need to start. I think you're pregnant."

"What did you say?" She pushed up onto her elbows and looked at him. She hadn't really been paying attention before, but now she was totally focused. *Did he just say I'm pregnant?*

Alex removed his arm from beneath her. "I said, I think you're pregnant. Actually, I'm pretty sure you are. Your scent changed and is getting stronger. That means you've conceived."

Kiesha thought about it for a moment. She searched inside for any feelings of panic, any traces of reluctance. She found none. Actually, she was cool with the idea. She loved him. He loved her. She wasn't getting any younger and her biological clock was ticking. What could be more natural than having a child with the man you love? "Okay."

"Okay? That's all you have to say?" He rose up onto one elbow. "Shouldn't you be upset? Where's the panic? The outrage and recriminations? You're being way too calm!"

"I'm okay with it." She wondered what the big deal was. Obviously, she wasn't reacting the way he wanted her to. Men!

"That's *it*?!"

She took a really good look at him. That's when she noticed the fear in his eyes. Oh, poor baby. Her big, strong alpha was afraid she wouldn't want his child. Kiesha pushed him onto his back and rolled over on top of him. Allowing her knees to fall to the sides, she sat up and leaned over him. With her forearms on his chest, she lowered her face until they were eyeball-to-eyeball with their noses touching. "I love you." She hoped he saw the sincerity in her eyes. "How could I not love any child that we create?" At her words, his penis, which was trapped between them, hardened.

He rolled them until he was on top, and then braced his body on his forearms. His nose touched hers, mirroring what she'd done to him. "And I love you. I've waited a long time for you. I'm absolutely ecstatic at the knowledge we've created a child." One of his hands slid down over her stomach possessively, covering their child where he lay. His arousal nudged at her opening. As she angled her hips to receive him, she arched her eyebrow in disbelief. "Again?"

He smiled in answer to her question. "With you? Always."

Epilogue

Alex had been true to his word.

Within a couple of days, Shannon was moved into his parents' house, which sat on the outer edge of his property. As far as she knew, only one other house was on the road past her own. Some of the wolves from the Raven pack had escorted her home, helped her collect her things, and move. Her brother had shown up to watch the proceedings, not saying a word.

She had formally resigned both of her positions. As well as being the pack's accountant, she was also the alpha-fem, second only to her brother. Rory had accepted it without complaint, but the look in his eyes had let her know things were not finished between them.

Shannon, however, had bigger problems to worry about.

She had a new home and job, but something felt wrong with her body. Something was different, and had been since the night of the attack. She couldn't put her finger on it; she just knew something was off. She was waiting for Alex to return to make an appointment to see him.

He and Kiesha had traveled to Florida to pack her things and to put her condo up for sale. Shannon was scheduled to begin work when they returned. Kiesha didn't anticipate them being gone for more than a week or two, since she already had a buyer for her condo—her cousin Shayla. In the meantime, Shannon took advantage of the break to get settled into her new home.

There was something strange going on. She felt as though she were being watched.

It happened mostly at night. She would look around, but no one would be there, at least no one she could see. She couldn't detect anyone with her senses either, yet she couldn't shake the feeling. It caused the hairs on the back of her neck to stand up. Her wolf self felt it, too, and was getting agitated because it couldn't determine the source of the threat.

As if that weren't enough, she'd been having these really intense sexual dreams, her body aroused into a sexual frenzy. They all featured the same man.

She couldn't see his face, no matter how hard she tried, but she could hear his voice. It haunted her throughout the day. No doubt about it, she couldn't wait until Alex got back. Maybe he could fix what was wrong with her. If he couldn't, she was afraid that she would lose her mind.

~ * ~

NIKOLAI'S WOLF

Chapter One

"Shannon! Shannon! Where the hell are you?"

The door closed with such force, it rattled the whole house. Shannon rolled her eyes and kept logging figures into her spreadsheet. He'd find her soon enough. She was in the same spot every day.

Her brother, Rory, stormed into the office. "I just spoke to MacDougal. He said you turned him down. That's the third one this week!"

She didn't even glance away from the computer screen. "If you would stop setting them up for failure, we wouldn't keep having this problem."

He pounded his hand on the desk, causing the monitor to shake. "I have to do *something*. If I left it up to you, you'd never take a mate. You're twenty-nine. Most females your age are mated and have several cubs."

Oh, great. Time for another one of those discussions.

Shannon sighed, saved her spreadsheet, and finally turned to face him. "I'm not most females my age. If I decide to take a mate, it will be one of my own choosing. Stop shoving men at me. All you're doing is pissing me off."

Rory growled in frustration and began to pace. "Shannon, you have a responsibility to mate and produce pups. It's for the continuation of our species. As the alpha-fem, you have to set an example for rest of the females, no matter how few of them there are."

Her eyes narrowed. "Cut the crap, Rory. You could care less about 'the continuation of our species.' Don't you mean the continuation of our family line? God, I never thought I'd hear myself say this, but you're starting to sound just like Dad."

"Well, he was right about this at least. We are the last of the McFelans. If we don't have pups, the line will die with us. Then who's going to lead the pack? Do you want that to happen, Shannon? Do you?" He planted his hands on the desk and leaned forward aggressively, getting into her space.

God, he is laying it on thick. Shannon relaxed back into her chair and crossed her arms over her chest.

"Rory, quit trying to lay a guilt trip on me. It's not going to work. If you don't want the McFelan name to die out, produce your own pups." As soon as the words left her mouth, she inwardly winced.

Her brother had been spreading his seed around like water since he was old enough to know what to do with it. As far as she knew, there wasn't a female in the pack over the age of consent he hadn't fucked. None of it had taken root. He had to be thinking he was the first infertile McFelan in generations. Maybe that's why he was becoming obsessed with her lack of a love life.

Rory grew completely still, and his face turned red, then white. Supernatural power spiked, raising the hair on her arms. His flesh rippled, and his eyes turned golden. *Crap!* His wolf was rising to the surface.

Shannon eased away from the computer, calling forth her wolf as she did. She didn't let it out but held it ready, waiting to see what he would do next. She didn't want to fight with Rory, but she would if his wolf attacked. She wouldn't be dominated by anyone, not even her beloved big brother.

Minutes passed as he visibly struggled with his beast, trying to push it back down. Finally, he regained control of his temper. "I don't want to fight with you. You *will* take a mate. I've called a gathering for tonight. Be there, and for once in your life, try to remember that you're supposed to be a bitch, not butch."

The door slammed behind him as he left.

* * *

A big, bright, and full yellow moon dominated the night sky. Despite making her best effort to get there on time, Shannon was one of the last to arrive. The gathering place, little more than a large clearing in the woods a couple of miles outside of town, was already packed.

The minute she joined the others waiting, her gaze connected with Rory's. *Oh shit, he's planning something.* Something she knew in her bones she wasn't going to like. A glance at the other members of the pack showed they sensed it as well. They stood in groups, talking quietly, throwing uneasy glances at the alpha.

As Rory climbed to the raised natural platform in the center of the clearing, his red hair glowed in the moonlight, and his power flowed outward like waves. All around him the silence grew and swelled with expectancy.

No longer was he her brother. The McFelan, alpha of the Sparrowhawks, stood before them. Allowing his power to continue to rise and surround him like an aura, Rory began to speak. "Tonight, we *hunt*!"

There were gasps and murmurs all around. Shannon stood still as shock waves rippled through her body. He'd called a hunt. *Sneaking, conniving, manipulative bastard.*

He waited for the pack to settle down before he continued. "All of the eligible, unmated she-wolves will be given a five-minute lead. Unmated males will begin hunting on my say. Once you've captured and subdued your mate, bring her before the council for formal recognition. All challenges will be settled by combat. In the case of a draw, the female will decide. No killing."

He waited, giving the rules a chance to sink in. "Let the hunt *begin*!"

Shannon took off running, cursing Rory with every step. Hunts were archaic, even for packs as locked into the past as the Sparrowhawks. He said he was trying to bring the pack forward. *Damn it! What was he thinking?*

In ancient times, once a year she-wolves of a certain age were gathered on the night of a full moon. They were given a head start and then the unmated males of the pack were set loose. If two or more males trapped the same female, the decision of which male claimed her was settled by combat and most often resulted in death. Once the male subdued his female—and by that, they meant fucked into submission—

the couple was brought before the council to have their mating formally recognized.

There were only two ways to avoid being claimed. The first was to make it to daybreak without being caught. Sunrise ended the hunt. The second was to keep from being subdued. Shannon hoped not to be captured, but if she was, it was a bet that she wasn't going to be mounted. She'd fight the whole damned pack before she'd allow a mate to be chosen for her this way.

She ran as fast as she could with the rest of the fleeing females, then veered off in the opposite direction. There were ten unmated females who fit the age requirements, and about thirty unmated males. Those were three-to-one odds, at best. Because she was the alpha-fem, none of the omegas—the weakest of the wolves—would give chase. Unfortunately, that still left the betas. Get enough of them on her tail, and she'd have a serious fight on her hands.

She ran uphill, through the toughest terrain she could find, hoping to slow her pursuers. When she'd gained a comfortable lead, she stopped and stripped, knowing she'd make better time in her wolf form. Unfortunately, her scent would also be stronger, but she couldn't afford not to shift. She needed all the help she could get.

She backtracked a bit and threw her pants in one direction, then came forward and threw her shirt in the opposite direction, hoping it would confuse them and buy her more time.

Rory howled. A chorus sounded with him, echoing through the night. The males were coming. If she could just make it to the ridge, there were places to hide and water to cover her scent. Damn, why hadn't she figured out ahead of time that he would do something like this? She'd been caught flat-footed and off guard, never good when dealing with Rory.

When she began, the wind had been in her favor, carrying her scent away from the pack. Now, she was running into the wind, her scent trailing like a beacon behind her, announcing her whereabouts to any shifter who wanted to know.

She could hear them behind her, gaining on her. She couldn't tell how many, but it was definitely more than one. Crap, she wasn't going to be able to outrun them. That meant she had to fight.

Shannon altered her course, already knowing the perfect place to make her stand. According to the rules, if more than one male cornered her, they had to fight with each other to determine who got to claim her. She couldn't escape while they were fighting, but it would give her time to catch her breath and gather her strength while she studied her opponents.

She rushed into the small clearing and turned to face her pursuers, hackles raised. At her back was a rock-faced wall where the mountain soared above them. It was surrounded by dense forest on three sides, forming a natural arena.

As they entered the clearing, she wasn't surprised to see Caleb Jones and Michael MacDougal, Rory's second and third. What absolutely floored her was the sight of her brother with them. *What kind of trickery was this?*

MacDougal was a big, burly bear of a man who'd made no secret of his ambition to one day be alpha. He would have challenged her father if it hadn't been for Rory. MacDougal was all right, but she knew he didn't see her as a person, just a means to the end. Mating her would automatically boost his position and prestige within the pack. She would be no man's stepladder to success.

Besides, MacDougal was old-fashioned and dominant as hell. With her petite build and small stature, he was sure to try to intimidate her, just like her father had her mother. The first time he tried to forcefully bend her to his will, she'd kill him. There was no way he would be her mate.

Caleb, she actually liked. He was a good man and a strong wolf, not to mention extremely attractive with his dark skin, lean, muscular build, and long, carefully maintained dreadlocks. He would have been a consideration, except he didn't move her. The thought of mating with him left the woman in her cold. There was no spark of attraction, no passion, nothing. She didn't want to fight him and risk damaging their friendship, but she would if necessary. This was *her* life they were messing with. She couldn't afford to throw away her future because her soft nature got in the way. There was no choice. No matter which man won, she would face off with the winner.

She sat back on her haunches and rested. She studied them as they trod into the clearing. Rory was the massive red wolf with a large barrel chest. In wolf form, he was the size of a small pony. As a man, he was short, standing only five-nine, but stocky, thick with muscle.

Michael was equally large. His fur was a dull grayish black that reminded her of mud. She'd seen him fight before and knew he used sheer brute strength in combat. Caleb was the smaller of the two suitors. His coat was the gray of a timber wolf, complete with all the traditional markings. Of the three, he was the only one who could pass as a regular wolf. He was also the most vicious. He never quit, and he didn't give an inch. A fight between Michael and Caleb should be interesting. Maybe they'd kill each other and save her the trouble. On second thought, that's probably why Rory was there—to make sure no one died.

Instead of confronting each other as she expected, her brother and Caleb sat down on their haunches on the side of the clearing, out of the way. Michael approached with his head and tail high, his steps oozing confidence. The fool actually thought she'd submit. She crouched in challenge, ears straight, and growled. Something was wrong. This wasn't the way things were done. Even her wolf knew and was angry.

Her brother's words about acting like a bitch came back to mind. It was suddenly obvious. He had handpicked one of these men to be her mate. These were the two he had thrown at her most often. Tonight, he was hoping one of these men would leave the clearing victorious.

She looked at Rory and snarled again, low in her throat, expressing her displeasure. Michael growled in return. She knew her refusal to simply drop and present herself for mounting would infuriate him. He would see it as a challenge to his manhood. They circled each other warily, watching to see what the other would do. She waited, knowing Michael would use his size to try to overpower her.

Suddenly, he sprang. Agile on her feet, she rolled out of the way. In the process, she caught him with a quick nip to his sensitive underbelly, drawing first blood. Spinning around, she crouched, already waiting when he landed and turned.

She'd surprised him. No one, with the exception of Rory, knew how well she could fight. MacDougal thought she'd be an easy victory. Now he was pissed. Although with his ego, he more than likely thought she got in a lucky blow.

He came at her again, using the same attack, confirming her low opinion of his cognitive ability. Wanting this over, she pulled every dirty trick her brother had ever taught her and defeated him quickly with only a few scratches to show for it.

Michael would have continued to fight, no doubt unable to believe that a woman defeated him, but her brother called him off. It was either stop as commanded or face the McFelan.

As MacDougal skulked away, Caleb entered the clearing. She felt like a wrestler being tag-teamed by her opponents.

Caleb was closer to her size. He was also fast and could think on his feet, which was why he was Rory's second. She watched Caleb closely, knowing he'd had time to sit and study her fighting techniques. She wouldn't catch him off guard like she had Michael.

He stalked slowly into the clearing, giving her time to submit. When she didn't turn and present herself, he growled, low and vicious. She'd hoped when he realized she wasn't interested that he would let it go. But for some unknown reason, he seemed to want her just as badly as MacDougal did.

She was tired, and Caleb was fresh. She couldn't let him draw this thing out or her weariness would work against her. She took the initiative and charged. The only thing she had working for her right now was that he wasn't trying to kill her. She wasn't in a fight for her life, just her virtue. Of course, being mated to a man she didn't want could be deemed as fighting for her life.

Caleb was ready for her and only sheer determination got her away from him without being pinned when his jaw locked around her throat. He was patient, toying with her, waiting her out. He knew time was on his side. He harassed her just enough to keep her on the move and from catching her breath. Sheer desperation gave her the strength she needed to defeat him, that and timely interference from her brother. Rory must have realized how determined she was not to submit, and called Caleb off.

As she stood there with her tongue hanging out and her sides heaving, Rory approached her. By this time she was ready to drop from pain and exhaustion as the adrenaline began to wear off. There were deep gouges in several places where she hadn't moved quickly enough. Had Caleb actually been trying to kill her, no doubt she'd be dead. She wanted to shift back and heal herself, but she refused to be naked in front of these two, especially after tonight.

She needed to close her eyes and rest, but that would have to wait until this entire fiasco was over. She couldn't afford to show any weakness, not now. She waited uncertainly to see what would happen, for the rules as she knew them had seemingly been thrown out the proverbial window. She felt like she was playing a game where she was the only player who didn't have a copy of the rule book. She'd always hated being left in the dark.

Rory was pissed. This was not going as planned. Shannon was too strong and stubborn for her own good. No shifter in the pack would have her now, not after she'd defeated two of their strongest males. She would never find a mate.

Look at her, bleeding and exhausted, but still proud.

When he came toward her, he did so as the McFelan. She should show him proper respect—ears, tail, and head down—especially in front of others. Though she knew how important it was to him to maintain a proper image, she stood there tall and proud, unconsciously issuing a silent challenge he couldn't afford to ignore now that his men knew just how strong Shannon really was.

The Sparrowhawks weren't ready to deal with an alpha she-wolf. Their way of thinking was too backward. He was trying to bring them out of the dark ages, but it would take time. Time, thanks to Shannon, he no longer had.

For the well-being of the pack, he knew what he had to do. Rory attacked.

Though he'd caught her by surprise, she responded instinctively, just the way he'd taught her. Had this been a real dominance fight, he'd have shown no mercy, but this was about teaching his baby sister a lesson—to show her alpha the proper respect.

As they circled each other, another plan came to his mind that was so genius in its simplicity, he didn't know why he hadn't thought of it before. Shannon needed a mate, one who was strong enough to tame her wolf, yet gentle enough to treat her with the love and respect she deserved. His wolves had already proven themselves too weak, but his was not the only pack in the area.

Just a few short miles away as the crow—or bird shifter—flew was another pack full of strong, unmated males, including Alex Wolfe, their alpha. The Ravens had twice as many unmated males as the Sparrowhawks, including some alphas.

He needed to get his sister to the Raven pack.

Concentrating on Shannon once more, he attacked with a controlled savagery. He knew just where to bite to inflict the most pain but the least amount of permanent physical damage, and he used that knowledge ruthlessly.

Shannon didn't have much fight left. He lashed at her until her wolf took control, turned, and ran. With his betas at his back, he herded her east toward the Raven pack, nipping at her heels whenever she tried to retreat to the safety of their home.

He kept her fleeing until she reached the Raven pack's territory. To ensure she stayed there, he took a chunk out of the tendon in one of her hind legs. By now, she was bleeding profusely. He ran her until she collapsed. Then he backed off, letting her think he'd gone away. She immediately dragged herself until she could go no farther.

When she was down, Rory sent his betas back to the gathering place. He let out a howl of triumph, one guaranteed to be heard, hoping Alex Wolfe came to investigate. Then he sat and watched her from a distance, protecting her from predators and any human seeking to do her harm.

Hearing a sound, he backed into the shadows. He was upwind so he had no fear of his presence being detected. He watched carefully as an unfamiliar male approached his sister. Rory sniffed the air. The male smelled like a wolf-shifter and was moving slowly, so as not to alarm or startle her.

Once he was sure the shifter was there to help Shannon, he headed home. He would miss having his baby sister around, but it was for her own good. After tonight's events, the council would have made her life a living hell. They were already saying she was unnaturally strong, and they hadn't even seen the true extent of her power. By defeating two of the highest-ranking males in the pack, she'd done the unforgivable. As the alpha-fem, her actions would set an undesirable precedent with the other females, one which the council, with their outdated ways, would not tolerate.

The Raven pack was run the way a pack should be. Their alpha was an honorable man and a strong wolf. Alex Wolfe was one of the few alphas Rory's father had respected. If Shannon had to go to another pack, he couldn't have picked a better alpha to entrust her to. They would be good to her, or he would truly become his father's son and kill them all.

Chapter Two

The strong scent of shifter blood hit Nikolai Taranosky's nostrils. Normally he kept to himself, but something about the smell called to him, and his beast rose in response. Giving in to impulse, he shape-shifted into a raven and went to investigate the source of that divine smell.

After circling the area, he found the injured shifter on the ridge overlooking the river. He landed out of sight a few feet away and shifted back into his natural form. Before stepping into the clearing and revealing himself, he disguised his appearance and scent to that of a shifter from the Raven pack, just in case any of the wolf's brethren were close.

Nikolai approached carefully. Though it appeared to be half-dead, he knew appearances could be deceiving. As he drew closer, he tried scanning the creature's mind but was blocked. This shifter was strong and possessed a natural barrier, making it difficult for him to connect with it, even in wolf form.

When he was close enough to touch it, he slowly lowered to the ground to see how badly it was injured. At its most vulnerable, the wolf launched at him, aiming for his throat. Nikolai was caught off guard. He reflexively threw up an arm to protect his face.

The enraged wolf locked down on his arm, its bite savage as it attempted to snap the bone in two. He sensed the moment the wolf swallowed some of his blood. The protective barrier vanished. Nikolai instantly seized control.

“Be at peace. Sleep.” He buried every ounce of compulsion he could within the commands.

The wolf immediately lost consciousness. Nikolai gently pried its mouth open and removed his arm, examining it to see the extent of the damage. It was nasty looking and painful, but the wound would heal quickly.

He turned his attention to the sleeping wolf, their minds still firmly linked. The she-wolf bled profusely from several wounds, which appeared to be fairly recent. She should be healing or at least shape-shifting back into her normal state to speed the process. That she hadn’t revealed the seriousness of her condition.

Knowing he couldn’t just leave her, Nikolai picked her up and flew with her to the one place where he knew she would receive the medical attention she needed. Alex Wolfe lived nearby. Not only was Alex the Raven pack’s alpha, he was the doctor all local shape-shifters used. Nikolai wouldn’t say that they were friends. They shared the natural wariness of two predators residing within the same territory. They each recognized the other’s power and had no desire to test to see which one of them was stronger.

He landed in the yard and walked slowly, in a nonthreatening manner, to the door. From the looks of things, Alex was entertaining. No telling how many shifters were inside. They should be alerted to his presence any minute now.

He was surprised when he made it as far as the porch without being noticed. The smell of blood was overpowering. Both he and the she-wolf were covered in it. Though her bleeding seemed to be lessening, it hadn't completely stopped. He walked up onto the porch and called out, "Alex, it's Nikolai. Open up."

The door opened immediately. With one all-encompassing glance, Alex took in the sight of Nikolai and the bloody, wounded wolf in his arms. "Please enter, Nikolai."

Pushing the door open with his shoulder, Nikolai strode past Alex. He barely acknowledged the other people in the room. "I found her down by the ridge. She must have been attacked. She's lost a lot of blood."

"Place her over here. Carol, go get my supplies while I take a look at her." Sweeping the throw off the back of the couch, Alex laid it on the floor in front of the fireplace.

"You say you found her out by the ridge?" The question came from the other male wolf.

"Yes. You won't find any sign of her attackers there now. I checked before bringing her to you. From what I could see, she must have dragged herself quite a distance before her strength gave out." Nikolai's gaze never left the wolf being examined on the floor. He had been strangely reluctant to put her down. His body was tense, waiting, for what he didn't know.

The female wolf that must be Carol came back with the requested supplies. As Alex moved to clean her wounds, Nikolai gave warning. "Be careful. I had to place her under compulsion before I could get close enough to her to help.

She was very defensive and half-crazed with pain." He watched closely as Alex tended to her injuries, ready to snatch her away should the doctor make a wrong move.

"While many of her wounds are severe and need stitching, none are life-threatening. She's already beginning to heal," Alex informed them.

"Do you recognize her? She doesn't smell like pack," the other wolf asked Alex.

"Yes, I know who she is," Alex said. "She's not one of ours. Her name is Shannon. She belongs to the Sparrowhawks. Her brother's the alpha."

"Are you going to contact him? Tell him what's happened?" Carol questioned.

Alex shook his head. "We don't know what happened, but until I do, this stays between us. We'll keep an eye on her and protect her while she's healing. She would heal faster if she could shift, but she's lost too much blood."

Nikolai approved of Alex's answer. Any brother who would allow something like this to happen to his sister didn't deserve to be contacted.

"We have got to keep this from getting out," Alex continued. "The pack wouldn't normally be a problem, but this is a small area and news travels fast. We can't take a chance on word getting back to the wrong ears."

Alex stitched up the worst of her injuries and poured some kind of liquid on them. Then he injected her with a shot of something. Finally finished, he removed his gloves as Carol quietly began to clean up. "She needs to be watched for a few hours."

Putting what was left of the supplies back in the bag, Carol responded, "She can come home with us. She'll need clothes and stuff. If we're keeping her presence a secret, we won't be able to send someone to her home to pick up her things. If necessary, I'll tell the pack I need some more items for Kiesha. Let them believe you got her size wrong."

"Do whatever you think best." Alex turned to Nikolai. "Is there any way that she could be tracked here?"

"No, but I'll backtrack and make sure."

"Thank you. You have the gratitude of the Raven pack for bringing her to us." It was a formal way of saying that the pack was now indebted to him.

Nikolai nodded, not particularly concerned with vamp/shifter politics and shifter protocol at the moment. He took one more lingering glaze at the she-wolf he'd rescued before striding out the door.

Outside, Nikolai breathed in deeply of the night air. Opening his senses, he gathered information from the wind. The evening was quiet, the animals of the forest still as if they recognized the predator in their midst. Other than himself and the people in the house, the woods were empty.

He shape-shifted into a large raven, flew back to the spot by the ridge where he'd found the she-wolf, and made sure her whereabouts couldn't be traced to Alex. Then, compelled beyond all reason, he tracked the she-wolf to the home where she was resting, using her mental signature as a guide. Masking his presence from her caretakers, he turned into mist and entered the home, reforming himself at her bedside.

He gazed at the she-wolf who'd managed to spark his interest after all these years of ennui and wondered what she looked like in human form. Not one to deny himself anything he truly desired, he fully connected to her mentally and commanded her to shift. She flowed seamlessly from a wolf into a beautiful redhead. He studied her naked form, surprised to realize that his penis was hard. It had been so long since he'd felt real physical desire, it took him a moment to recognize the sensation.

While he luxuriated in the forgotten pleasure of arousal running through his veins, he tried to figure out what it was about her that called to him. He'd seen beautiful women before, ones with better figures. She was a bit too petite for his taste. He liked tall women to complement his own six-four stature. He'd be lucky if this one came to his chest. She had to be five-two, maybe five-three if she stretched herself.

The word "pixie" came to mind.

His gaze followed the slight curve of her stomach to the apex of her thighs. The sight of the red curls there caused his cock to jerk in his pants. *How interesting!*

As he stared at those curls, he imagined himself parting them with his tongue and tasting her essence. Lost in his fantasy, he didn't immediately notice her breathing had sped up. Nikolai glanced at her face. Seeing that she was still asleep, he let his gaze wander again. Her breasts caught his attention. Where before they'd been lax in her drug-induced sleep, her nipples were now pointed little beads, proclaiming her arousal. He could smell her desire. It amazed him that she was so attuned to him.

Nikolai closed his mental link with her, stepped away from the bed, and backed himself into a corner of the room. He wanted to determine if it was his thoughts or his presence to which she was responding. He looked away and willed his body to cool down. He thought of the mundane and kept his gaze off the bed until he was in control again.

As his arousal subsided, he glanced once more at the woman. Her nipples were still peaked, and the curls between her legs glistened as the juice of her arousal dampened them. The beast within him rose, and he lost a good deal of the control he'd just attained.

Unable to resist the temptation, he crossed to the bed and dipped his finger in her honey-dampened curls, being careful not to touch the flesh below. Once his finger was coated in her juice, he brought it to his mouth. The taste of her caused his fangs to explode in his mouth as his beast jerked on its leash. In this instance, retreat was the better part of valor.

Nikolai quickly streamed out of the house and headed home, tightening the leash on his beast as he left. His sense of fair play wouldn't allow him to take an unconscious woman. Had he stayed any longer, he'd have taken her, right or wrong. It didn't help knowing that on some level of her consciousness, she'd been aware of his presence and her body had responded, welcoming his. He needed to research what that meant.

* * *

Rory took his time returning to the pack, not wanting to face them just yet. Sometimes being their leader was a real pain in the ass. All around him, the sounds of howling, yipping, and growling could be heard as males found and subdued their mates.

He entered the clearing as others began returning from the hunt. First, the unsuccessful males filed in. Then, little by little, the newly mated pairs arrived. He was glad to see some of the troublemaking females had been mated. Those females were cock-teasers. Having so many males to choose from had made them prima donnas, holding out, always waiting to see if someone better was going to come along.

One female, Yana, was a particular thorn in his side. She'd made sure everyone knew she had her sights set on being his mate, as if he'd have her or any other female in this pack that kept throwing herself at him, trying to attract his attention. He hadn't touched any of them since his father died. He hoped all of them had been claimed. It would be one less headache for him.

As he'd expected, Rory was immediately confronted by the members of the council. The council was made up of three of the older men in the pack. Their job was to advise him and to help enforce pack law. Among them were Graham, the pack's historian; Bertram, a former alpha of one of the packs his father had taken over who had been allowed to step down, a rarity since his father normally killed them; and Wesley, newest to the council and the most arrogant.

"Where's Shannon?" Graham demanded.

"What do you plan to do about her? This can't be tolerated. A female that refuses to do her duty and submit? What if word gets out?" Bertram added.

"The problem's been dealt with." Rory hoped his tone told them this discussion was closed.

Wesley was unwise enough to push the issue. "How do we know it's been sufficiently dealt with? She should be brought before the council. We'll make sure a suitable punishment is devised. After all, Shannon's your sister, and you've always been protective of her."

"Are you questioning *me*?" All the anger and pain that he was feeling burst loose. Rory shifted and attacked. Quicker than a blink, he had Wesley on the ground, his teeth locked down on his throat.

"No, alpha. Forgive me." Wesley pleaded for his life while the acrid scent of his fear rose.

Having sufficiently made his point, Rory released Wesley and shifted back to his human form. His power swelled until it filled the air around him, and he angrily demanded, "Does anyone else have any more questions?"

People dropped to their knees, assuming a submissive position before him until only he was left standing. No one said a word.

"Then I suggest we turn our attention to formally recognizing the newly mated pairs. Let the ceremony commence."

* * *

Shannon paced her room, waiting to speak with Alex for the second time that day. When they'd talked earlier, she'd been reluctant to share the private details of her battle with Rory. At the time, she'd only known he was alpha of one of the most feared and respected packs around. She'd also believed the man was looking for a mate.

Now, she knew better. She'd met Kiesha, Alex's true mate. According to Kiesha, Alex hadn't settled for just any female but was willing to wait however long it took for the right one. Not only that, but his second-in-command was a female beta named Carol, who was also mated to her true mate. This gave Shannon hope he'd understand her stance on not mating with anyone because it was expected, and her refusal to submit during the hunt.

Unlike Rory.

As she paced, she noticed she was feeling better and stronger than she had last night. She wondered what was in the shot Alex had given her. Whatever it was, it had sped up her healing process. She'd never healed this fast in her life.

A knock sounded at the door. "Shannon, it's Alex."

"Come in."

Since she knew Alex wasn't interested in her, she allowed herself to study him. He was a very handsome man. He had the kind of rugged good looks that you expected in action-adventure movie stars, with his deep brown eyes and his cropped black hair with just a touch of gray at the sides. He was in his early forties, about the same age as Rory.

"Kiesha said you wanted to speak with me?"

"Yes, there's been a misunderstanding. I didn't know you were mated when we spoke earlier."

He looked puzzled. "I fail to see why that would make a difference."

"Rory's been pressuring me to take a mate. Last night, he called a hunt."

Shannon could see Alex's mind working as all the pieces fell together. "I think you'd better start from the beginning. You mind if I sit down?"

"No, go right ahead." They both sat on the bed, and Shannon told him everything about the hunt and the events that led up to it.

When she was finished, Alex asked, "Will there be any repercussions for your actions within your pack?"

Shannon shrugged. "I don't know. There might be some tension. Until the other night, no one except Rory really knew how strong my wolf was. Rory's trying to bring the pack into the twenty-first century. It's been an uphill battle all the way. There are a lot of males that took issue with what I did and how strong I am. It's okay for me to be the strongest female; that just means my cubs have a better chance of being alphas. But to be the strongest wolf, second only to Rory?" She shook her head.

"Then there's Caleb and Michael. I'm sure they're not too happy with me right now. If our pack was more progressive, MacDougal would be right to fear for his position. He's always been power hungry." The more she considered it, the more she began to dread going back home.

"Don't be afraid."

She knew then that Alex could smell her fear.

"I know from the dealings my father had with yours, and my own when I became alpha, that your father was archaic. Magnus followed the old ways faithfully. I still can't believe he forced his own son to kill him to prove he was strong enough to lead. If your brother's trying to bring the pack forward, he's got his work cut out for him." Alex paused, then asked, "How familiar are you with the inner workings of the Raven pack?"

"I know the Raven pack doesn't have dominance struggles that most packs do. You have several alphas in your pack that have no desire to lead. Rory said he admired the way that the Ravens operate more like a corporation than a pack of wolves."

She leaned back against the headboard. While the Raven pack wasn't an enemy of the Sparrowhawks, neither were they allies. Alex *had* helped her. She needed to consider her words carefully. "The first thing Rory did was change the way omegas were treated. When my father was alive, omegas were little more than slaves to the rest of the pack. Now they're treated with much more respect. He appointed the two strongest shifters as his second and third to help run things. They meet regularly to discuss leadership issues."

"That was smart, giving his closest contenders positions of power and then using their skills. Cuts down on discontent."

Thinking of MacDougal, Shannon wasn't sure how correct Alex's analysis of the situation was. "Rory's opened several business enterprises and put the pack to work, for the betterment of us all. He gave the elders a voice, banned dominance fights to the death, and got rid of the hunt. Well…until the other night," she finished ruefully. "He also wants to garner equal opportunity for the women, but the males of the pack, particularly the council, aren't ready for it. In their narrow minds, women are for mating and breeding, nothing more.

"The council watches Rory like a hawk. They've always been a thorn in his side, but he can't simply disband them. A lot of them feel he's much too lenient with me. That he should have put his foot down and put me in my place a long time ago," she finished tiredly.

Alex questioned her further about the Sparrowhawks, the council, and the men she'd fought, asking what type of reception she thought she'd receive when she returned. Then he explained how the Raven pack operated, its hierarchy, and the duties of the various pack members.

In an effort to reassure herself and Alex, she questioned, "How bad can it get? I'm the alpha-fem. Magnus was my father. I'm supposed to be strong. The alpha's my brother. He won't let them do anything to me."

"Don't worry about it. I hereby formally offer you the protection of the Raven pack. No one knows that you're here, and if you want to stay, you'll be more than welcome."

He raised his right foot and propped it on the bed rail, then linked his hands around his knee, studying the floor as he continued. "I've never agreed with the practice of forcing our women to take mates. It's archaic and distasteful. It sounds like your brother picked up the practice from your father. If you decide to accept our protection, I'll make sure you have an escort when you go home to pack your things. I'm not asking you to pledge your allegiance to the pack. I would offer the same protection to anyone in your situation. By going back, you may be returning to a potentially life-threatening situation, depending on how much of an example your pack's council wants to make of you and on which side of the issue your brother falls. At the very least, your life is going to become extremely difficult."

It's one thing to think she might have FUBAR'd the situation. It was totally different to have someone else confirm it. Damn it, she didn't want to stay here. She wanted to go home but highly suspected that was no longer possible.

"You don't have to decide now," Alex said, almost like he'd read her thoughts. "Take your time. If someone comes looking for you, we'll assure them you are safe but only allow them to see you on your say-so, and that includes your brother."

Shannon didn't need time to think about it. She'd already made her decision. With the Ravens, she wouldn't have to hide how strong her wolf was. It wouldn't be an issue.

She hated being the alpha-fem, hated the responsibilities and restrictions it placed on her life. She would be happy to be one of the pack. There would be no one looking up to her, no one holding her responsible for setting an example, and no one judging her because of her position. She would be giving up all that was familiar to her, but that could be a good thing. After all, she was almost thirty years old and still lived at home with her brother.

Maybe it *was* time for a change.

"Staying here was not the course of action I was seeking, but a clean break is probably for the best. Consider me the newest member of the Raven pack."

They ironed out the rest of the details, and then Alex took her into the kitchen where Kiesha, Carol, and her mate, Mark, were waiting. Carol was tasked with providing Shannon with an escort when she went to retrieve her belongings. Kiesha just happened to need a CPA to handle the accounts for her consignment stores, which was fortunate since Shannon doubted she'd be allowed to continue to handle her former pack's accounts.

As Alex and Kiesha were leaving, Kiesha pulled Shannon to the side. "I'll get with you tomorrow with more information about the job." Then she followed Alex out the door.

Within a couple of days, Shannon moved into his parents' house, which lay on the outer edge of the property. As far as she knew, there was only one other house farther up the mountain, though she didn't know to whom it belonged.

Alex refused rent. He argued that the place needed a live-in caretaker. Since her new home was also the pack's safe house, she could expect to occasionally share it with fellow pack members as the need arose. For the most part, she'd have the place to herself. That was fine by her.

When Shannon went home to get her belongings, some of the Raven pack, including a deputy sheriff, went with her. Rory watched the proceedings. He didn't say a word the entire time she was there, nor did he offer to help. She knew this wasn't over between them. Sooner or later, they were going to have to work out their differences. She was willing to do a lot of things, but spending the rest of her life estranged from her brother was not one of them.

Chapter Three

For the last hour, Shannon had been poked and prodded by Alex and now sat in his office waiting for the results of her tests. She knew what they would reveal. Both she and her wolf were losing their collective minds.

A whole month had passed since the night of the hunt, and she still couldn't remember what happened after she'd run from Rory. Neither Alex nor Carol would tell her who'd found her. Hell, she'd even asked Kiesha. They were mum on the subject, saying it was better that she remembered on her own.

Tired of pacing, Shannon began leafing through one of the health and fitness magazines when Alex breezed in. He dropped into the chair behind his desk and tossed her chart on top. "Have you ever heard of a condition called polycythemia vera?"

"No. What is it? Is this poly—whatever you called it—what's wrong with me?" She was vaguely alarmed, and she didn't even know what it was yet.

"PV is a blood disorder in which the body produces too many red blood cells, thickening your blood. It's extremely rare, but it explains a lot of the symptoms you are experiencing."

"Are you sure? I mean, if it's so rare, how would I have it?" This was not what she was expecting. Shape-shifters didn't get sick. Their rapid healing prevented everything from paper cuts to the common cold.

"I'm not a hundred percent sure. I would need to run more tests. Your red blood cell count is higher than normal, which caused your blood to thicken. I noticed it when I drew blood. In conjunction with your other symptoms, and after a little research, this is the diagnosis I settled on."

"So I have PV and that explains the problems I'm having," she slowly repeated, trying to let it sink in that she wasn't actually crazy. There was a medical explanation for what was going on inside her body.

"Not entirely. This is only a part of it. It would explain the tingling in your legs, itchy skin, and your lack of sleep. Insomnia wouldn't normally be a major issue, not in its milder stages like what you have, but there are complications. Something has thrown your body into a second heat. You're not mistaken. You are going into heat, and that's going to create a problem."

"Ya think?" Once a year was bad enough. Twice was mind-boggling.

"There's more. Do you take birth control of any kind?" Alex looked downright grim as he asked the question. She suddenly had a bad feeling about where this was headed.

Many she-wolves took birth control to regulate their heat. That was when a female was most vulnerable. The instinct to mate and reproduce could have her, literally, acting like a bitch in heat, accepting any and all comers.

"Yes, I'm on the Pill."

"You have to come off of them."

Her mouth dropped open, and she bit back the urge to rail at him. Did he understand what he was asking her to do? "Alex, you know I can't do that, especially not now." If she did, she might as well lie down in the street naked and hang a sign around her neck that said FUCK ME.

"Shannon, I'm sorry, but you really don't have a choice in the matter. I hate to sound melodramatic. It really is a choice between your virtue and your life. With the extra blood your body is producing, the Pill can dramatically increase your chances of forming a blood clot, which I don't have to tell you is deadly. That's not a chance I'm willing to take with your life. You need to come off the Pill and any other natural substances you're taking. All of them have the same threat potential."

She had never gone without some type of buffer. She didn't know how. Only mated females went through the heat unmedicated. Wouldn't Rory get a kick out of this? "If I can't control the heat, I could end up mated to any wolf that was cunning enough to get to me, whether I want to be or not."

"I know the risk, but would death be preferable? I don't want your choices taken away from you any more than you do. This is serious business. Look, this is the problem: The thickening blood in your veins, the hormones in your birth control pills, and the surging hormones in your body caused by the heat all exponentially increase the likelihood of blood clots forming in your body. I can't control the PV because there is no treatment or cure. All we can do is monitor it and take measures as needed. I can't stop the heat because I don't know what's causing it. Of the three, the only factor in this equation that is in our power is the birth control pills you take. Anything we can do to decrease the potential for clotting needs to be done."

"Is there anything you can do about the pack? Make the unmated males leave me alone or something?"

He looked at her sorrowfully and shook his head. "Under normal circumstances, I could try, but your season is scheduled to hit its peak during the week of the blue moon."

She stared at him as the implications set in.

Oh shit!

A blue moon was a second full moon falling within the same month. It only happened once every two years. Weak shifters had little to no control over their beasts during a regular full moon. Blue moons were worse because they triggered a sexual frenzy. Males referred to the week of the blue moon as the fuckfest because the urge to mate was all-consuming. Everyone was affected, even the alphas. There were always more pregnancies after a blue moon phase.

"It will be all right, Shannon. We'll figure something out, okay? I promise. In the meantime, let me give you something to help you sleep at night."

"Thanks, Alex," she said as she took the bottle of pills. "I appreciate your help. Do me a favor. Don't say anything to anyone about this, please?"

"I couldn't. It would violate doctor-patient confidentiality. Try not to worry. The last thing you need right now is stress. At least now you know you're not going crazy." He smiled at her, but it wasn't much of one. Shannon could tell he was worried.

"I would prefer crazy. I'd probably handle it better. I'll see you later. Thanks for the sleeping pills."

Shannon left Alex's office and sat in the truck, trying to get herself together. *Think, Shannon, think. This is no time to panic.* She had a brain. She was an intelligent woman. There had to be something she could do.

What was that serenity prayer? Something about not worrying about the things she can't change. To focus on what she could. All right, what about this messed-up situation did she have power over?

She couldn't do anything about her blood. Ditto the heat. The PV whatever took away any control she might have had over it. If she didn't want to jump on the first penis she saw, she was going to have to make it difficult for the penises to get to her.

Leaving was out of the question. Shape-shifters were everywhere, and the last thing she wanted to do was be surprised by some out-of-area wolf-shifter. What she needed was a way to keep the males from getting to her. She might not be able to control them, but she could limit or prevent their access to her body.

Realizing she was on to something, she let that thought play out in her mind. If she could make it difficult enough to get to her, she might just make it out of this heat unmated and in one piece. She needed a secure place, like a panic room, 'cause Lord knew she was going to be in a panic when the blue moon rose.

She backed out of the parking lot and drove to the house. She was sure Alex wouldn't mind. He'd probably help out if she told him what she was about to do. Now she needed to find a room that suited her purpose. She was grateful she'd spent so much time helping Rory with his construction business. Every bit of knowledge she'd gained was going to come in handy.

* * *

That night, Nikolai materialized next to the bed of the she-wolf he'd rescued after scanning first to make sure she was asleep. Fascination was quickly becoming an obsession. It was increasingly difficult to stay away from his wolf.

Just the mere thought of her essence was enough to cause his fangs to throb. He wanted to devour her, to gorge himself in her feminine cream, and then satiate himself with her blood.

Every night he came to see her, sometimes more than once. With each visit, he pushed the limits of his control. Merging deeply with her mind, he would psychically stroke and caress her body, arousing her mercilessly. He couldn't seem to help himself. Every time she was close to the edge, her wolf took control. She'd start to shift, and he'd have to leave. While the blood bond he'd formed with her gave him some control over her mind, he couldn't control her beast. It was too strong.

Nikolai psychically pulled down the bedsheet, baring her naked body to his view. Though he'd scrutinized her thoroughly many times before, he still could not determine what fascinated him so.

There was something different about her tonight. Something wrong.

He expanded his senses until he found the source of the problem. There was a faint metallic scent of medicine emanating from her body. With their mental link engaged, he searched deep. Whatever she took, it didn't hinder his ability to connect with her subconscious mind, but it rendered her beast defenseless.

A wicked smile slowly crossed Nikolai's face.

Her beast sensed him and tried to stir, but the medication was too powerful. It knew he was there but couldn't do a thing about it. Not one to look a gift horse in the mouth, he took advantage of the opportunity Shannon had unknowingly provided him with.

Using phantom fingers, he gently stroked the brow of her eye, gliding his hand down her cheek. Her full lips parted beneath his touch. He ignored her obvious invitation in favor of exploring elsewhere. His fingernail ghosted down her neck, causing her to arch in response. Goose bumps pebbled her flesh.

He continued his exploration to her ample breasts. Her flesh cried out to him, demanding that he cease with the mind games and touch her for real. For a second, he considered giving in to temptation.

He toyed with her breasts, and her nipples puckered. Using his mind, he played her body like a master musician, touching her all over simultaneously. Multiple mouths suckled on her nipples and between her legs while ghostly hands stroked and caressed the rest of her body. He kept a firm grip on her mind, having no fear she would awaken and catch him toying with her.

Her body began to undulate. She opened completely to him, legs spread wide as her fingers gripped the sheet. Her heartbeat raced. The heat of her excitement caused her blood to cry out to him, begging him to taste it.

His beast stirred as bloodlust rose. His gaze traveled over her, noting every detail: the rapid rise and fall of her chest; her tightly puckered nipples; the rosy flush of her skin as the blood rushed through her veins and arteries; the glistening red curls covering her mound. Her swollen clit begged to be touched. He could see the clutch and release of vaginal muscles as invisible fingers thrust relentlessly in and out of her foaming pussy.

The more he stared, the more he hungered. *A taste*, temptation whispered, *just a nibble. What can it hurt?*

Yes, he thought, just one small taste. Maybe if he tasted her this one time, he could discover just what her hold over him was.

He planted a knee on the bed, followed by one hand and then the other, like a great big cat stalking prey. His gaze was completely focused on his target—the glistening flesh between her legs. A fog of lust covered his mind. One sample. That's all he wanted. One taste, then he could leave and never return.

Bracing himself above her undulating body, he timed his movement just right. Quick as a cat, he swiped at her slit with his tongue. The flavor of her caused his fangs to burst out of his gums and lock into place as his vision bled to red.

Unable to resist, he went back for more and more until his face was mashed against her, his nose buried in her pubic hair, mouth wide open against her flesh. His lethal teeth nicked the fragile skin of her outer labia, drawing forth a bead of blood.

His bloodlust took control.

Like a snake he struck, sinking his fangs deep into the femoral artery running beneath the skin of her inner thigh. He drew strongly, her rich blood rushing through his body and bringing a surge of power with it.

He was barely aware of her convulsing beneath him as orgasm after orgasm streaked through her body.

Her blood was addictive—thick, rich, and powerful. He wanted to gorge. Some small part of his mind screamed at him to pull back. He was taking too much.

He closed the wound and yanked himself away from her. Then licked the last bit of blood smeared on his mouth. His chest fell and rose sharply as he fought against the urge to take her, mark her, and claim her as his own for all eternity.

He stood rigid beside the bed, eyes closed, hands balled into fists as he struggled to rein in his body, fighting his instincts. He broke the link between them, knowing the distance was necessary, but hated losing contact with every fiber of his being.

After a period of quiet meditation, he was able to gain control. His fangs retracted, and his eyes returned to their natural black color. His fists loosened. His breathing evened out to a slow and steady rate. When he was ready, he opened his eyes and focused on the woman lying before him. Steely determination entered his gaze. He wanted her, and he would have her. No one would stand in his way.

Nikolai walked around the bed until he was closer to her head. Once more linking his mind with hers, he placed her under compulsion as he brought his wrist to his mouth and ripped a hole in his skin with his fangs, causing the blood to flow. Pressing his wrist against her mouth, he compelled her to drink.

When she'd drunk enough of his blood, he commanded her to stop, then licked the wound closed. Instinctively, he started a mating ritual so old it was imprinted on his DNA. Two more blood exchanges, and she would be his. Giving her one last lingering look, he dematerialized and left the house.

Soon. Very soon, he would claim her.

* * *

Rory wanted to know how Shannon was doing. He hadn't heard from her since she'd left, which was understandable under the circumstances. Still, he was used to watching over her, making sure she was safe and sound. He knew he needed to let go and let her be her own person, but it was hard to turn off his protective instincts. He was her big brother, although he felt more like her father.

He swiveled his chair around to look out the office window. She'd only been gone a month. It was too soon to go and check on her, not without a valid reason. While he was wondering what excuse he could concoct that she would believe, his phone rang.

"McFelan Construction. McFelan speaking. How can I help you?"

"Mr. McFelan, this is Kyle Wilson. I used to work for you."

Rory remembered him. He'd been a good worker. "What can I do for you?"

"Well, sir, I was just calling you to let you know that I ran into your sister over in Colbyville. It seems she's moved to Refuge and needs someone to help her with some remodeling. I still do odd jobs from time to time, so I told her I would help. The thing is, sir, I was just wondering why your sister would need to hire anyone when her brother owned a construction company and did stuff like this for a living. I don't mean to pry, but Miss Shannon was real nice to me when I worked for you, and I liked her a lot. I just wondered if you knew what was going on."

"No, I didn't know that she needed help. Thanks for letting me know. You know how independent little sisters can be. Did she say what she wanted done?"

"She didn't go into a lot of details. I'm supposed to meet her at her house tomorrow morning around ten. She has a truck scheduled to deliver the supplies she purchased around that time. I know she ordered a lot of studs and drywall, and a couple of steel doors. That's really all I can tell you."

"Tell you what, Kyle. You go ahead and show up. Whatever Shannon offered to pay you, I'll double it. I'll meet you at her house, and you can work with me to accomplish whatever it is she's trying to do. I appreciate you calling me to tell me what was going on. I love my sister, but sometimes she takes this independence thing a little too far, you know what I mean?"

"Yes, sir, Mr. McFelan. I sure do. I have a baby sister too. Drives me crazy."

They worked out the rest of the details before ending the call. Rory sat with his hands steepled underneath his chin. This was just the excuse he was looking for.

* * *

Shannon rolled over and stretched. What she wanted was another hour or two of sleep, but one look at the clock assured her that she wouldn't get it, at least not today. She rolled out of bed on legs that wobbled before getting her equilibrium. Then she made her way into the bathroom, stretching in a yawn as she went.

There was a strange taste in her mouth. It was probably from the medicine, but it tasted like blood. She wondered if she bit the inside of her mouth while she slept. As for the medicine, it had worked wonders. This was the most rested she'd felt in weeks; even her legs were relaxed. Usually she woke several times during the night, her wolf agitated, never able to determine the cause. Last night it hadn't happened. She didn't intend to make the pills a habit, but it was nice knowing she had them to fall back on whenever necessary.

The delivery truck would be here in about an hour. Certainly enough time to cook breakfast. As she headed into the kitchen, she heard a familiar vehicle in the drive. What did *he* want?

She opened the door and stepped onto the porch. Rory exited the blue crew-cab truck he used for business.

"To what do I owe this pleasure?" She was a little wary, considering all the unfinished business between them.

He walked up to the porch like he owned the place, sliding his shades on top of his curly red head. He nailed her with a hard look. "If you're needing help, why didn't you call me? I'm still your brother, aren't I?"

Oh hell. Kyle had blabbed. "I take it you ran into Kyle."

"You could say that, but you'd be wrong. Man called, wanting to know why my sister had to hire help when her brother owned a construction company. Same thing I'd like to know. Any reason why you didn't call me?"

Hell, he was pissed. His accent was showing. *Come on, Shannon. Think fast.* "This is Raven pack business. It doesn't concern the alpha of the Sparrowhawks." Maybe that would make him back off.

"As long as it affects my baby sister, it affects me. I'm here as your big brother. I ask you again, why didn't you come to me if you needed help?"

Because I didn't know if I could trust you, Shannon thought. Despite their differences, he was blood, and she'd never do or say anything to deliberately hurt him. In the heat of an argument was different. They both tended to be a little loose with the lips when angry. But to deliberately say words she knew would cut? She couldn't do that. She had to find a reason to give him that wasn't the full truth. He would smell a lie.

As much as she loved Rory, this was one thing she couldn't tell him. There was no telling what he'd do, what level he'd sink to "for her own good." They already fought over his interpretation of what was good for her. She wasn't giving him ammunition to use against her. "I'm building a safe room for Alex. The Raven pack doesn't have one. The alpha's mate is human and hasn't gone through her first full change yet. The beta just had a cub. A place will be needed for his first time as well. Since I'm living here rent free, I volunteered to create one for the pack."

It was logical, and Rory couldn't fault her reasoning, but it didn't make sense, not with who he knew her to be. While every pack had a safe house or room, Shannon had never liked the idea of them. She thought they were little more than nicely decorated jail cells.

No, there was something else going on. Something to do with the change in her scent. She stood before him, defensive and defiant, daring him to say something. "Then it's a good thing I brought my tools. I'll assume you made all the necessary measurements, and you ordered everything that we'll need?"

Defiance gave way to confusion. Rory almost smiled.

"Yes, I took measurements. The supplies should be arriving in about an hour. Since you're here, and you don't appear to be leaving anytime soon, come on in. I was just about to fix breakfast." Shannon turned and walked into the house.

"Sounds like I arrived just in time." He entered behind her and looked around with interest. *So this is where Alex placed her*. Not bad, even though he knew it was only temporary. As he helped Shannon cook, he updated her on what had been happening within the pack since she'd been gone, such as the newly mated pairs, but didn't mention the council. They were his problem, not hers.

While she was relaxed and off guard, he made his move. "You know, things are starting to back up since you've been gone. Vendors aren't getting paid, money's not being posted to the account, or it's posted incorrectly. No one else has your level of expertise, and I don't have time to go looking for another accountant. Think you can help your brother out? You know how much of a mess I make when I try tangle with them." It was a patent lie. He was more than capable of handling both his own and the pack's business accounts.

"I won't come to Sparta. You'll have to bring the books to me." The hint of temper in her voice said she knew she was being manipulated.

"That's fine. Whatever paperwork we have that can't be transmitted electronically will be hand delivered or mailed." Until things settled down, her being in Sparta wasn't a good idea anyway. He could tell his agreement made her suspicious. Before she could ask the question he knew was forming in her mind, he said, "Show me the room."

"Actually, it's the basement. I think it's perfect for what we've planned."

"I'll let you know how perfect it is after I've seen it." He followed her to the door off the kitchen that led below. "What are you going to do about this door?"

"I ordered a steel-reinforced one to replace it. Actually, I purchased two. I plan to put one here and the other one at the bottom of the stairs."

She opened the door and led the way down. "Right now this is open, but I intend to close in this stairway and put the second door right here for extra security."

"So if someone gets past the first door, they'll still have to get past the second one."

"Yes, that's exactly what I was thinking."

He walked around the basement. "There's a bathroom down here. That's good. It looks like someone started remodeling this area and then stopped midway. The walls need finishing. What about these windows?"

"They're relatively small. I bought some steel netting to cover them. I don't think they are big enough for anything to get through, but you never know."

"The netting won't keep anything in unless you spray it with silver. It's not sturdy enough. A shifter's claws will go right through it. You need to install bars on the outside."

"Wouldn't anything trying to get in simply pull the bars off of the window?"

She'd told him they were trying to keep something from getting out. If that were the case, she shouldn't be worried about something getting in. He gave her a look that spoke volumes, but didn't comment on her slip. "We'll put the netting on first, then put the bars over the netting and spray both down with silver paint. The smell alone should be enough to deter any shifter from using the window. By putting everything on the outside, you'll still be able to open the windows. You don't want to cut off your air supply."

While she was studying the windows with a worried look on her face, he continued looking around. "Have you located the breaker box?"

"Yes, it's over by the washer and dryer. The shut-off valve for the water is down here too, along with the furnace."

"Good. This would be a good location for a panic room. It can also work as a safe room, but it will function better at keeping people out."

She looked at him sharply. He stared at her knowingly. She neither confirmed nor denied his suspicion, and he didn't push the issue. He knew what she was doing, just not why, but he was determined to find out.

His sharp ears picked up the sound of an approaching vehicle. "Your supplies are here."

"I hear them. Did Kyle say if he was still coming?"

"Yes, he'll be here. I changed the time of his arrival. When he gets here, he'll be working for me. I've already set up payment arrangements."

Kyle showed up just in time to help with the truck. They unloaded it, piling everything in the basement for easy access. Under Rory's direction, they removed the basement door and framed the stairway first. Then Rory and Kyle drywalled the interior while Shannon prepared lunch.

After eating, Rory had Shannon prep the wall for painting while they installed the first steel door. He worked like a man possessed. He didn't know what the threat to

Shannon was, but he wasn't leaving until he had done all that he could do to ensure her safety.

If he hadn't known it would piss her off, he'd put a guard on her and assign some of the pack to watch over her, day and night. Problem was, if she caught on, she'd rip them a new asshole, then come looking for him to do the same, or at least give it a good try. The last time he and Shannon had seriously tangled, it had taken them both a week to recover.

Because he'd made her wolf so strong, she was past the age when most she-wolves mated. It wouldn't bother him so much if she were happy. Despite what she said, he could see the loneliness in her eyes. He saw the way she watched the cubs in the pack.

His sister wanted a mate, but her stubbornness wouldn't allow her to admit it.

For the last year he'd been pressuring her to find a mate for herself and the cubs he knew she wanted. He'd hoped she would become so sick of his matchmaking that she would get out there and look for her own man, if only to get him off her back. He'd pushed hard. Maybe too hard. It was the only thing he knew to do. His actions had created a wall between them, and he knew it. He'd rather have her mad at him and doing something about changing her situation than wallowing in her loneliness.

Maybe here with the Raven pack she could find a mate. He hoped so because otherwise all his hard work would have been for nothing. Surely one of them would be strong enough for her.

By the time he left late that night both doors were installed, the studs had drywall on them, and the windows were secured. Though she hadn't asked, he'd be back tomorrow to install motion sensors and security cameras. By the time he was finished, this room would be tougher to get into than Fort Knox.

As he drove away, he decided it was time he and Alex had a little talk. If the man was going to be his baby sister's alpha, Rory was going to make sure she was being well taken care of. The first thing they were going to discuss was whatever the hell it was that scared her so much.

Chapter Four

Shannon walked into the diner and paused, her gaze scanning past the occupied seats at the counter and searching the tables beyond, looking for her friends. When she'd arrived at Kiesha's store this morning, there'd been a note on the door directing her to come to Moe's. Spotting Kiesha and Mary Elizabeth in the back corner, she started forward only to stop as an attractive young wolf with a lecherous expression on his face stepped directly in front of her, blocking her path. He had to be drawn to the scent of her burgeoning heat.

Eyes narrow, Shannon told him, "Move out of my way."

The young wolf smiled confidently, secure in his irresistibility. It might have been charming, had she been in the mood. When he still didn't move, choosing instead to allow his gaze to wander over her body, she snapped.

Allowing her wolf to show, she looked him dead in his eyes and allowed her power to flare. She was an alpha, and she wasn't in the mood to deal with his crap today. "Move out of my way before I rip out your throat," she said in a low growl.

The acrid scent of fear rose in the air as the young wolf realized his mistake. As an omega, he should have known he didn't stand a chance against an alpha, even if that alpha was a small female. Especially when said female was in the early stages of the heat. Alpha-fems tended to be ferocious on a good day. Add the heat to the equation and they became downright vicious. He quickly lowered his eyes in a sign of submission and mumbled an apology as he slunk away.

Shannon's gaze skimmed over the rest of the diner's male patrons, lingering on those her nose identified as unmated wolves. She issued out a silent challenge that went unanswered. Even those who'd previously been interested turned away, directing their attention elsewhere. Others actually got up and left the diner. When Shannon was satisfied she'd gotten her point across, she turned off the flow of power and called back her wolf before continuing to the table where Kiesha and Mary Elizabeth were waiting.

"What?" she snapped defensively when she saw how her friends were staring at her.

Holding her hands up high in front of herself, Mary Elizabeth looked at her innocently. "Nothing. I like my throat just where it is. I've had enough trouble lately."

Kiesha fanned herself with her hand. "Whew, you've got some serious mojo going on. What was that all about? As soon as you walked in the door, half of the guys in this place stared at you like you were sex on a stick and they couldn't wait to get a lick. I swear I saw one guy drool. I don't remember you getting that kind of reaction at the party two weeks ago."

Shannon slid into the booth next to Kiesha and grimaced. "I'm going into heat," she mumbled under her breath.

Kiesha and Mary Elizabeth exchanged puzzled looks. "Pardon me?" Kiesha asked. "I didn't quite catch what you said."

Shannon huffed and then said a little louder, and with a lot more attitude, "I said, I'm going into heat."

Mary Elizabeth's mouth dropped open. "You mean the way dogs… *Ouch*!" She glared at Kiesha. "What did you kick me for?"

"You were being rude. Shannon is not a dog, and I'm sure she doesn't appreciate you calling her one."

Mary Elizabeth vehemently protested. "I didn't call *her* a dog. I only mentioned them as a frame of reference so that I could understand what she was talking about. I swear, you better hurry up and have that baby because it's eating your brain cells."

When Kiesha opened her mouth to retaliate, Shannon cut her off. "Ladies, please! This is difficult enough as it is. Yes, Mary Elizabeth, to answer your question, it is similar to when female dogs go into heat."

Turning to include Kiesha, she briefly explained what the heat was like and the impact it was having on her body. Her friends sat in stunned silence as they absorbed the impact of her words.

Mary Elizabeth was the first to recover. "Isn't there anything you can do to prevent that from happening? Any medicine you can take that will control it and not leave you so…" She floundered, obviously searching for a word that fit.

"Helpless," Kiesha finished for her.

"Normally, yes, there would be, but your mate just pulled me off of everything I usually take to help get me through this," Shannon told them glumly, still a bit pissed about the whole situation.

Fire flared in Kiesha's golden brown eyes. "Why in the hell did Alex do that? Didn't he know how it would affect you?"

Mary Elizabeth echoed her.

Shannon, who'd thought she'd never find anything about this situation funny, was amused and touched that they were so firmly on her side, considering the short time they'd all known each other. "Don't blame Alex. There's other stuff going on that literally meant I was taking my life into my own hands were I to continue taking them."

"Man, that sucks," Mary Elizabeth said sympathetically.

"Damn," Kiesha said. "Since he had a good reason, I guess I don't have to rip into him as soon as I see him. What are you going to do? I know you're not going to just sit back and hope for the best."

"Don't worry. I have a plan," Shannon assured them before changing the subject. She'd come here to get her mind off her problems. Talking about them was just bringing her down. "How is Hugh? I haven't seen him since you left on your 'business trip.'" Business trip was a euphemism for Mary Elizabeth's freak-out when she discovered she was mated to Hugh and not just having an affair as she'd originally believed.

Mary Elizabeth rolled her eyes. "The man hasn't let me out of his sight since I returned. If he knew I was in the diner, he'd be over here right now. I had to talk fast to keep him from driving me to work this morning."

Shannon laughed because "work" was only two blocks away.

Kiesha smirked. "I'm surprised the man let you out of bed. You took off for five days without a word to him. You're lucky he lets you out of his sight."

Shannon nodded her agreement. Shape-shifters were extremely possessive, especially when newly mated.

"You don't know the half of it," Mary Elizabeth told them. "When I got home Saturday, there was a surprise waiting, and not a good one."

Interest piqued, Shannon said, "Well, don't hold back. Tell us what happened."

Mary Elizabeth looked around to see if anyone was listening and then motioned them closer. Quietly, she stated, "Charles came to visit."

Kiesha sucked in her breath sharply. "Are you serious? Why didn't you tell me about this before?"

"Isn't Charles your brother-in-law?" Shannon asked.

"Mary Elizabeth's *needy* brother-in-law who's been trying to get her to move back home," Kiesha explained.

"How did Hugh react?" That's what Shannon wanted to know. You do *not* mess with a shape-shifter's mate. Trying to convince Mary Elizabeth to leave Refuge, and subsequently Hugh, qualified.

Mary Elizabeth looked at them both, obviously trying to decide which question to answer first. "I haven't had the opportunity. And Hugh's still pissed, so please don't mention this in front of him. By the way, Charles is dead. Oh, and I shifted into a bear."

Shannon and Kiesha stared at her, eyes and mouths wide open.

Mary Elizabeth looked around awkwardly, then tucked her long brown hair with blonde highlights nervously behind her ear. "How long do we have to sit here before we get any service? Someone should have been over by now to take our order. They could have at least asked if we wanted coffee. I'll go and get us some." She slid out of the booth.

"Move another inch, and I'll sic Shannon on you," Kiesha threatened.

Shannon nodded. If Mary Elizabeth thought they'd be satisfied with the tiny piece of information she'd thrown at them, she deserved to be bit. She growled at her for good measure, flashing a glimpse of her canines. Mary Elizabeth narrowed her brown eyes at Shannon but sat back down as directed.

"Okay, now start again from the beginning," Kiesha commanded.

"And this time, don't leave anything out," Shannon added.

"And what was that bit about shifting into a bear? You *shifted*?" Kiesha's voice rose. "I've been mated for over a month now, and I haven't fully shifted."

Mary Elizabeth shushed them, waving her hands for silence as she looked uneasily around the diner. "Keep your voice down. I don't want everyone knowing what happened."

"Start talking, or it's going to get ugly," Kiesha threatened.

Mary Elizabeth relented and explained in greater detail. She finished with, "I got so mad at the things Charles was saying that I saw red. I didn't know I'd shifted until Hugh told me. Apparently strong emotions bring on the change. I don't know how Charles went from being in jail to crashing his van on the road out of town. And to be frank, I don't want to know. I'm just glad the man's finally out of my life."

"I always knew there was something wrong with that man." Kiesha nodded her head in an "I told you so" manner. "How did he find out where you were living? I thought you hadn't given the folks your address."

Mary Elizabeth sighed. "I hadn't. He used my mother against me. She called begging me to come home for a visit. When I said I couldn't, she guilted me into giving her my home address. Charles must have been sitting right there with her when she called."

Shannon looked at her. "Aw man, that's deep."

"You're telling me."

"I can't believe your mother helped Charles like that. Then again, knowing her and the way she's always treated you, I shouldn't be surprised," Kiesha acknowledged. "Sorry, but you know it's the truth."

Mary Elizabeth gave her a smile of understanding. "I know, and it's okay. I've made my peace with Mother. She is who she is. She couldn't have gotten away with half of the things she did if I hadn't enabled her. I could have broken free a long time ago. I guess that I wanted to feel needed and connected to my family, no matter what form that connection took. With Hugh, I'm finally starting to understand what a real family is supposed to be like. Coming here was one of the best decisions I've ever made. I don't know about anyone else, but I'm getting hungry. Since we can't seem to get any service, I'll go and get us some coffee. Does anyone need a menu, or do you know what you want to eat?"

Both Kiesha and Shannon knew so Mary Elizabeth got one of the order pads, wrote down their orders, and stuck them in the window. While she was standing there, the swinging door that led into the kitchen opened, and Hugh came out. He grabbed Mary Elizabeth by the hand and tugged her back through the door.

Kiesha gave Shannon a knowing look. "Think we'll get our food anytime today?"

Shannon smiled. "Only if there's another cook back there."

They laughed as Kiesha got up to get the coffeepot and some cups. When she returned to the table and they'd both fixed their coffee, she asked, "How's things going with your brother? He still driving you crazy?"

Shannon rolled her eyes. "Is he still breathing? 'Cause the only way he couldn't make me crazy was if he were dead, and even then I'm sure Rory would find a way."

"Why has he suddenly begun hanging around so much? That's what I don't understand. You've been here for almost a month with no contact, and suddenly he's here every day."

"He knows something is going on with me, but I won't tell him what it is. It's put him into full-blown big brother role, which for Rory is taking protectiveness to the nth degree."

Kiesha winced. "While I never had any siblings, I'm learning through Alex that a male shifter in protective mode was no little thing. It has the power to drive any self-respecting, independently thinking, mature woman positively batty. Do you think he'd let up off of you if he had something else to do?"

"He *has* other things to do. The man owns a construction company, for God's sake. You'd think he has enough to do without bothering me all the time. I can't even work in my own home because he's always underfoot. I didn't see this much of him when we lived in the same house."

Kiesha pounced on her statement, eyes gleaming with excitement. "He owns a construction company? You think you could get him to do some finishing work for me at the store? The contractor I hired went to another project he'd committed to prior to his accepting my bid. I knew it was a possibility, but I was hoping we'd be done by now so that it wouldn't be an issue."

"All you can do is ask. I'm sure he won't turn you down, if for no other reason than that it gives him the opportunity to check you out," Shannon said ironically.

Mary Elizabeth came back to the table with her lips swollen and a glow on her face. Neither Kiesha nor Shannon mentioned the scent of arousal that lingered around her. She heaved a sigh of relief and motioned to the coffee cups in front of them. "Oh, good, you already got coffee. Sorry, I got…detained. The food will be out in a few minutes. What did I miss?"

Kiesha rolled her eyes. "We were discussing overprotective men of the shifter variety." Shannon nodded in agreement.

"Are we referring to your brother? Or are you complaining about the way Alex has been hovering since you became pregnant?"

"Don't even get me started about Alex," Kiesha said with a groan. "The man makes me crazy. He's a doctor. There's no telling how many babies he's delivered over the course of his career. You'd think this child I'm carrying was the first baby in all of creation with the way he's been carrying on."

Shannon laughed. "It may not be the *first child of all creation*, but it is *his* first. From what you told me, he's been waiting a long time for you and this baby. Cut the man some slack. At least you're still leaving the house and going to work every day. Some women can't even do that much."

Kiesha narrowed her eyes. "If you only knew what a battle *that* was. I had to put my foot down. He wasn't against my working, but he wanted to have one of the wolves in the pack follow me around when he couldn't be with me."

"How did you convince him otherwise?" Mary Elizabeth asked. "Hugh threatened me with the very same thing. I need all of the pointers on dealing with stubborn males I can get."

Kiesha's smile was smug. "I told him if he did so it would make me *extremely* unhappy. It would place unnecessary stress on me, and stress wasn't good for the baby."

"You played the baby card," Shannon said, feeling a bit envious of the loving relationships her two friends had found, despite their complaining.

Mary Elizabeth laughed. “You better use it sparingly. Only pull it out for the big arguments, the ones you feel yourself losing. Lord knows, I lose more than my fair share of arguments with Hugh. Almost makes me wish I had a baby card of my own to play.”

Kiesha winked at them. “Don’t worry. I only use it in times of extreme emergency. The rest of the time, I play the sex card. It’s amazing what an alpha male will agree to when he’s sated and relaxed after a good round of sex.”

“Hear! Hear!” Mary Elizabeth said in agreement, and the three ladies laughed.

Hugh brought their food out to the table while they were still laughing. “Do I even want to know what you ladies find so amusing?” He placed the tray on a nearby table so that he could distribute their food.

They looked at him and then at each other, and they laughed again, harder. Hugh smiled ruefully. “I’ll take that as a no.” Shannon noted he’d brought food for himself as well. Nudging Mary Elizabeth over, he slid his huge body into the booth beside her. All conversation ceased as they focused on satisfying their hunger.

When they were finished, Hugh cleared the table and returned with more coffee. Seated once more, he placed his arm on the back of the seat and began playing with Mary Elizabeth’s hair as she leaned against him. “How’s Alex? I haven’t seen nor spoken to him since the night I came to your house looking for Mary Elizabeth.”

“He’s made it his mission in life to see how crazy he can make me before this baby is born, but other than that, he’s doing fine. He should be here soon. He had a meeting this morning that must have been pretty important. He was very hush-hush about it. I told him we would be meeting here at the diner before going over to the store."

While Kiesha was still speaking, the door opened, and Alex walked into the diner with Rory trailing close behind. It was apparent from their manner that the two were together.

Shannon took one look at them and muttered under her breath. "He didn't. He *wouldn't.*"

But it was obvious that he had.

Rory had gone to Alex looking for answers to his questions that Shannon refused to give.

Chapter Five

The two men crossed the diner headed for the back table where the women and Hugh were sitting. They were a study in contrasts, in appearance and personality. Though they were both alphas, their backgrounds and upbringings vastly differed. Alex, with his dark eyes rimmed with gold, black hair splashed with gray at the temples, and his long, lean, muscular body, was the more laid-back of the two. Then there was Rory and his hazel eyes that were constantly changing color. He was shorter in height, but much bigger by comparison with his barrel chest and stocky build topped off with his head of fiery red hair and a temper to match. Both men were attractive enough to star in any female's fantasies. Definitely drool worthy, and not just because of their looks. If any of the males Rory had thrown at her had been like these two, or even Hugh, she wouldn't be in the predicament she was in now.

Shannon studied them carefully, worried. Although Alex had promised not to disclose anything about her condition, she knew how tricky and resourceful Rory could be. He excelled in conning people into revealing more than they had intended. There was no doubt in her mind he had pulled every trick in his repertoire hoping to get the information he wanted from Alex. She looked from Rory to Alex, trying to read the expressions on their faces. It was like trying to read a rock and just as informative. Neither man was giving away anything.

Alex called out to the waitress for some coffee and a couple of menus before bending down to give his mate a kiss. As he lifted his head, he looked at Shannon and shook his head slightly. She gave a small sigh of relief, even though in a couple of days it wouldn't matter. Rory would be able to smell what was going on with her, if he couldn't already.

Rory snagged a table and dragged it closer to the booth in which they were sitting while everyone exchanged greetings. Alex introduced Rory to the group, one by one. Shannon waited for the inquisition to begin. He'd spent the last few days grilling her for information on her friends and her life in the Raven pack. Now was his opportunity to discover firsthand.

"Shannon tells me you own your own construction company," Kiesha stated after an encouraging nudge from Shannon. "You wouldn't happen to be interested in gaining a little extra business, would you? My contractor had to start on another project."

Rory frowned. "He committed to doing a job for you and then left to go work on something else?"

Shannon hid a smile. Kiesha's question had effectively sidetracked Rory, just as she'd hoped.

Kiesha appeared to be puzzled; then her expression cleared. "Oh no! I knew about this other project. He committed to it prior to accepting my bid. I went with him because he had the best reputation of all the commercial contractors I contacted. I was lucky he agreed to take me on. He's a very busy man."

Seeing that Rory was effectively hooked, Shannon allowed her thoughts to drift as Rory asked more questions about who Kiesha's contractor was, the work she was having done, and what remained to be completed. She tuned back in just as Rory stated, "I usually only do residential work, but since you're a friend of my sister as well as her employer, I'll do it for you. When do you want me to start?"

"Probably in another day or two. Shayla should be here by then, and she can tell you what her requirements are."

Alex and Mary Elizabeth groaned in unison.

"Your cousin Shay is coming here?" Alex questioned in apparent dismay.

"Shay's coming?" Mary Elizabeth asked at the same time.

Kiesha looked at them in surprise. "Alex, I told you Shay was coming to set up the computers and get everything operational. And Mary Elizabeth, I'm sure I said something to you about it."

Mary Elizabeth rubbed her forehead. "Kiesha, I'm trying to remember, but I'm coming up blank. When exactly did you tell me Shay was coming?"

Shannon smirked, always ripe for an opportunity to give Mary Elizabeth a hard time. "She told you on the same day you decided to take off on your little *business trip*."

She laughed when Mary Elizabeth gave her an evil glare as Hugh clutched her a little tighter, a small growl rumbling out of him.

"Besides, what's wrong with Shayla?" Shannon asked. "Why the big fuss?" Shannon had never met Kiesha's cousin but had spoken with her on the telephone a few times to give her input on the necessary system requirements.

"I've got to admit, you've piqued my curiosity. What's this Shay like, and why the groans?" Hugh had never met Shayla either. She glanced at Rory, but he was busy noting something in his planner.

"Shayla cannot be described," Alex said. "She can only be experienced. All I can say is you're in for a treat. Shayla's a hoot."

Mary Elizabeth agreed with a laugh. "Amen to that. Shay is beyond description. You'll just have to wait until she gets here to see for yourselves. When are you expecting her?"

Kiesha lightly popped Alex on the arm. "Cut it out. Shay's not that bad. I will admit she can be a little bit out there, but don't let her manner fool you. The girl's a certified genius. I think a lot of what she does is just a front to hide how intelligent she is. She used to intimidate people."

Shannon hadn't known that little tidbit.

"Honey, she still intimidates people. She threatened to hack into the FBI's most wanted files and add me to the list if I didn't treat you right. After she took my picture with her camera phone."

Shannon burst out laughing. Mary Elizabeth snorted, then covered her mouth to muffle her laughter.

Kiesha's mouth dropped open. "She did what?"

Alex smiled. "You heard me. She's very protective of you."

Shannon smirked and raised her coffee cup in a toast. "I like the sound of her already."

"Good." Kiesha grinned. "I already told her she could stay with you."

Shannon shrugged, expecting nothing less. She was living in the pack house, after all. Being newly mated, Kiesha wouldn't want Shayla staying at the house with her and Alex, even if she was family.

"You never said when you were expecting her?" Mary Elizabeth reminded Kiesha.

"Oh, she should be here sometime late this evening."

"Good. I was hoping I would get a chance to see her before we left."

"You two going somewhere?" Alex asked.

"Unfortunately," Hugh replied. "I can't talk her out of it, and I won't let her go alone."

"Going where, and why don't you want her going alone?" It was Rory this time with a question.

"I'm going back home for a funeral," Mary Elizabeth said.

Before Shannon could offer her condolences, Hugh spoke, "No, you're not going back home. Your home is here, with me. Say it! 'My home is with you now, Hugh.'"

"My home is with you now, Hugh. Squawk, squawk. My home is with you," she said in her best parrot imitation.

Hugh hooked her around the neck and dragged her closer to him. With his other hand, he took his knuckles and rubbed them against her forehead while she shook with laughter. "Smart-ass."

Watching the two of them, Shannon felt a twinge in the region of her heart. Long-forgotten dreams of a loving mate of her own rose up to haunt her. The combination of the heat and the blue moon stole any chance she'd ever have of experiencing what her friends had. No, she couldn't think like that. She had a plan. A good one. It would work. It had to. Failure was not an option.

Kiesha suddenly gaped at Mary Elizabeth. "Please tell me you are not going back for Charles's funeral. Not after what he tried to do. I'm sure your family would understand if you couldn't make it."

Shannon kicked Kiesha under the table and hissed, "She told us not to say anything."

"Oops, my bad. But still, what the hell is wrong with your thinking?" Kiesha continued to scold Mary Elizabeth.

Instead of the anger Shannon expected, Hugh merely shook his head and sighed, his expression that of a man who had fought hard and lost. "That's what I said. You try and convince her not to go because I tried and got nowhere."

"Guys, I *have* to go. My parents have no idea what happened, and I have no intention of telling them. He was a good son-in-law to them, no matter how crazy he was. I'll let his secrets go to the grave with him where they belong. Besides, his lawyer called and said Charles recently changed his will, making me the executor of his estate. I'm obligated to be there for the reading of the will, which will be the morning after the funeral."

Shannon privately agreed with Kiesha and Hugh. Mary Elizabeth was a little too nice for her own good, especially where her family was concerned.

Hugh glared at Mary Elizabeth. "You didn't tell me *that*. Exactly when were you planning on revealing it?"

"I wasn't. I knew how you would react, and I didn't want to hear it."

Shannon interrupted. "He made you the executor of his estate?"

"Who's Charles?" Rory wanted to know.

Mary Elizabeth and Hugh were still glaring at each other. Kiesha appeared to be in a daze. Shannon was still waiting for an answer to her question so Alex answered Rory. "Charles is Mary Elizabeth's brother-in-law. He recently showed up in Refuge, trying to get her to move back home."

"Wait, how did you know? Mary Elizabeth just told me about it a few minutes ago," Kiesha stated to her mate.

"Because I'm alpha, and my men were involved."

"Why didn't you tell me? As your mate, I'm alpha too," Kiesha exclaimed.

Mary Elizabeth finally answered Shannon, dragging her attention from Kiesha and Alex and the argument brewing, the whole while maintaining eye contact with Hugh. "Actually, he did a bit more than that. He left half of his estate to me. I won't know all of the details until the will is read."

Hugh's eyes got big as a vein in his temple began to throb. Shannon could actually see it pulsing.

"*Oh! My! God!* He left you half of his estate? Do you have any *idea* how much money we're talking here?" Kiesha exclaimed.

Not a clue, Shannon thought, but I definitely want to find out, and mentally urged Kiesha to continue.

Mary Elizabeth started cursing under her breath. "Damn, I was hoping to keep that bit of information to myself for as long as possible." She glared at Kiesha.

Hugh stood up so fast the table jolted. Shannon grabbed a glass to keep it from toppling over as Hugh reached over and dragged Mary Elizabeth out of the booth. "Excuse us. We need to talk." He towed her behind him. When she didn't move fast enough, he swung her over his shoulder before disappearing with her through the swinging doors that led to the kitchen.

Shannon looked at Kiesha and said dryly, "This is just a wild guess on my part, but I don't believe he knew."

Kiesha dropped her head onto Alex's shoulder. "Oh damn, she's going to kill me. Of course, he didn't know. That's not something she would have told him unless she absolutely had to. I was so shocked that I didn't think. I just blurted it out."

Rory asked what they all wanted to know. "How much money are we talking here?"

Kiesha looked up and her eyes grew unfocused as she made a mental tally. "There's the main house, the cars, the vacation house, and the condo. I guess in personal assets alone he's worth several million. Then there's the family business, plus a few subsidiaries that Charles owned. He and Babs, Mary Elizabeth's sister, never had children, and as far as I know, Charles didn't have any siblings. There are a few cousins and some aunts and uncles in the way of relatives. I've never heard Babs mention his parents so I assume they are no longer living. I do know that he comes from old money, the kind you don't hear much about. I was surprised when he gave in to Babs's demands and had a home built in Pirate's Cove so she could be close to her parents."

Shannon's jaw dropped lower and lower as the list of assets went on and on. No wonder Kiesha was shocked.

Just then they heard a loud roar, the sound of an angry bear. Right on its heels they heard Mary Elizabeth yelling, "Don't you roar at me, Hugh William Mosely!" The women smiled while the men grimaced. Hugh was in for it now.

"Mary Elizabeth must have just told him about the money," Kiesha stated.

Mary Elizabeth came storming through the swinging doors with Hugh right behind her. "I refuse to talk to you while you're being unreasonable," she raged at him.

Hugh didn't give a verbal response. He scooped her up in his arms again. A moment later, they all winced as the office door slammed behind him.

"Looks like they'll be discussing things for a while," Shannon said. "How long is Shayla going to be here?"

"She said it shouldn't take her more than three or four days to get everything set up and running. Then a couple more days to download the programs and verify all of the computers are connected and running properly. I'm going to make sure she has things set up so that you and I can both work from home without any problems."

Shannon did some mental calculations and then frowned. "That will put her here at the start of the blue moon. I hope that won't be a problem."

Rory looked at her sharply. "There's a blue moon this month?" He sniffed the air, making no attempt to hide what he was doing. "Dammit, Shannon! Are you telling me there's a blue moon coming right when you're coming into heat?" he bellowed at her.

Shannon looked around the diner. Thank goodness they were the only ones in the place. The last thing she needed was for that bit of information to get out. "Jeez, Rory. It's not like I planned this. And could you have been just a little bit louder? I'm sure the folks over in Colbyville didn't hear you."

Rory didn't respond to her comment, but he did lower his voice. "Is that why you're building a panic room? Why aren't you taking something to control the heat?" He fired the questions at her rapidly. "Wait, you already went through your heat cycle this year. Why are you going through it again? What's going on with you that you aren't telling?"

She saw Kiesha open her mouth to interfere, probably hoping to take some of the pressure off her, and Alex motion for her to keep quiet. "This is a family squabble," he murmured. "As her alphas, we can only interfere if things begin to get out of hand."

Shannon clammed up. It wasn't like there was anything Rory could do. She would handle this. She didn't need big brother riding to the rescue. When she didn't say anything, Rory turned to Alex and demanded, "What's going on with my little sister?"

Alex shook his head. "While I understand your position and would feel the same way if I were in your shoes, I can't help you. Shannon will have to tell you."

Rory stood and slid into the booth opposite Shannon, reaching for her hands. The concern he felt was visible on his face. "Come on, little bit, tell me. I can't protect you if I don't know what the threat is."

Shannon flushed to the roots of her scalp. Rory hadn't called her by that name since she'd become an adult. Hearing it brought back all the times she'd run to him as a child, wanting him to soothe her hurt. She studied him carefully. The fact that he was making no effort to hide what he was feeling let her know exactly how worried he was.

"You might as well tell him, Alex. I really don't understand everything well enough to explain it correctly."

"About damn time," Alex muttered, obviously relieved. Still, he hesitated. "You sure? I'll keep your secret if you want me to, but I really feel that this is something Rory needs to know."

"I'm sure. Go ahead. He won't let it drop until you do."

Alex explained about her medical condition and the complications it was causing. As he spoke, Rory fired questions at him, his face becoming redder and redder in proportion with his growing anger. Shannon tried not to fidget under the weight of his glare. Only Rory had the power to make her feel like a guilty teenager.

"That does it!" He slammed his hand down on the table. Kiesha startled. "You're coming home with me where I can keep you safe."

"Keep me safe? You're more likely to throw me to the wolves."

His eyes widened in unfeigned shock. "Throw you to the wolves? Where do you come off with an idea like that?"

"Rory, you've been throwing men at me for the last couple of years. Why wouldn't I think that you would take advantage of this situation?"

His chest rumbled as he growled in frustration. He dragged his hands across his face and up into his hair, then folded them on the table, leaning as close as he could get. "Shannon Fioana McFelan, listen to me and listen well. I threw those men at you hoping it would make you get up off of your arse and do something about claiming a mate for yourself and birthing the children you want. Don't you think I see the look on your face every time a mated pair is formally recognized, or the longing in your eyes whenever a newborn is introduced into the pack? I'd hoped you would go after what you wanted and make it happen. What I do not want is a choice being forced on you because you're in heat and can't protect yourself."

"What about Michael and Caleb?" she asked suspiciously.

"Caleb's a good man. He would have made a decent mate if your wolf had accepted him. He's my second-in-command, loyal to the pack. He's always had feelings for you, and I didn't have to worry about you with him as your mate. MacDougal was just there as a diversionary tactic. I knew you could beat him with one hand tied behind your back."

"Then why did you attack me?"

He gave a long sigh and looked at his hands folded on the table. "You had gone through all of the unmated males in our pack. I knew the Ravens had unmated alphas and betas,

Alex included. You would have never left the Sparrowhawks on your own. You're too loyal. I had to do something. I just didn't know Alex had found his one."

It all made sense, in a Machiavellian kind of way.

She was touched *and* angry with him. Touched that he'd gone through all of this to get her to go after what she wanted, and angry at the manipulative way he'd gone about it.

"I've met some devious people in my time," Kiesha said, "but *you* are a mastermind. Hell, I can't even be upset that you tried to set Shannon up with Alex." Kiesha's gaze drifted over Shannon in a manner she wasn't sure she liked. "And you're right. Shannon would have made a fine mate for Alex. She's strong enough, and she already has what it takes to lead."

Alex shook his head. Whether at Rory or Kiesha, Shannon wasn't sure.

"One day I'm sure I'll appreciate all that you've done in an effort to get me mated, but I'm still not coming home with you. For the first time in my life, I'm standing on my own two feet. I'm not going to run home at the first sign of trouble. The blue moon will only last for a few days. I can lock myself in for that long. You've made sure that nothing human or otherwise is getting into that room unless I want it to, and I've set up a few precautions of my own to make sure that doesn't happen." She ignored the small voice of uncertainty lingering at the back of her mind. She could do this without Rory.

"Fine. If you won't show any sense and come home, then I'll be moving in with you until this is over. They'll get to you over my dead, broken body."

At his words, she fought to keep the relief she was feeling from showing. Yes, she could handle this without her big brother's help, but it didn't mean she wanted to.

"What's so important about the blue moon?" Kiesha asked. "And why is everyone so concerned?"

"You know that a blue moon is a second full moon in the same month, and that it only happens about once every two years, right?" Alex asked.

Kiesha nodded.

"The full moon is the one time of the month when we're ruled completely by instinct. Since the beast within us operate primarily on instinct, it's at its strongest during this time. In all but the strongest of us, the beast takes over completely. This is the one part of shape-shifter lore that is actually true."

"The blue moon is also a time when we're at our most fertile," Shannon added. "Shifters are driven by the need to mate and procreate. It affects everyone, mated and nonmated. Mated couples have been known to hole up for days on end, neither eating nor sleeping, driven by the need to copulate over and over again until conception occurs."

"Unmated females usually hide or lock themselves away to keep their male counterparts from rutting on them until they conceive," Alex continued. "In Shannon's case, because her peak is going to coincide with the blue moon, her wolf will take over and could force her to rut with any male that manages to get within touching distance. Even if she is strong enough to keep from going to them, her scent will drive them to hunt for her until they manage to catch her."

"What about Shayla? Should I be worried about her? It's too late for me to call her and tell her not to come."

"Your cousin is human, right?" Rory asked. Kiesha nodded. "Then she should be fine. Shifters know better than to go after humans during a blue moon. They usually stay with their own kind."

"Maybe, maybe not. There are exceptions to every rule," Alex said. "Kiesha has shifter DNA. Her cousin may too. If she does and it's strong enough in her, she may be targeted, especially if she happens to be ovulating—the human version of the heat. If she meets up with her true mate during the blue moon, the combination of the mating fever and the blue moon fever may overwhelm her. How are you related to Shayla, Kiesha? On your mother's side or your father's?"

"Our fathers are brothers. Twins, actually. Why? What difference does it make?"

"Shifter DNA is usually strongest in males. That being the case, the odds are higher that you got it from your father, which means Shayla did too."

"Alex, you've got to do something. Shay has no idea what she's letting herself in for by coming here. I don't want anything happening to her. She's more than my cousin; she's like a sister to me."

Shannon was a bit concerned as well, for different reasons. The safe room was built for one, not two. Especially not a human who didn't understand the danger and might balk at being cooped up in close quarters for five days with a woman she didn't know. That brought up another question. "Does Shayla know what we are?"

"I don't keep secrets from Shay. She knows about me and Alex, and I explained a little bit regarding true mates. I didn't tell her about the pack or anyone else. I'm not even sure she believed what I said."

Well, that was something, Shannon thought. How much it would help, she didn't know.

"Was that wise?" Rory asked. "In general, we frown on outsiders knowing about our existence. It's safer that way. People still fear the unknown, and what they fear, they usually try to destroy."

"Shay's cool," Alex said. "Besides, she and Kiesha *are* so close, she would have realized something was amiss sooner rather than later. Better to tell her ourselves than have her figure it out on her own. Cuts down on confusion."

Shannon turned on Rory as yet another thought occurred. "Just where are you planning on sleeping? The house only has two bedrooms since one of them was converted into an office. Shay will be in one. I'll be in the other one."

"Nice try, little bit. I'll sleep in the basement."

Just then, Mary Elizabeth returned to the table, a triumphant expression on her face. Hugh, lagging behind her, had the fatalistic yet determined look of a man who had lost the battle but still hadn't given up the war.

Glancing around the diner, Mary Elizabeth said, "The lunch crowd is starting to come in. Are we staying here, or should we head over to the store?"

"Let's go," Kiesha said. "I can show Rory what's been already been done and give him an idea of what still needs to be completed."

* * *

As the five of them walked back to Kiesha's store, Sheriff Rome Barrio drove by in his police cruiser. They all lifted their hands in greeting as he beeped the horn.

Seconds after the sheriff passed, Shannon felt the hairs on her neck rise. Someone was watching her. She tried to look around without drawing attention to herself. The last thing she wanted was Rory or one of the others to notice. She didn't feel threatened. Quite the contrary, in fact. Her nipples puckered, and her vagina moistened. She knew it was a male. But who was it, where was he hiding, and why?

Rory noticed the tension she was trying not to show. "What's wrong with you? What are you searching for?" he asked her under his breath. The man had eyes like a hawk. He didn't miss a thing.

She really didn't want to tell him what she was sensing, but Rory would press until he knew, and he wouldn't be quiet about it. He'd probably scare off whomever it was before she had a chance to identify him.

"I feel like I'm being watched," she whispered. "I'm trying to figure out who's doing it. Don't do anything to alert him."

"Him? Do you feel threatened?"

"It's definitely a male. And no, I don't. It's just a really intense, focused stare. This is not the first time I've felt him."

She paused. "I can never locate the source. I don't hear anyone, and there's no scent. It's really starting to spook me."

As she continued her search, she noticed a large black raven sitting on the roof of the diner. Though it was hard to tell from this distance, it appeared to be looking straight at her. She'd seen that bird before. It usually coincided with the feeling of being watched, but that was just coincidence. It *had* to be. As far as she knew, there were no bird-shifters in the area.

She asked Rory, "Do you sense anything?"

He was still scanning the area, making no attempt to be subtle about it. "No, I can't sense a thing. Are you *sure* it's a male, and can you still sense him?" he asked, keeping his voice low.

"Yes, he hasn't left, whoever he is, but the feeling's not as intense." It was like he'd gotten distracted.

"How often does this occur? Is there any pattern to it? Maybe it's a male that's attracted to you and too afraid to come forward." Rory actually stopped and turned in a circle, looking in all directions.

Shannon grabbed him by the arm and tugged, hissing, "Keep moving. You'll scare him away."

Rory scowled at her but obeyed her directive. "I don't like this. While I want you mated, I don't like the idea of you being stalked."

"Off and on for the last month or so," she admitted. "At first, I thought it was my imagination. It was happening rather frequently and then suddenly it stopped. This is the first time it's occurred in over a week." She fought the urge to squeeze her legs together, hoping Rory wouldn't smell her growing arousal.

She'd never been this stirred by a male. Her shadowy dream lover didn't count. If she had, maybe she wouldn't still be a virgin, then this whole heat-moon thing would be a nonissue.

Nikolai sat within the body of the raven and watched his mate walk down the street with a male who closely resembled her enough to be her brother. It was a blustery, overcast day, and the wind brought the scent of his mate's budding arousal to his nose. Good, she was aware of his presence. He took note as she glanced around, trying to locate him. She looked directly at him, although he knew she had no idea that it was he she was seeking.

She said something to the male. Judging by the way he suddenly went on alert, that's exactly what she had done. From his manner, Nikolai could tell that it was going to be a real test to get past her protector. *Excellent!* He hadn't had a decent challenge in years. It would increase his pleasure exponentially to steal his mate right out from under her guardian's nose.

Spreading his wings, he flew off and headed for home. He had a she-wolf to capture and claim for his own.

Chapter Six

Shayla Morgan hummed to herself as she set up the computers in her cousin's store. The mind-numbing beat of techno music pumped into her ears via the headphones attached to the MP3 player she had tucked into the waistband of her pants. Bending at the waist, she twisted and turned, hooking connections and putting everything in its proper place, then dropped to her knees and crawled under the desk to plug the equipment in.

While she worked, she thought back to the night before. It had been late when she'd arrived, much later than anticipated. Her flight into Fort Knox had been delayed by the freaky weather hitting the northeastern seaboard. A late-spring cold front was the forerunner of a northeaster that had dumped snow and rain across the country.

She'd had no problems getting from Jacksonville to Atlanta. It was her connecting flight out of Atlanta that was the problem. By the time her flight landed and she'd secured a rental, it was past midnight. She'd arrived at Kiesha's an hour later and collapsed into the offered bed. Tonight, she'd be bunking with Kiesha's friend Shannon.

When Kiesha had first asked her to come, she'd told her cousin she'd book a room at one of the local hotels, only to be informed there weren't any. The closest hotel was in Colbyville, a forty-five-minute drive from Refuge.

Her cousin had stated she should stay with them until Shay had bluntly informed her she had no intention of lying in bed listening to her and Alex humping and bumping their way through the night. She often teased Kiesha about her stuff drying up for lack of use, but now it was her own stuff she was worried about.

She spent more time on the road than at home and still had several more trips lined up. While she didn't mind getting her freak on, she wasn't a big fan of one-night stands. A girl couldn't be too careful nowadays, and she was as safety conscious as the next person. Besides, she was too smart to lay up with a stranger simply because she was feeling a little horny. That was a good way for your picture to land on a milk carton.

If things kept going this way, she'd have to invest in a little self-gratification. Not that she believed anything store-bought could compare with the feel of a big, thick cock. Until she settled down long enough to find her a boy toy to play with, she'd just have to make do with the next best thing.

Her musings were interrupted when she backed into something solid as she maneuvered from under the desk. She glanced to see what obstacle was blocking the way. A pair of large, man-sized construction boots attached to thick, denim-covered legs standing way too close caught her eye. She hated being loomed over. Since it wasn't Kiesha behind her, she wouldn't feel guilty for what she was about to do.

Casually pulling her knee forward, she suddenly kicked up and back, aiming for his kneecap. That ought to bring him down to her level.

He twisted away at the last second, but the force of the kick was enough to throw him off balance, allowing her room to come out from under the desk. She did so swiftly, turning to face whoever was stupid enough to get in her way. She ripped the headphones off her ears and verbally blasted him. “Dude! You ever hear of personal space?” She blocked the area off around herself with her fingers. “Three feet. Any closer, and you’re a target. Got it?”

Rory stared in shock at the demented little woman standing before him with her hands on her hips. She’d actually *kicked* him! Him, one of the most feared and respected shifters in the region. He watched in growing anger as she slipped her headphones back onto her head, then walked out of the office, effectively dismissing him as though he were no more than an annoying fly.

He stormed after her, ready to take her down a peg or two. A few seconds later, he clamped a heavy hand on her shoulder, halting her departure. “Wait a minute, you little she-devil! What the hell is your—”

Seconds later, he was clutching air as she suddenly dropped low, twisted out of reach, and spun around to face him with her hands raised in a boxer’s fighting stance, murder in her eyes.

“Hands off.”

"Oh, good, you found her." Kiesha's cheery voice grated like fingernails on a chalkboard, doing nothing to alleviate the rising tension.

Shay quickly lowered her fists when she heard Kiesha's voice, but continued to glare at him.

They sized each other up like prizefighters confronting each other for the first time in the ring. It was a wonder that Kiesha couldn't see the sparks flying between them. Or maybe she knew the evil troll was crazy, and was ignoring it. Her next words seemed to confirm his theory. "Shay, this is Rory, the contractor I hired to finish the rest of the work. He has questions about what you'll need to set everything up."

"What I need is for wolf-boy to mind the personal zone and keep his hands to himself," Shay said, her tone harsh. She watched him warily, as though expecting him to spring at her any second.

Only sheer will kept him from going for Shayla's throat.

Kiesha's smile disappeared as at last she appeared to realize something was amiss. "Uh, Shay? Why did you call Rory 'wolf-boy'?"

Shayla gave a "duh" look. "It's obvious the man's not human," she said as though even a simpleton should be able to figure it out.

"Why do you say that?" Kiesha laid a hand on the witch's arm while casting worried glances in his direction.

"I have a nose. I *can* smell. He smells the same way that Alex does, human with an underlying hint of something…wild." She stared at him, her hands twitching like she wished she had something in them. A weapon, maybe?

Rory felt his eyes narrow. His fists clenched as he fought for control of his temper, unable to believe he'd allowed this…this…*thing*…to get under his skin. "You can smell what I am? That isn't possible. Humans don't have noses that sensitive. Only another shifter should be able to recognize what I am by scent alone."

"Yes," Shayla answered slowly, as though speaking to someone incredibly simpleminded. "I can smell what you are, and it's not pleasant, let me tell you."

Rory growled low in his throat and took a step forward. This woman was beyond annoying. *Look at her, with her strange hair and clothes. Who color-coordinates their hair with their outfit?* She wore short navy blue leggings that clung to her shapely thighs and firm, tight ass. The top half of her body was covered by a skintight dusty blue T-shirt. He could see perfectly the shape of her braless breasts. Suddenly he realized her nipples were hard. *Was the little she-devil cold…or aroused?*

Taking a closer look, he silently acknowledged that while Kiesha was a biracial beauty, with her mocha-colored skin and curly golden brown hair, Shayla was a perfect blending of East meets West. She had the height, round face, deep brown eyes, and silky black hair of an Asian woman. Although it was a little hard to tell about the hair because of the short punk cut and blue spikes. Her complexion reminded him of butter toffee, making him hungry for a taste. He caught the faintest hint of her arousal and felt his cock tighten in response.

Rory closed his eyes and prayed for mercy. This little troll doll could *not* be his mate. He wouldn't accept it. He knew true mates were a gift from the Creator, but if she was his, this was one gift He could keep. He'd happily pay the postage to send this little package back.

"Shay, I've always known your sense of smell was strong, but how can you smell what he is?"

"Maybe she's not as human as you think. She certainly acts like a bitch," Rory told Kiesha, smiling grimly as he got revenge for Shayla's crack about how he smelled. Maybe if he was nasty enough, she'd keep her distance. If she *was* his mate, he wouldn't stand a hope in hell of staying away from her. He already wanted to touch her despite, or maybe because of, her attitude. Other than Shannon, no woman had ever stood up to him the way this one did.

Oooo! He's going to pay for calling me a bitch!

With a hiss, Shayla opened her mouth, choice words on the tip of her tongue when Shannon walked up.

"Morning, Kiesha. Shay, finally we meet, face-to-face." She held out her hand and Shay shook it. "Rory, spreading love and sunshine around as usual, I see." Shannon's voice was laced with laughter. She must have heard them as she was coming up the stairs.

Shayla looked at Shannon, then back at Rory, noting the strong resemblance between the two. No one had to tell her they were siblings. Pasting a sorrowful expression on her face, she said in her most solemn voice, "You must be Shannon. I am *so* sorry."

"Shay…." Shayla ignored Kiesha's warning tone, determined to get even.

Shannon's amused countenance changed to confusion. Rory looked suspicious. "Sorry about what?"

Kiesha groaned and covered her face with her hand. "Don't encourage her," she wailed.

"Sorry you had to be stuck with this Neanderthal as a brother. It must be very painful for you." *Gotcha!* She shot a triumphant look at Rory.

Shannon nodded in agreement, a very sincere expression on her face. "It is. So few people actually understand just how much I suffer," she said as she wiped imaginary tears from her eyes. Then she gave a subtle sniff, just for effect.

"Oh, for the love of…" Rory muttered, glaring at the two of them.

Out the corner of her eye, she saw Kiesha roll her eyes to the ceiling, mouth moving in a silent prayer for divine help.

"You just hang in there," Shay told Shannon and patted her on the arm. "It *will* get better. After all, nobody lives forever."

"This is so true." Shannon and Shayla grinned at each other like lunatics that had successfully escaped from a mental hospital.

Rory opened his mouth, then seemed to think better of what he was about to say before turning and storming down the stairs. Moments later, the front door slammed.

Shayla fluttered her eyelashes. "Gee, was it something we said?"

Shannon and Shay fell all over with laughter while Kiesha stood there staring at them, a bemused expression on her face.

"Did you see his face?" Shannon asked, tears streaming down her face. "I've never seen him look like that. You rock!" She held up her hand for a high five.

Shayla slapped it, still giggling and wiping her eyes.

"All right, playtime's over," Kiesha said after this had gone on awhile. "There's work to be done. Shay, I'm going to be pissed if you ran off my contractor."

"Don't worry. He'll be back," Shannon reassured. "Once he commits to a job, he'll see it through. Besides, his pride won't allow him to admit he let two harmless females get under his skin."

Kiesha snorted in disbelief. "Shayla hasn't been harmless since the day she was born, and I have a feeling Rory would say the same about you."

They discussed computers and programs as they headed back into Shannon's office.

"Shay, are you *sure* you have what you need to set up? I know you can't stay long," Kiesha asked.

"I've already inspected all of the stations, and everything I need is present."

Kiesha murmured to Shannon, "That's good. I don't want to force Rory and Shayla into contact with each other any more than necessary."

Shay ignored the comment and got back to work.

* * *

Later that afternoon, Shayla was downstairs in the main part of the store hooking up the computerized registers when Mary Elizabeth walked in. She already had the workstations in the offices up and running but still needed to download the store's operating system onto the computers, then install the inventory program.

"Shayla, how's it hanging?" Mary Elizabeth jumped up on the countertop and swung her legs back and forth next to where Shayla was crouched.

"Life's good. Can't complain. What about you?" she asked as she gave a stubborn cord a vicious yank.

"Getting better every day. Kiesha around?"

"She's upstairs with Shannon going over the store accounts. Hey, I'm sorry to hear about your sister. You know I would have had your back at the funeral if I'd been local. By the time I heard the news, she was buried, and you were on your way here."

"Kiesha said you'd been doing a lot of traveling. She was glad you were able to fit her into your busy schedule."

Shayla smiled and said in a mock-gangster accent, "Yuz gotta take care of family. Besides, Kiesha's good people. She's always had my back."

Mary Elizabeth laughed. "Girlfriend, no one seeing you or listening to you speak would believe that you have two doctorate degrees and a IQ out of this world."

Shayla laughed with her and said in the extremely proper tone of the British upper crust, "That is precisely the point, my good friend. It serves the purpose of keeping people off balance. If a person doesn't realize how intelligent you are, they make the mistake of underestimating you." And if they understand just how intelligent you really are, they treat you like a freak, she thought to herself. "So, what, you're in the big leagues now and setting your own hours?"

Mary Elizabeth laughed. "Actually, I guess you could say I'm on bereavement leave. I'm headed back to Pirate's Cove for my brother-in-law's funeral. We're leaving tonight."

"I can't say I'm sorry dickhead is dead, but I offer you my condolences anyway." It *was* the polite thing to do.

Mary Elizabeth waved them away.

"I take it that your Hugh is like the others I've met around here?"

Mary Elizabeth looked confused. "Others? What others? What are you talking about?"

"I meant that Hugh is a...shape-shifter...like Alex, Shannon and her brother, and now Kiesha."

"How did you guess?"

"I can smell him on you."

"Shay, if you can smell Hugh on me, then you'd better be very careful while you're here, or you'll find yourself mated to one of these shifters. Believe me, there are a lot of them. You're exactly the type of female they're looking for. With your sense of smell, I'd say this shifter gene is strong in you. She did explain to you about true mates, right? About how it works?"

"Yeah. Well, actually, she told me what happened to her. I pieced the rest of it together myself. The only thing I don't understand is what triggers the initial change. You know, what started the ball rolling." She'd been thinking about it a lot and finally concluded that she didn't have enough information. Apparently, Kiesha left out some of the details of her experience, or I'd have figured it out by now, Shayla thought.

"I'll let Shannon answer you," Mary Elizabeth said as the other woman walked into the room. "I'm still new at this, and there's a lot I still don't understand."

Shannon shrugged. "Okay. Since I don't know how much Kiesha explained, I'll give you an overview of the whole mating process."

"Wait," Shayla interrupted, "let me get comfortable first." She shoved the cables and cords out of her way and sat on the floor, leaning against the wall behind her.

"What's going on?" Kiesha asked as she stuck her head through the doorway.

"Shannon's getting ready to explain the mating process to us."

"Oh, good. I want to hear this too. I have yet to get a definitive answer out of Alex. He always tells me it depends upon the couple. Shannon told me more when she was explaining things to Mary Elizabeth last week than both Alex and Carol put together."

"Wow! I feel like I'm teaching a class with the way you three are sitting here staring at me, but that's okay, 'cause these are the things you need to know, especially you, Shayla. Ignorance is not bliss when it comes to the mating process. The only way to protect yourself from being taken advantage of is to have as much knowledge as possible. Most males won't hesitate to use a female's ignorance against her if it would gain them what they want most—a mate."

Shannon took a deep breath before continuing. "Among shifters, the mating process is simple. The male marks the female during sex, which both signifies that he has chosen her as his mate and warns other males away. If the female marks him in return, they go before the council or pack elders to have their mating formally recognized. Or at least, that's how we did it in my former pack. Not sure what the procedure is with the Ravens."

"What happens if she doesn't want him as a mate and doesn't mark him in return?" Mary Elizabeth asked.

"What do you mean by 'mark her'?" Shayla asked. "I sincerely hope you don't mean the way dogs mark their territory."

Mary Elizabeth and Kiesha burst out laughing. Even Shannon grinned. "The mating mark is a bite that one shifter gives to another. It's located on the tendon where the neck meets the shoulder. It's not visible to humans unless the shifter giving it was unusually aggressive.

"If the female does not mark the male at that time, he has two weeks to court her and change her mind. At the end of that time, if he is unsuccessful, the mark on her shoulder fades, and she is once again considered fair game by other male shifters. This keeps males from being able to force females into relationships they neither want nor desire.

"True mates are a tad bit different. Between shifters, there is no question that the female will accept the male's mark and mark him in return because they both instinctively recognize the other as their one. Things change when one of the mates is human because humans are not as in tune with their instincts as shifters are. There may be a struggle while one mate waits for the other to accept their destiny. That's where the mating fever comes into play. Because there is such a strong attraction between the two, they usually can't keep their hands off of each other long enough for one or both of them to fight the mating bond growing between them."

"What's a mating fever?" Shayla asked.

"Since I've only heard about it, I'll let the experts answer your question." Shannon pointed to Mary Elizabeth and Kiesha.

"It's a lust that defies imagination," Kiesha said. "You literally cannot keep your hands off of each other, and the more you fight it, the stronger it gets."

"No matter what your mind says, it's your body that's in control. I fought against my desire for Hugh, to no avail. It just got stronger and stronger until it literally erupted between us," Mary Elizabeth added.

"But that's just lust, right? I mean, sex is sex. Sure, sometimes it's really good, mind-blowing, out-of-this-world sex, but it still all boils down to sex," Shayla said, trying to understand what the big deal was.

"It's more than just sex," Kiesha said. "On a physical level, once you've been marked, every time you exchange body fluids, be it something as simple as a kiss or as complicated as sex, the human partner's DNA changes, becoming shifter like their mate's. With each mating, a soul-deep connection forms that only gets stronger and stronger until, like it says in the Bible, the two literally become one soul."

Shannon continued, "Once that happens, the mate bond rite takes place. This part varies from couple to couple, but it refers to that point in the relationship where the human party accepts the shifter as their one and marks them in return."

"What would have happened if Alex had marked Kiesha, and she refused to accept him?" Shayla didn't intend to get herself into that kind of situation, but if she did, she wanted to know her options. She believed in planning ahead and being prepared for any eventuality.

"The first thing she would have needed to do was get as far away from Alex as she could to try and stop the bonding. With enough time and distance between them, it's possible that mating fever would lessen in intensity, but it would never truly disappear, not once you've been marked. Getting away is the trick. It's almost impossible since shifter males are obsessive about keeping their mates once they find them. Even if you manage to escape, I'm not sure you can break the bond once the process has started. I've never heard of anyone succeeding."

"So, if I were to find myself extremely attracted to a shifter and wanted to indulge, I could do so as long as I didn't let him bite me?" Shayla asked.

"Shay, *don't* even think about it," Kiesha warned. "If you're attracted to one of them and you don't want to find yourself mated, don't let them close to you. A strong physical attraction is a major sign of a true mate. It's not simply a matter of not getting bit. If you have sex with one, you'll be so caught up in the pleasure that you'll never notice him biting you, not until it's too late. This is no time to indulge your curiosity."

"They're that good in the sack?" Shayla asked as her neglected libido raised its head in hunger.

"Shay, really, this is *not* something to play with. These guys are *serious*. They play for keeps. They won't put up with your games."

"Kiesha, chill out. I was just asking a question. I won't be here long enough to get into trouble. Besides, the only male I've met here besides Alex is Shannon's dickhead brother. Sorry, Shannon."

Shannon laughed. "No offense taken. He *is* a dickhead, among other things. I'm just glad I'm not the only one who sees it."

"Don't worry, Kiesha. If I meet someone here that looks like he could really rock my boat, I'll run long and hard in the other direction," Shayla said.

After I get myself a taste first, she finished in her mind.

* * *

In a few hours, the moon would rise. Tonight was the first night of the full moon—a blue moon. Shannon felt hot and itchy, as though something were crawling under her skin. Her sex was swollen and sensitive, her pussy weeping for the cock it was being denied. Her heat was at its peak. If she had any sense, she'd be home right now, locked in her panic room where it was safe.

Her body was broadcasting "come and get me" signals. Fortunately, there weren't any males around to receive it, which was the only reason she'd ventured out of the house. Shayla was done with the computers at the store. Last night she'd worked on Shannon's computer, getting her networked so that she could work from home. She was driving Shayla over to Kiesha's so that she could do the same to hers. She said it would only take her about thirty minutes to get the system up and running.

That was a good thing. There were about three hours until moonrise. Fifteen minutes getting there, thirty minutes on the computer, and then another fifteen-minute ride home. That gave her two hours to make it to the basement and safety.

Rory had said she was crazy for leaving. "Stay home. Let Shayla drive herself to Kiesha's house. There's a capable adult in there somewhere, I guess, under all that weird hair."

That, of course, had led to yet another round of bickering between Shayla and Rory. The night before had been full of them. It seemed to Shannon that he went out of his way to antagonize Shayla.

After arguing for almost an hour, Shannon said, "Please, Rory. Stay here and make sure everything is secure. If Shay goes by herself, she may get lost. Do we really want her out there alone with a bunch of sex-hungry shifters on the prowl? If we aren't back in an hour, you have my permission to come get us and drag us back."

Rory finally relented.

On the way out of the door, Shayla placed a suitcase in the trunk of her rental. "Once I'm finished with Kiesha, I think I'll leave town for a few days until this blue moon madness is over and done with. You and that brother of yours have argued so much about it the paranoia is spreading."

"I think that's a great idea. I know you think I'm overexaggerating the seriousness of this, but if you're gone that's one less thing I have to worry about."

If Shayla didn't leave, the two of them would have to hole up together. The panic room wasn't really made for two people, especially when one of them was a shifter at the peak of her heat. Shifters didn't really tolerate confined spaces. They required the freedom of the outdoors with lots of space to move. If shifters had to be locked up, they needed to be distracted with lots of food or sex or both.

The sun was already sinking from the sky. Shannon looked at her watch as she pulled up in front of Alex's home. "Shay, please work as fast as you can. I'm already pushing it. Arguing with Rory wasted time I didn't have."

As they exited the car, Shay responded, "Don't worry. We'll be in and out before you know it."

Alex answered the door. His eyes grew round when he spotted her and he seemed disturbed, even dismayed, by her appearance. "Shannon, I didn't know you were coming with Shayla. Shouldn't you be home preparing for tonight?" He cast an uneasy glance over her shoulder to the yard behind.

"I couldn't let Shayla ride over here by herself. She's unfamiliar with the area. She might have gotten lost. We couldn't afford for that to happen, not tonight of all nights." She watched Shayla follow Kiesha into the den where she had her home office set up, then wondered what was wrong with Alex. He'd never seemed unhappy to see her before.

"Why don't you head on home? One of us can drive her back, or she can stay here tonight if it gets too late." Alex sounded a bit desperate. *What's up with him?*

She looked at him strangely. "That's not necessary. I'm here now, and Shayla said it wouldn't take long. There's no sense in you leaving your house when I'm already here. Besides, the only males in scenting distance are you and Rory. Otherwise I'd be more concerned. Most of the males live closer to town, and that's where they will be heading, where the females are most abundant." *At least that's what I hope they'll do.* That little bit of uncertainty was why she'd let Rory hang around.

Alex stalked off toward the kitchen muttering, "Stubborn females, always messing up my plans."

Shannon followed slowly behind him, wondering again what his problem was. She joined the ladies in the den, where Kiesha was watching Shayla work, asking the occasional question.

"Kiesha, what's wrong with Alex? He seemed upset to see me. In fact, he tried to get me to go home and let one of you bring Shayla back, or he said she could spend the night here and wait until tomorrow."

Kiesha's eyes narrowed in speculation. "He actually said that to you?"

Shannon nodded. "Not only did he say it, but when I pointed out that I was already here and that there was no sense in leaving, he stalked off muttering about 'stubborn women and messed-up plans.' What 'plan' was he talking about?"

Kiesha thought about it for a moment; then her eyes widened in alarm. "Shay, stop what you're doing. You have to get out of here. Both of you. He's trying to find a mate for Shayla! He *knew* she was coming tonight, and probably invited a few of the alphas from the pack to come over. He didn't say anything to me because he knew I'd be pissed."

Shannon's eyes rounded like saucers. "Oh, shit. Did you say *alphas?* Shay, *hurry*. We have to go. Now!"

"I'm coming," Shay mumbled, shutting everything down as fast as she could. "When I see that cousin-in-law of mine again, I'll have a few things to say to him. Too bad there's no time for it now."

She ran through the door on Shay's heels, giving her a gentle shove when Shay paused to throw a glare over her shoulder at Alex as they bypassed him in the kitchen.

Outside, Shannon ran for her truck, keys in hand, with Shay close behind. *Damn, I should have listened to Rory*. Then she wouldn't be in this mess. She hated that he was always right.

She started the truck and shoved it in gear before turning around in the yard to head back to the main road. "We have to get back to the house. The minute they catch my scent, they're going to be all over me. I wish I knew who he'd called, what time he expected them to arrive, and how they were coming—in vehicles or on all fours."

"From his reaction to your presence, I'd say he expected them to arrive at any moment, which was why he was trying to rush you out of there."

Shannon spun out onto the little two-lane dirt road that ran up the mountain and through the woods. They bounced up and down inside the cab as the tires navigated over ruts and dips, sometimes coming off the ground entirely. Shannon cursed as the truck began losing power, shuddering and shaking. She beat the dash. "Come on, you piece of shit. Don't do this to me now." Apparently it wasn't listening; the engine stalled, and the truck came to a rolling stop in the middle of the road.

"I should have replaced you when Rory wanted me to. This is how you repay my loyalty? Sentimental reasons! Hah! I should have dumped your sorry, sometime-working ass when I had the opportunity."

With one last hit to the steering wheel, she turned to Shayla. "Leave your laptop. We'll get it tomorrow. We're going to have to run for it. The house isn't that far if we cut through the woods. It's still light enough for us to see."

"Then what are we sitting here for? Let's go." Shay opened the door and jumped out.

Shannon slid across the seat, climbed out of the passenger side, then grabbed Shayla's hand before taking off. The light wouldn't be as good once they were deep in the woods. Since she was a shifter, she could move much faster than Shay. She didn't want to accidentally leave Shay behind because she couldn't keep up, although Shay was surprising her. She was running, jumping, twisting, and turning through the thick undergrowth just like a shifter.

The adrenaline pumping through her system was intensifying the heat. *Oh God, if the males are close, they'll smell me.* Just as the thought crossed her mind, she heard crashing in the undergrowth, headed in their direction. She could see the house in the distance. They stood a better chance of making it if they split up.

She dragged Shayla to a halt. “They’re coming. We need to split up. It’s me they’re after.” She pointed straight ahead. “There’s the house. Keep going, and you should make it. Tell Rory not to worry about me. I’m going to head upwind and try to lose them. If you get into trouble, scream for Rory and he’ll come running.”

While speaking, she’d been stripping out of her clothes. “I’ll make better time in wolf form. Wish me luck.”

Shayla shook herself and forced her legs to move. She could think about what she saw later, when she was safely behind closed doors. She fixed her gaze on the house and ran, thankful for the years she’d spent running track and the many times her father had taken her hiking as a child.

As the front yard came into sight, she heard a sound close behind—too close for comfort. She didn’t waste time looking behind her to see what it was. Instead, she screamed at the top of her lungs. “Rory!”

She hit the driveway just as the front door crashed open, and Rory came charging out. He paused at the top of the stairs, searching. When he saw her and then what was behind her, something savage came over his face. He roared, “Mine!” in a voice that couldn’t possibly be human, then cleared the porch, the steps, and a few feet of yard in one single bound.

Shay didn’t know what was behind her, nor did she care. She was focused on the open front door. All her energy was concentrated on reaching it and the safety it represented. She heard the sounds of growling and fighting behind her as she sprinted for the porch. As she prepared to leap up the steps, a huge wolf came from out of nowhere, directly in front of her. She stopped so abruptly she actually skidded and had to windmill her arms to keep from falling on her butt.

Oh damn, what to do now?

Nothing in her life had prepared her for this moment. She had two werewolves fighting behind her and one on the porch in front of her, blocking the way to safety. She could run to her car and try to lock herself inside, but would she make it? Would it do her any good? Maybe she could talk her way out of this.

It was worth a shot.

Before she could give that option a try, there was a heavy thud followed by a high-pitched yip, then total silence behind her. She really wanted to know who'd won the fight, but she couldn't afford to take her gaze off the wolf in front of her. She prayed Rory had been the victor. Her motto for the moment was better the devil—or, in this case, shifter—she knew than the one she didn't.

She sidled slowly to the side, a few steps at a time so that she could see what was behind her, but at the same time keep the wolf on the porch in her sights. Then she heard a god-awful growl behind her that she felt right down to her bones. The hackles on the wolf rose, and he crouched, fangs bared. She dived out of the way just as he sprang at whatever had issued the challenging growl behind her. She heard flesh meeting flesh as she scrambled to her feet and virtually flew up the porch stairs and into the house.

She opened the basement door, pushed it shut, then locked it behind her. Running down the steps so fast that she almost tripped, she rushed through the second door. Using her body to push it closed, she twisted the locks into place. Okay now, that was better, she thought as she propped her hands on her knees and tried to catch her breath. Supposedly the only way anything could get into this room was with a key. She was safe, but she wouldn't feel safe until she knew what happened to Rory and Shannon.

She wasn't sure how much time passed before she heard the door at the top of the stairs crash open. Shayla backed away from the entrance, looking around desperately for a place to hide. The measured tread of heavy footsteps sounded loud as they came down the stairs. She was hoping like hell that it was either Rory or Shannon on the other side as she heard the scrape of a key, the locks unlatched and the door began to silently swing open. If it wasn't, there was nowhere to run, no way to escape.

* * *

Shannon ran as fast as she could through the thick undergrowth and up the side of the mountain. Her goal was to climb high, then circle around and come back down behind the house and enter through the back door.

She'd told Shayla she would try to get upwind of her pursuers and slow them down. Under normal circumstances, that's exactly what she would be doing. However, she was hampered by her need to stay downwind of the males. With this traitorous heat racking her body, the last thing she wanted to do was catch the scent of hot, ripe male pheromones.

With a little luck, it wouldn't be long before she was safe and sound at home. She'd left Shay not far from the house. When Shayla arrived at the door without her, Rory would know something had gone wrong and come looking for her. Not that she needed his help. Still, it was nice knowing big brother would be running to the rescue.

Dusk bled into darkness as the full moon crested above the tree line. Its mellow light barely penetrated the forest in which she ran, but with every fiber of her being she could feel its presence. Thinking she had climbed high enough to avoid detection, she turned in the direction of home and began circling back. With her change of course came a shift in the wind, bringing the mouthwatering scent of male wolf to her nostrils. Her beast took over as instinct rose to the forefront, overriding human reasoning. She let loose a howl, a primal mating call that made the human part of her wince. The night air resonated with the melodious sound of howling wolves, as unmated males from miles around responded to her mating call.

Her beast firmly in control of her actions, she pranced around the area until she found a spot suitable for her needs and settled down to wait. She quivered with expectation as she felt them drawing closer to her. They entered one by one into the clearing where she stood, so excited she was almost dancing in place, stirring up the cushioning bed of needles and leaves beneath her paws with her antics, until there were three of them gathered. She sat down on her haunches, her ears tilted forward expectantly as she waited for them to settle which one would have the privilege of mounting her. She'd waited a long time for this moment.

She would only mate with the strongest. She needed a worthy male, one who could give her strong, healthy pups. He had to be strong enough to protect her and her pups. She was an alpha female. Only an alpha would suit.

She sat regal as a queen surrounded by suitors vying for her attention. They strutted and preened before her in all their masculine glory before settling down to the serious business of eliminating the competition. They'd already proven their ability to hunt by finding her. Now came the test of strength.

A large brown wolf with white markings aggressively came forward, head held high, ears and tail up, and teeth bared in challenge to his opponents. His chest vibrated with the almost-silent growls emanating from his being.

An equally large brownish black wolf met his challenge. He puffed up, bared his teeth, and crouched, prepared to fight for the right to mate.

The two males circled each other warily, each searching for an area of weakness, a lowering of the defenses in the other. As the minutes passed and nothing interesting happened, she yawned, bored with all of the posturing. Come on and fight already, she thought. You're burning moonlight. Can't you smell how ready I am? Can't you see how anxiously I'm waiting to be mated?

Finally the brown-and-white wolf made a move, charging directly at the other wolf, hoping to intimidate him into backing down. The brownish black wolf was prepared and leaped out of the way at the last minute, swiping at the flanks of the charging wolf as he passed, leaving behind a large gash that bled profusely. After a few more fruitless attempts, the brown-and-white wolf gave up in defeat and conceded the prize to the stronger, more determined male.

The brownish black wolf approached her proudly, head held high, ears straight up and tail high as he strutted to her like the champion that he was. When he stood before her, she came to her feet, and they licked muzzles in greeting. They rubbed their bodies against each other as they circled, sniffing and getting accustomed to one another. She stood still as he worked his way behind her. Once in place, he sniffed and licked at her sex, testing her readiness to be mounted as she stood patiently waiting.

Just as he positioned himself to mount her, a huge black wolf came barreling out of the darkness and into her potential mate, causing them to flip and roll in a growling and snarling tangle of fur, teeth, and legs. The black was ferocious in its attack, ruthlessly subduing his opponent and showing his willingness to kill to claim his mate. The brownish black wolf, sensing it was no match for the black, reluctantly surrendered his prize and slunk off.

At first, she was highly impressed. Here was a premium specimen, one worthy of her and capable of producing strong pups. She waited eagerly as he approached, the wind at her back ruffling her fur and causing it to stand on end. As he neared, she got her first whiff of his scent, and her hackles rose. She knew that scent.

Unnatural. Not wolf.

Chapter Seven

Nikolai gazed at the bristling she-wolf in front of him and sighed. He and this beastly side of his mate's nature would eventually come to terms with one another, but not tonight. He shifted into his natural form and, with a strong surge of power, commanded Shannon to sleep.

Without the support of her human side, the she-wolf stumbled, off balance and disoriented. Taking advantage of its momentary distraction, Nikolai spoke in a sharp, compelling tone, "Change!"

The she-wolf, turbopowered by the strength of the blue moon, fought hard, unwilling to give up its control, but had no choice. He'd infused his decree with so much power that the beast found itself forced back into the innermost being of the sleeping woman before it was fully aware of it happening.

The change was fluid and seamless, and over in a matter of seconds. His mate lay on her side, slumbering deeply on a bed of cushioning leaves, the wolf buried within. Random pockets of moonlight filtered through the trees, highlighting the fragile beauty of her naked body.

Nikolai breathed deep, savoring the scent of his chosen. With a casual wave of his hand over his lower body, he clothed his legs in a pair of well-worn, loose-fitting denim jeans before bending down to scoop her up into his arms. He carried her through the woods to his home, a massive two-story structure built out of stone near the top of the mountain.

He walked up the stairs to the huge double-door entrance, through the foyer, and into the library until he reached the secret elevator leading to the lower level of his home. As the lift settled onto the basement floor, he turned the key to lock it in place so that there was no danger of them being disturbed by anyone. When he stepped out of the elevator, the doors closed behind him and a section of wood paneling glided into place, completely hiding its existence.

He walked through the sitting room with its enormous fireplace and into his bedroom; low-level lights from the evenly placed sconces on the wall flickered as he passed, lighting the way. He strode over to the massive four-poster bed in the center of the room and laid Shannon in the middle of the bed. He stood back for a moment and just basked in the satisfaction of finally having his chosen here, in his lair.

The room was done in shades of green and brown, reminiscent of the forest he loved so much. The wall dividing the sitting room from the bedroom wasn't really a wall at all. It was an open fireplace that, when not lit, allowed one to gaze from one area into the other. With a flick of his hand, the fireplace roared to life, the heat removing the lingering chill from the room.

Now to prepare his woman for mating.

He went to the highboy dresser and pulled out some scarves, a blindfold, and restraints. He'd thought long and hard about the problem of her beast rising to the surface. If her wolf was allowed to come forth, he might have to hurt her in order to subdue her, for her beast would not easily submit to his dominance. He would bind her, at least until she became used to his passion and had better control over her own.

Nikolai went to each corner of the bed and secured extralong scarves to the posts. After tying them in place, he gave them a good, hard yank, putting his considerable strength into it. The knots held, and the posts didn't budge. *Good.* The bed had been handcrafted out of the strongest wood available—live oak—and should be able to withstand an angry werewolf bent on gaining her freedom.

He put the silk wrist and ankle restraints on his mate, ran the scarves through the specially made attached loops, and gently pulled until she lay spread-eagle on the bed. He knotted the scarves to keep her in position, then stood back, admiring his handiwork.

He walked to the top of the bed and removed the pillows. Sliding one hand under her hips, he lifted her and positioned one of his fluffy, fat pillows under her, elevating that portion of her body for easier access and maximum penetration. Then he gently blindfolded her, careful not to snag her hair in any way. No matter how much she twisted and rubbed her head against the mattress, it wouldn't come off until *he* removed it.

One thought and his clothes vanished from his body. He walked to the foot of the bed and gazed at her as he absentmindedly stroked his aching arousal. He climbed onto the high bed, crawling between her legs until his body hovered over hers, his weight supported by his forearms. Leaning down, he placed his face directly over hers, his mouth mere centimeters above her own so that her first breath would be scented with him.

"Shannon, awake!"

* * *

Rory walked down the basement stairs, struggling with every step to leash his beast and shift back to human form. He was a strong alpha, but his beast fought harder than it should, even with adrenaline from the fight still pumping through his veins and the rising blue moon strengthening it.

The sight of Shayla in trouble had brought every primitive instinct in his body roaring to the forefront. The impulse to protect and defend had crashed over him, blocking out any attempt at rational thinking. Now that he had fought for and won her, the urge to claim her, mark her, and breed pups with her rode him hard.

He'd had no intentions of mating the troublesome woman, even though he highly suspected she was his one. He'd decided long ago he'd never mate *or* breed. There was too much of his father's nature in him. He'd never inflict the mental and physical agony on any child that his father had wreaked on him. Staying alone was the only foolproof way to guarantee it didn't happen.

Even though Shayla irritated him to no end, he didn't want to scare her. Knowing what he was and seeing it were two different things. Unfortunately, the most he'd been able to manage was a partial shift. He was still in his wolf-man form—part wolf, part man—but he'd managed to even out his facial features enough so that he looked more man than wolf. He could do nothing about his size or his height, which now was a little under seven feet.

He opened the door slowly, not knowing what to expect. She was probably hysterical after being chased by two werewolves. Most women would be. The scent of hot, sweaty female hit him in the face and rushed straight to his cock, driving every thought from his mind except for the need to procreate. Heaven help them both—Shayla was in heat!

* * *

Shannon woke to darkness, totally disoriented. The last thing she remembered was her wolf surging to the forefront and taking over. She'd been totally helpless to prevent it. She hadn't lost control of her beast like that since puberty, before Rory began training her. Her mind ran in circles. Where was she? What trouble had her beast caused? Dear God, was she mated, and if so, to whom? Before she could get her bearings, the powerful scent of aroused male entered her nostrils. Her mind blanked, and her flesh went haywire.

There was a hard male body on top of her.

His naked chest brushed against hers, lightly rubbing her tight, puckered nipples with each breath that he took. His stomach pressed against her mound. Shannon's body turned to liquid, and she arched into him, trying to get closer.

She reached out to touch him, draw him nearer, but couldn't. Something was stopping her, holding her back. *Why can't I…?* Her hands were bound. Lust forgotten, she stiffened all over as anger and fear washed over her. *No!* She jerked hard, pulling and tugging to free herself. How dare he bind her! A growl rumbled out of her chest as her beast responded to her skyrocketing emotions. First she'd rip free; then she'd kill this male who dared to do what no other had.

Before she could summon her beast to the surface, a deep voice commanded, "Be at peace, little one. The restraints are for your protection. The blindfold is merely a tool to enhance your pleasure. This is your first time, and I don't want to hurt you. If I am to remain in control, I can't allow you to touch me."

At the sound of his voice, she stilled, shock overriding her wrath. *I'm blindfolded too?* She turned her head from side to side, testing the truth of his words. Then it dawned on her. *I know that voice. I've been hearing it in my dreams.* "Do I know you?"

"Nikolai Taranosky, at your service."

The rational side of her mind tried to understand what was happening, but her body was being bombarded by male pheromones, short-circuiting her ability to reason. Her breath quickened as her passion once again rose to the forefront.

She tugged uselessly at the restraints on her wrists, needing to touch him.

"Be still."

She struggled all the more, arching wildly beneath him. "Please, let me touch you."

He let out a husky laugh that set her nerve endings on fire, stroking her from the inside out, and she shivered as he promised in a silky voice, “Oh, I fully intend to. Please you, that is.”

Dimly, in the small portion of her brain that could still reason, a tiny voice was screaming. *Shannon, resist! Stop this before it’s too late. You don’t know this male. He could be like your father, or worse. Do you really want to bind yourself to this stranger for the rest of your life?*

That last thought pushed through the heat and hormones fogging her analytical abilities, and her mind began to clear. Knowing it was futile, she tried to bargain with him. “Please, don’t do this. Let me go. Give me the opportunity to get to know you when my mind’s not so clouded. If we’re to spend the rest of our lives together, let’s not begin it like this.” She breathed through her mouth, not wanting to lose the bit of ground she’d gained over her body.

“You know me,” he countered. “And before this evening is through, I’ll be engrafted into your very soul.” Then he ended all pending arguments by blowing a stream of air directly into her nostrils, and Shannon was lost.

Nikolai locked his mouth onto hers, kissing her deeply. In all of the toying he’d done with her body over the last few weeks, not once had he kissed her. The taste of her made his gums ache. He fought to keep his fangs from dropping into place. If he accidentally nicked her and got a taste of her blood, he wouldn’t be able to restrain himself. Bloodlust would take control.

He intended their first time to be, for her, a mating initiation that she could look back on with joy. He withdrew from her mouth and hissed in pleasure, fighting to restrain himself. He'd been arousing her fiery passion for too long without satisfying his own. Now that she was in his possession, he was dangerously close to losing all restraint. He couldn't allow that to happen. His mate's needs must come before his own.

That thought firmly in mind, he nibbled and tasted his way to her ear. Running his tongue delicately around the rim, he toyed with it before sucking on her earlobe. She turned her head and arched her neck, granting him access as she shivered with pleasure. "More," she moaned.

The pulse beating in her neck drew his attention, and he allowed his mouth to travel there. He nuzzled her lightly before dragging his teeth back and forth, scraping the skin as he fought the urge to bite and feed. There would be time for that later.

He continued with his exploration of her body. Previously, he'd touched her only mentally, except for the night he'd lost control and fed. Tonight, they were skin to skin, no powers involved, just the way it was supposed to be between chosen. He lightly stroked her nipple with his tongue, licking it back and forth as she whimpered and arched her back.

"Harder. Give me more."

He smiled to himself. Virgin she might be, but his woman was no shy miss.

"Is this what you want?" He latched onto one nipple and drew it into his mouth using deep suction. He squeezed the other one hard between his fingers, pulling and tugging on its taut peak. He suckled as though there were milk inside and if he just pulled hard enough, he could draw it out. He was going to indulge his every fantasy, even if it took hours. After all, they had all night. Here, deep in his lair, there was no one to disturb them.

He leisurely switched to the other side, suctioning deeply until half her breast was in his mouth. His fangs pressed against her skin, and he could smell the engorged veins just beneath the surface. Again the temptation arose to bite down and drink his fill.

Bloodlust whispered seductively in his ear. *Was she not his? Did not the very blood streaming in her body belong to him? Take. Drink.*

Nikolai clamped down on it. He was no fledgling vampire to be ruled by his instincts, but a fully mature one in control of all his urges. To prove it, he pulled back until only her nipple was in his mouth and bit down until his teeth broke the surface, enough to hurt but not to bleed, a move he knew she'd find pleasurable. Shifters, like vampires, relished biting and scratching in their love play. Their very natures demanded that sex be rough.

His mind fully merged with hers, he was aware of Shannon's every thought, every reaction of her body to his actions. He smiled when, with a keening cry, she shook as pleasure shot straight to her core, causing her pussy to spasm in need. Just the response he'd anticipated. When she planted her feet flat on the bed with the little bit of leeway the restraints allowed and rubbed her mound against his hard-muscled stomach, he knew she sought to soothe the ache building there.

"Answer me. Is this what you want?" He switched to the other breast and bit down on that nipple as well.

"Yes," she growled out, her beast beginning to rise to the surface.

"*No!* You *will not* shift. Control your wolf."

When he backed away, removing all physical contact, she struggled to do as he commanded.

"Every time I feel your beast rising, I will cease giving you pleasure. Do you understand?"

"Yes," she moaned, and his nostrils quivered as her body released a torrent of fluids at his demand. The scent of it permeated the room. Her wolf was pleased by his dominant behavior. It was only to be expected, he mused. She was an alpha. She needed a mate strong enough to tame her.

"Good."

Because his mind was linked firmly with hers, he knew she was keeping a lock on her beast, at least for now. He worked his way down her torso until he reached her mound, licking, nibbling, and biting, careful not to break the skin. He lingered there at the sensitive flesh of her belly just above her mound.

"Nikolai, I need…" Shannon's voice faded as her hips lifted, silently telling him what she wanted. Her thighs glistened with fluid, the pubic hair slick with dew.

The aroma of her essence was strong, beckoning him to come and taste. He resisted, remembering what had happed the last time he'd given in to temptation. Instead, he drew his fingers along her slit, moistening his fingers and teasing her entrance. Slowly, he eased one finger inside her virgin sheath. Shannon moaned and arched her hips, clamping down on his finger.

She was hot and tight. He was going to have to loosen her before he could mount her. Nikolai eased his finger in and out, spreading her juice and increasing her arousal before adding another digit. He blocked out the sounds of her whimpering and pleading, concentrating fully on preparing her for penetration. When she could handle two with ease, he gently added a third.

Her head was thrashing about. She abruptly began to growl as her climax neared. Feeling her beast once more attempting to rise, he stopped what he was doing, withdrew his fingers completely, and left her hanging on the edge of climax.

"Noooo!"

"Control your beast," he said calmly, though he was anything but. His cock was so tight he thought it would explode. It was taking every bit of control to keep *his* beast in check.

She fought a battle within herself as anger and need clashed. Anger that he had stopped what he was doing when she was so close warred against the need to do whatever he asked to make him continue. Her strong emotions were fueling her beast, and she struggled to control them, knowing he wouldn't continue until her wolf was once more in its cage.

She understood and appreciated what he was doing even as the necessity of it pissed her off. If allowed, her beast would challenge and force him to prove his dominion over it, in whatever form that took. She'd seen female shifters scarred and broken, almost beyond repair, because their inner beast challenged a dominant male at the wrong time. That he cared enough to prevent that from happening to her went a long way toward calming her anger and gave her the control she needed to leash her wolf.

Once again, he stroked her, rebuilding the fire within. This time, it flamed higher for having been denied. He started again with the one finger and built to three, giving her body time to adjust. Her muscles tensed, and she began to shake but stayed in control of her beast. As a reward, he took his thumb and stroked her clit, increasing her pleasure.

Fire shot through her body, and her fingers sprouted claws, which bloodied the palms of her hands as she fought to keep her beast in its cage. Her hips pumped, driving him deeper, yet it wasn't deep enough. "More," she growled.

"Not yet."

"Now," she snarled. "Need…more!"

"No." Firm and implacable, his tone let her know that he wouldn't budge from his course.

She switched to pleading. "Please, Nikolai." She heard his heart jump and smelled his arousal increase when she called his name.

"It's too soon."

"Nikolai." She panted his name as she rotated her hips in a circle.

He cursed under his breath, and the hand gripping her thigh tightened.

Oh, he liked that, did he? She did it again, calling his name at the same time. "Nikolai, please. Need…deeper…harder."

"Don't want to hurt you."

He was weakening. Shannon pushed the advantage. "Nikolai, please. Nikolai." She chanted his name, her voice throaty in her passion. She was drowning in pheromones, hers and his, as lust permeated the air. If he didn't break soon, she was going to scream.

"Now, Nikolai!"

He gave her what she demanded, adding the fourth finger while thrusting as deep as his fingers would go. The scent of her blood-tinged vaginal fluid was making him crazy. He didn't know how much longer he could hold on. He balanced on his elbow and leaned over her to suck on her nipple. The added sensation pushed her over the edge. Her neck arched sharply as she howled her release.

His fangs dropped into place. He removed his hand and grabbed his throbbing cock, lining it up with her entrance. With a hard thrust, he plunged into her, past the fragile barrier of her virginity, until he was seated deep inside. He planted his hands on the mattress beside her, elbows locked into place as he threw his head back and fought for control.

"Shit. Shit. Shit. Shit!" He struggled not to savage her like the monster that he was. She was so tight. Her hungry vagina milked his shaft, trying to pull his seed from his body. Her blood called to him, beckoning him to gorge himself.

He groaned as he slowly withdrew until only the head was seated at her entrance, and then he slid his way back home, this time not stopping until he hit the opening to her womb. Her cervix contracted around him, making him hiss and curse in pleasure before he withdrew and did it again and again, until he found his rhythm.

“Yes! Yes! Harder!”

Nikolai shook his head, still trying to take it easy on her, but she was having none of it.

“Harder, damn you! Don’t hold back!” Then she snarled at him, and the leash on his beast loosened the slightest bit. He picked up the pace, hammering into her over and over.

The force of his thrusts caused her breasts to bounce as she matched him. A red haze covered his mind as his fangs throbbed. He heard the beating of her heart. Felt its rhythm increase as it sought to keep up with the demand being placed on it. He smelled the rich scent of her blood as it rushed through her veins. When she screamed her release, his control snapped. Quick as a snake, he struck, driving his fangs deep into her breast and sucking ravenously on her blood as his seed exploded from his body, flooding her waiting womb.

* * *

Shayla jumped as the door crashed open, bouncing off the wall. Rory stood in the opening, but it was a Rory she’d never seen before. *This* Rory was huge and covered from the chest down in very fine red fur. He was so tall, he had to duck to get through the doorway. He'd been large, but now he looked like a bodybuilder on steroids.

As he stepped into the light, she got a good look at his face. Something was off, something wrong with his jaw and his eyes. They were the eyes of a wolf.

She glanced over his downy body only to come to a jarring halt when she reached his crotch. The bulge there was as massive as the rest of him, and it strained against the fly of his tattered jeans, fighting to be free. She licked her lips as her body came alive. *Down, girl*, she told it. *This is Rory. We don't like him, remember?*

Her body wasn't listening.

As she stared, transfixed, Rory reached down and casually ripped the jeans from his body. He wasn't wearing underwear. Shayla almost fell to her knees at the force of the lust that surged through her at the sight of his cock, primed and ready for action. It was so long, reaching almost to his navel, and so thick she knew she wouldn't be able to close her hands around it. Its bulbous head was purple with the volume of blood engorging it. Her pussy contracted at the thought of getting it inside her, and she began to pant.

"Mine," Rory growled as he stepped toward her. She reluctantly looked away from his cock to his face, her breath catching at the lust she could see there. "Mine," he repeated, coming steadily closer. "Fought. Won. Claimed. *Mine*!"

Yes, he had fought to protect me and won. Doesn't he deserve a reward? "Yours," she confirmed.

His eyes flared in satisfaction.

There was a niggling voice at the back of her mind warning her that this was a mistake. Shut up! All I want is a taste, she thought. Just one little taste to satisfy my curiosity. As long as I don't let him bite me, everything will be fine. I'll have some fun and no one will be the wiser. Besides, she consoled her conscience, this is Rory. He doesn't like me any more than I like him.

She stood still as he stalked toward her, not the least bit afraid at this proof that he wasn't human. Seeing his beastly side actually revved her arousal. She wondered what it would take to make him lose control. She gasped when he shredded the clothes from her body, and her pussy gushed in response to his savagery.

He grabbed her under the arms and tossed her onto the bed, over six feet away. She shrieked as she flew through the air, landed with a bounce, and slid to the top of the bed, arms and legs splayed in an effort to catch herself. Before the bed had stopped rocking, he leaped after her and landed on his hands and knees over her.

She looked down the line of his body to his cock bobbing between them. Curious, she wrapped a hand around its head and squeezed. She watched him to gauge his reaction. He growled in pleasure, and his eyes began to glow. Pleased with his response, she shimmied underneath him until she could take his cock into her mouth.

Holding his shaft firmly, she delicately licked the precum leaking from his slit before engulfing the head with her mouth. It was a tight fit, but she managed and began to suck firmly. With her other hand, she slid her finger into her pussy to lubricate it and began stroking her clit.

He pumped into her mouth as she stroked herself faster and harder. She was so excited it wouldn't take much for her to come. Her mouth involuntarily clamped down around him, giving him a little too much teeth as her pussy contracted. Orgasm rushed through her body. That hint of violence must have excited him because he shoved his cock to the back of her throat as he spurted cum down her esophagus.

He pulled out, and before she had time to notice that he was still hard, he'd dragged her back to the head of the bed, spread her legs, and plunged inside. His cock was so big that for a minute she saw stars as her body struggled to adjust. It was a good thing she liked a bit of pain with her pleasure, or the agony shooting through her right now would have killed her desire. She forced her vagina to relax. She could do this. It was just a matter of mind over matter.

After he entered her, he planted his arms on the sides of her, balancing on his forearms. She took advantage of her freedom and clamped her legs low on his thighs, restricting the depth of his penetration. He snarled at her, and she snarled right back. She was the one whose future ability to walk was being jeopardized.

He tried to pry her legs open. She reached up and grabbed him by the ears, dragging his face down to hers. "Do it, wolf-boy, and you won't get any of this pussy. I'll close my legs and leave you hanging."

He stared at her, as though gauging her level of determination while trying to intimidate her into relenting by growling, showing plenty of fang. She gave an extrahard tug on his ears and squeezed her legs together, slowly forcing him out. He released her leg when he felt himself sliding out, eyes narrowed in disbelief.

She smiled wickedly and relaxed her legs. "Good boy."

Rory growled again, eyes narrowed and focused on her curving lips, but said nothing. He rotated his hips, working his way inside once again. Her arousal increasing with each stroke of his cock, Shayla opened her legs and allowed him complete access. He immediately took advantage. His thrusts became deeper, longer, and smoother until he was nudging against her cervix.

Shayla dug her nails into his back and shifted her legs until they were wrapped around his waist. She tilted her hips and raised her cradle, aiming for maximum penetration. "Harder," she demanded.

When he didn't comply with her demands, she dragged her nails down his back, then bit him on the arm. "I *said* harder!"

He smiled at her savagely right before he came to his knees with his hands locked around her waist, lifting her hips onto his lap while keeping her impaled on his pistoning cock. With considerable strength, he hammered inside her.

Shayla purred. *This is more like it.* She let Rory have his way. His cock pounded against her cervix, sharpening her pleasure with a small bite of pain. Her legs tightened around him in a death grip, and her head thrashed from side to side on the mattress as a powerful orgasm ripped through her body. He fucked her through one orgasm right into another.

She was just coming down from the second when Rory suddenly lunged forward, teeth bared, gaze locked on her neck as his body began convulsing in release. She dropped her arm from his shoulder and managed to block him just in time, his teeth clamping down on her forearm.

"We can fuck all you'd like, but no marking," she told him firmly, despite the pain she felt as his teeth broke the skin and dug in deep.

Rory's eyes narrowed in anger as he snarled, his lips and chin bloody from the blood flowing from the wound on her arm, but she'd stopped him from marking her. That was all that mattered. She felt a brief flicker of worry when he released her forearm, licked his lips clean, and then gave her a wicked grin.

What the hell was that about?

Chapter Eight

Shannon shook like a person with palsy as each suctioning draw caused an answering contraction in her womb, prolonging her orgasm and propelling it higher. Vampire, she thought with the last remaining functioning brain cell that she possessed. Nikolai's a vampire.

Her instincts screamed out warnings. There was something important…something she was supposed to remember, just beyond her reach…oh man, sex was good. Why had she resisted doing this for so long? She shook her head and tried to breathe through her mouth. What was…umm, she inhaled deeply through her nostrils. He smelled so good. She needed… *THINK! You have to focus, Shannon.*

Later.

Right now, she wanted to rub her hands all over him and wallow in his scent. She reached forward, and her hands jerked to a stop as she reached the end of her leash. It shocked her out of the daze she was in.

Oh God, my mate's a vampire.

Shannon lay beneath Nikolai, stunned by the realization.

Not mate. Other, her wolf said firmly in denial.

Shannon agreed. A vampire couldn't be her mate. It wasn't possible; at least, she'd never heard of it. Vampires and shifters didn't mix. They certainly didn't copulate, not to her knowledge, and yet, here they were—together.

Somehow, this *vampire* had invaded her dreams and incited her lust. "You're the reason I'm in heat."

"Am I?" he questioned languidly as he gently sucked and licked the breast from which he'd fed.

"Don't play games with me." She gasped as the heat rose again in her body. "What have you done to me?" She didn't have time for vampire tricks. She had to figure this out before she lost the ability to reason…again.

"I mated you. You are my chosen."

Shannon shook her head in denial; whether it was in response to the claim he made or the fire building in her body, she couldn't say. Chosen was the vampire equivalent of a true mate. "I'm a shifter. I can't be your chosen. You're mistaken."

He ripped the blindfold off her face, and she got her first good look at him. He was so handsome, it made her heart hurt. He was everything she found desirable in a man, and she couldn't have him. It wasn't allowed. Even if it were, her wolf would never accept him. She could feel it bristling at his proximity.

"Does this feel like a mistake?" He pumped his hips, plunging his shaft in and out of her vagina.

Shannon closed her eyes against the intensity of the pleasure. "No, it doesn't feel like a mistake, but it has to be." She cried out as her body caught his rhythm.

"Look at me," he commanded.

As she opened her eyes, he continued, "Feel me. *Know who I am.*" The last thought was spoken from his mind to hers.

Shannon was beyond caring who he was. He could have been old Slewfoot himself as long as he kept fucking her. She undulated beneath him, trying to take him deeper. Her eyes stared into his, mesmerized by the red flame glowing within. Deep in her belly a force was gathering, building in intensity until she began to fight, sure it would destroy her.

"Let it come, love."

"I can't. It's too much." She thrashed back and forth, neck arched until it felt like it would break, but still she maintained eye contact, unable to tear her gaze away.

"Yes. Come. NOW."

Flames expanding until they filled her entire field of vision, the pressure suddenly exploded into an inferno of ecstasy, ripping a keening cry from her throat.

Nikolai hammered into her, pushing her into another howling orgasm, this time feeding from her jugular vein as she came, and marking her as his mate. Then he tore a hole in his wrist and held it to her mouth, compelling her to drink while she was too out of it to be fully cognizant of what she was doing.

Once she'd drunk enough for a true exchange, he removed his wrist from her mouth and licked it, instantly healing it. Releasing her from the compulsion, he gathered her close and drove for his own completion, but not before giving her satisfaction one last time.

When he'd recovered and could once again function, he commanded her to sleep. As her eyes closed, he scanned her mind to make sure she was really asleep. She was. Unsheathing himself from her body, he climbed off the bed and went into the bathroom. He took a washrag, wet it with warm water, squeezed out the excess, then went back to the bed and tenderly bathed the blood and semen from his mate's body.

When he was done, he tossed the rag back into the sink and released her body from the restraints, leaving them dangling down the sides of the bed. He lifted her up, pulled the cover down, and placed her on the sheet before climbing into bed beside her.

Dawn was approaching. He could feel it dragging on his senses, weighing him down. He scanned the house and the surrounding area to make sure everything was secure before placing safeguards around the perimeter. Any person approaching would trigger an alarm. Reinforcing his command for her to sleep, he added an additional compulsion for Shannon not to awaken until he told her to do so. That done, he pulled her close and allowed himself to sink into the deep sleep of his kind.

* * *

Shayla woke the next morning facedown, sprawled on top of Rory, ready for another round. He'd fucked her hard, all through the night, and she'd loved every minute of it. She'd made up for several months of abstinence and was raring to go at it some more. Who knew when she'd get the opportunity to indulge again?

She lifted her head off his chest, took a look at her surroundings, and blinked.

At first glance, the place looked a wreck. She took another look and realized it wasn't the whole room that was trashed, just the area around the bed. The pillows were shredded. The bedspread was on the floor tangled with the sheets. The mattress hung drunkenly, one side on the box frame, the rest on the floor. The bottom sheet was loose, and what wasn't shredded was trapped underneath their bodies.

She looked down at Rory and realized he'd shifted back to normal. Some men looked boyish while they slept. Not Rory. His face was all rugged masculinity, even while relaxed in sleep. She planted her hands on either side of his torso and prepared to lift herself off him. Needing more leverage, she slid her legs up his body so that she straddled him. As she locked her elbows and lifted her upper body, his hands clamped down on her hips, cradling her slit against his morning erection.

Her eyes flew to his as he asked in a sleep-roughened voice, "Where do you think you're going?"

"I need to pee," she responded as he rubbed his cock back and forth against her slit, the head of his penis rubbing against her clit.

"Later," he told her as he canted his hips and surged upward, impaling her with his cock with one mighty thrust.

She moaned, her bladder forgotten as she rocked against him, hungry for the satisfaction only he could give her. Their movements caused the last remaining corner of the bed to give up the fight and it too crashed to the floor.

Rory's eyes bled to wolf as he watched her, craftiness in his gaze as he waited for an opening. All through the night, each time they'd mated he'd attempted to mark her and been denied each time. Shayla's arms were a mass of teeth marks. It was becoming a contest of wills to see who would prevail.

In reality, he could have marked her by now and been done with it, but each time she'd managed to evade him, his respect for her increased. He couldn't ask for a stronger, more passionate mate. She wouldn't grovel like his mother. Shay would stand toe-to-toe with him, demand his respect, and command his attention. Controlling her would be a challenge, one he would relish.

She cried out, her nails digging into his chest, head thrown back as her pussy clamped down, milking him with her release as she rode him to completion. Hoping to catch her off guard, he lunged forward, his eyes focused on his target—the tendon that connected shoulder to neck.

When the heat of his breath neared her shoulder, Shayla jerked back, causing his teeth to graze her from shoulder to chest, leaving a trail of red. He bit her on her breast just for the hell of it as he followed her down, forcing her back to the floor. In retaliation, she popped him upside the head.

He grunted in satisfaction, cupped her hips, and plunged back inside her waiting sheath. Her movement had dislodged him as he hovered on the edge of completion. Giving up his intent to mark her for now, he rode her long and hard until he came bucking with a howl. He collapsed on top of her, panting.

Shayla wiggled beneath him, causing his cock to harden inside of her. "No! No more nookie, not until I pee and get something to eat."

With a grumble, he rolled off her and allowed her to get up. "Hurry and come back. I'm not finished with you."

Shayla jumped to her feet and then stood for a moment, gazing at Rory, who lay sprawled on his back like a red-haired Adonis. She let her gaze travel over his body, admiring his physique until her bladder issued another warning call. Pee here or in the bathroom; either way, it was coming out. She rushed to the bathroom, almost crying in relief as the pressure eased.

Once that was over, she hopped into the shower. She smelled like Rory. Well, she smelled like Rory *and* sex. She stood under the shower and watched as the water turned green, washing yesterday's gel out of her hair. She'd dyed it green to match the army green outfit she'd been wearing. One she wouldn't be wearing again since Rory had clawed it off her body. She washed all over, taking special care with the tender area of her sex.

When she was finished, she exited the shower, then rubbed her head with a towel and wrapped another one around her body. She'd have to go upstairs to get clothes to wear. She found a spare toothbrush and brushed her teeth before leaving the bathroom, hoping to find something good to eat. She was starving.

As soon as she opened the door, Rory was on her. Her head bounced off the wall as he pressed her forcefully up against it. Lifting her to eye level, he growled gutturally. “You washed my scent off of your body.”

Before her mind finished deciphering what he said, his tongue was in her mouth and his cock in her pussy. All thoughts of food forgotten, she wrapped her legs around his waist and hung on. She shouldn't want any more sex after last night and then again this morning, but her body didn't agree. It couldn't get enough of him.

The more he fucked her, the more she craved him. She was sensitized to his touch. She'd never get enough of him. No one else would ever be able to please her the way he did. He'd ruined her for anyone else. She pushed that disturbing thought from her mind, then relaxed and let the orgasm take her as he gave one final lunge and flooded her with his seed.

She unlocked her legs as he let her slide against him until her feet rested on the floor. Well, she thought ruefully, she *had* been clean. He'd definitely accomplished what he'd set out to do. Once again, his scent was all over her body.

Rory sniffed her and smiled in satisfaction. Shayla shook her head. It must be some kind of freaky wolf thing.

He kissed her lightly on the lips. “I'll fix breakfast as soon as I come out of the bathroom.”

Before he could turn away, she asked, “Is it safe for me to go upstairs? I want to get my clothes.”

“What's wrong with what you have on?”

She gazed down at her naked body before looking back at him and arching her brow. “I don't have anything on.”

"Exactly," he said, smiling in satisfaction. His smile faded as he said, "It's safer for you to stay down here. Don't go upstairs unless I'm with you. If you have to cover up, put on one of my shirts. That way you won't be upset when I rip it off of you later."

* * *

Kiesha opened one eye and looked around, trying to figure out where she was and why the bed was so hard. The kitchen. She—no, *they*—were in the kitchen. *What happened?* One minute she was ripping into Alex for trying to set Shayla up on the sly, the next they were tearing the clothes off one another. Everything else was a blur.

She heard a groan and looked over to see Alex struggling to stand. "What happened? Why are we on the floor?"

"Blue moon," he answered, as though that explained it all.

"I didn't think it would affect us since I'm already pregnant."

"We didn't get the full effect. If you weren't pregnant, we'd still be going at it," he told her as he helped her to her feet.

If this isn't the full effect, I don't want to see the real deal. That made her think of Mary Elizabeth. *She isn't pregnant. I wonder how she's handling things.*

* * *

Mary Elizabeth shuddered as another orgasm rocked through her body. "Hugh, please." She panted. "We've got to stop."

They'd been making love all night long. It was ten in the morning now, and Hugh showed no signs of slowing. They'd just barely made it into the room before the sexual frenzy had started.

"Can't stop," he responded, changing the angle of his thrusts until she was once again pushing back into him as the heat of arousal roared through her body.

"The funeral." She panted and then moaned as he hit a particularly sensitive spot. "We have to be there." Her fingers clenched on the bedding. She whimpered with pleasure and arched her back as Hugh plunged into her from behind, his body covering hers.

"What time is it?"

"What?" she asked, her mind hazy as it started to separate from her body.

"What…time…is…the…funeral?" He punctuated each word with a thrust of his hips.

"Two o'clock." She gasped, on the edge of another orgasm.

"We'll make it," he told her as he drove her up and over another peak.

They did…barely. Hugh took her in the shower as they prepared for the funeral. Her panties came off in the elevator when he took her against the wall, scandalizing an old couple who had tried to enter when it stopped on their floor on the way down to the lobby. Well, the old woman was scandalized. The man looked like he wanted to watch.

Their bout in the elevator satisfied them all the way to the church, where they went at it again in the parking lot as the coffin was being escorted inside. Mary Elizabeth couldn't blame Hugh for that one because she'd initiated it, releasing his cock and straddling him as he sat in the driver's seat. He'd hurriedly released the catch on the seat until it lay all the way back when she accidentally leaned on the horn.

She managed to make herself fairly presentable, smoothing most of the wrinkles from her skirt and straightening her hair before entering the church on Hugh's arm. He escorted her to her seat with the family where they proceeded to embarrass her mother by barely keeping their hands off one another in the house of the Lord.

Once the funeral was over, Hugh hustled her out of the church and into the car with indecent haste. They didn't speak to a soul. He drove with grim determination back to their hotel. Mary Elizabeth tempted his self-control mightily as she wiggled and squirmed in her seat, trying desperately to keep her hands off him.

As they rode up in the elevator, they stood on opposite sides, neither one looking at the other. Once they reached the room, he ordered the startled housekeeper out as he began ripping the clothes off his body. She took one look at his face and ran. Hugh slammed and locked the door behind her, barely remembering to put out the DO NOT DISTURB sign before he fell on a naked and waiting Mary Elizabeth.

* * *

Kiesha picked up the telephone after she and Alex had eaten. “Come on, answer.” It just rang and rang. She hung up when voice mail came on, and called again. This time, when there was no answer, she left a message. “Shay, call me and let me know you're all right. If I don't answer, leave a message.”

She disconnected and dialed another number.

“Who are you calling now?” Alex asked.

“I'm calling Shannon to make sure she's okay and see if Shay is with her,” she answered distractedly as the phone rang and continued to ring. “Where the hell are they?” she asked, beginning to get worried.

She disconnected the call and tried again. When she still didn't get an answer, she hung up the phone and snatched her keys.

“Whoa,” Alex said, blocking her way to the exit. “Where do you think you're going?”

“I'm going to check on my cousin and my friend. Move out of my way, Alex,” she said, trying to push past him.

“Honey, I know you're worried, but you can't go over there. The moon will be out soon, can't you feel it?” He placed an arm around her to hold her in place.

“Alex, I don't *care* about the moon. Shay might be in trouble. I need to know that she's safe.” Kiesha was still trying to get past him, even though she knew it was useless. Alex was strong enough to keep her in the house if he didn't want her to go.

"Kiesha, look at me," he said firmly. When she reluctantly looked up, he asked, "How much of last night do you remember?"

"What does that have to do with anything?" she asked angrily, frustrated because he wouldn't let go.

"It has a lot to do with it. Now answer the question."

Knowing he was going to continue to push until she did, she told him, "Not much. I remember arguing with you, and I remember ripping at your clothes, but the rest is blank until I woke this morning."

Alex nodded, as if she'd confirmed what he suspected. "And why do you think that is?"

"I don't have time to play twenty questions. If you have something to say, then say it. Otherwise, get out of my way. If I hurry, I can get over there and back before the moon rises."

He shook her slightly, causing her eyes to widen. "You're not going anywhere. The reason you can't remember last night is because you shifted. *Your first change.* How much help do you think you're going to be to them if you change? Rory is there. He's an alpha. Shannon's an alpha as well. You go over there, and you'll do more harm than good. They're all right, and even if they're not, there's nothing you can do about it now."

Tears filled Kiesha's eyes. At the sight of them, Alex cursed and pulled her into his arms. "I'm sorry, baby. I didn't mean to be so harsh. You have to see that there is nothing you can do but wait it out. I know you're worried. I am too. We'll just have to be patient and hope for the best."

"I'm fine. It's these damn hormones. You're right, and I know it. It just seems like there ought to be something I can do. I hate not knowing what's going on." She thought for a moment, then asked, "I *changed?* You're sure?"

He laughed. "Yes, I'm sure. I was there, remember?"

"Why can't I remember? Shouldn't I?"

"Not necessarily. You were angry. Strong emotions bring it on."

She'd been beyond angry. She was furious with Alex at his deviousness, worried for Shayla's and Shannon's safety, and guilty because if it hadn't been for her, Shay wouldn't be involved in any of this mess. Add all those emotions together, throw in a blue moon, and it's no wonder she changed. "Will it happen again, tonight?"

"More than likely. Now that you've experienced your first full shift, you should begin changing more frequently, especially during the full moon. It will take some time before you are strong enough to resist its call. Let's go upstairs and get comfortable. I don't want to get caught in the kitchen again like we did last night."

* * *

Shayla lay sprawled on the mattress on the floor, hands above her head. They'd given up trying to keep the thing on the bed. She lifted her head and looked down at her body before dropping back to the mattress. A person would think she'd been attacked with all of the bruises, bites, and claw marks on her body. She smiled contentedly. She loved making Rory go primal on her.

Rory's hand slid leisurely up her leg to play with the folds of her sex. She widened her thighs, granting him full access. And to think they'd made such a big deal about the blue moon that she'd actually been nervous. This was wonderful. She would have to make sure she was in town for the next one.

Rory leaned over and suckled her breast. She ran fingers through his hair as thoughts continued to run through her mind. She should be sated. Actually, she should be unconscious. They fucked and ate, then fucked some more. He'd spent more time inside her than out. She never knew a man could maintain an erection that long and get hard again with that amount of frequency. Must be a shifter thing. Whatever it was, she was going to enjoy it as long as it lasted. Thoughts faded away as he moved over her and the passion between them flared again.

Chapter Nine

Nikolai awoke just before sunset. He scanned his surroundings, making sure all was secure before turning to his mate. As commanded, Shannon was still asleep. He had enough time to carefully wake her. If he did it too early, she would be in command of her senses and ask questions he was not prepared to answer. If he waited too late, her beast would gain control, strengthened by the full moon.

He walked a fine line. Because of the heat, he was able to claim her body. Her lust-filled mind offered no objections to anything he chose to do as long as he satisfied the passionate craving of her body. He was fully aware that the real battle to claim Shannon's soul would begin once the moon waned and her heat subsided.

She would try to reject him. He was a different species. Her wolf was hostile toward him. Her family and pack would not approve. Then there was the transformation occurring in her body because of the blood exchanges of which she was unaware. All these things would work against him. None of them mattered. She was his chosen, his true mate, his soul mate. Whatever you wanted to call it, the bottom line was she was his. Nothing she did or said would change that.

In her one lucid moment, she rightly suspected that he was the source, the reason her body had been thrown into heat. There were a lot of things that she didn't know, and it would be his pleasure to inform her, but not until he had physically bound her to him as tightly as he could. Time was not on his side. The moon would only be at maximum strength for another two nights. After that, he would have to let her go—temporarily.

Then the wooing would begin.

He had no doubt he would win her, despite the things conspiring against him. He would prevail because she wanted him as much as he wanted her, and because he'd never failed to obtain that which he desired most. He wouldn't fail now. He would bind her to him so tightly that she wouldn't know where she ended and he began. By blood and by passion, she would be his before she left his lair. Then he would work on owning her heart as surely as she already owned his.

He needed to prepare for his mate's awakening. He hungered, but his needs could wait. First, he would attend to his mate. Then he would satisfy his own.

He lit a fire to take the chill off the room. Going into his private bath, he filled the Roman-style sunken tub, large enough to hold four, with oil-scented water. While that was going, he went into the kitchen area and prepared a tray of food for his mate to satisfy her hunger and replace the energy she'd expended. Once everything was arranged to his satisfaction, he collected his mate and carried her into the bathroom.

Stepping into the tub, he cradled Shannon in his arms and sat on one of the bench seats lining the perimeter. With his arm supporting her back, he lifted her face to his. "Awaken hungry for me, my love," he commanded before covering her mouth with his own.

Her arms twined around his neck and her body sought his own before her eyes ever opened. The heat, freed by his command, swirled like a living thing inside her, seeking relief. Her body was a firestorm of need, and only he could put out the flames.

He positioned her over his cock. "Take what you need."

She sank down on him and began to move, instinct taking over where experience was lacking. She rose to her knees and rode him, the water making her movements languid in spite of the urgency he felt in her body. His hands explored while she took her pleasure, knowing that once she fed the hunger of her body, he would be free to feed his.

He cupped her breasts, their lushness filling his hands to capacity. He fondled them as he watched the intense concentration on her face. A quick tap into her mind showed she was focused inward on the sensations her body was feeling. Taking two fingers, he pinched her nipples and pulled, causing them to tighten and harden. As he tugged at them rhythmically, she gasped and her head fell back, giving him a tempting view of the veins in her neck.

"You like that," he stated, unable to resist nuzzling the spot where he would later feed.

"Yes."

"What about this?" He slid his hand down her stomach and parted her curls until his thumb was pressed against her clit. Using the oily water as lubrication, he rubbed back and forth.

She hissed in pleasure, her hips shooting forward to match his stroking. Her nails dug into his shoulders, the claws lengthening as her wolf began to surface. Her eyes began to change and glow as her climax neared.

"Control your beast, my love."

Remembering what happened the last time, she struggled to regain control. She was too close for him to draw back now. Her claws still dug into his shoulder, but her eyes returned to normal.

Nikolai smiled and placed his hands on her hips, guiding her movements as he matched her thrusts, adding an extra bit of force to the movements. He felt so good, she whimpered and closed her eyes. He was so sexy that she wished she had a camera to capture his image.

He pulled her closer so that her clit ground against his pubic bone. Her breasts rubbed against the light brushing of hair on his chest. Her fangs lengthened as the urge to bite and mark him as hers overwhelmed her.

Her wolf stirred in horror. *No! Not mate. Other! NO MARK!*

She jerked back just as her orgasm surged over and through her, driving every thought from her mind.

Shannon slumped against Nikolai, her body weak and trembling from more than just her release. She hadn't eaten since lunch yesterday. Her mouth was dry and parched from the blood he'd taken. A cup was pressed to her lips.

"Drink."

She grabbed the water and drank. When empty, the cup was removed and food was substituted in its place. The mouthwatering aroma of cooked beef assaulted her nostrils, causing her stomach to rumble. Shannon gulped down the meat, barely chewing. As soon as she swallowed, another bite-sized piece took its place, and another, until the edge was off her hunger, and she slowed down enough to actually savor the food.

Nikolai began alternating pieces of meat with bits of cheese and fruit. Now that she wasn't starving, Shannon noticed the tray of food stationed by his arm on the marble ledge of the tub. Feeling silly being hand-fed when she was perfectly capable of feeding herself, she reached for the food.

"No, my love. Allow me this small pleasure."

Shannon subsided against him without protest. She hadn't been fed since she was a young child. It was a novel experience. When she'd eaten her fill, Nikolai moved the tray out of the way and placed another cup of water in her hands. She needed to replace the fluids she lost before he'd feel comfortable enough to feed again. She finished drinking and handed him the cup, which he placed on the tray.

She leaned sleepily against him. "You didn't eat."

"Your needs come first." He turned her body and positioned her with her back against the tub, then pressed his body between her outspread legs.

Shannon abruptly became aware that Nikolai was still hard. "You didn't come earlier."

"No."

"Why?"

"It wasn't time."

"Why would you deny yourself?"

"That was for you. This is for me." He kissed her as he slid home. "Last night and earlier I held back, not wanting to hurt you with my passion. Now that you've eaten and been strengthened, I'll give you a taste of what I withheld before."

He held her legs open and back until they met her chest. He stroked deep, long powerful strokes that touched her womb. Her head fell bonelessly against the rim of the tub as the passion in her rose to match his own. Pressed into the side of the tub as she was, she couldn't move; she could only clutch his head as fire streaked through her body.

The water churned around them as the temperature rose. Nikolai kissed his way down to her throat and lingered there, scraping his teeth back and forth against her vein. He smiled as she clutched his hair and arched her neck, pressing his mouth more firmly against her skin in a silent appeal to bite her. He licked her and suckled the skin, pulling it into his mouth, toying with her.

"Bite me."

He released the skin and kissed his way up her neck to nibble on her ear.

"Nikolai, bite me."

He licked around the rim of her ear, briefly dipping his tongue inside before nibbling on the lobe.

Shannon dug her nails into his scalp. "Nikolai, please. Give me what I need."

"Are you sure?"

"Yesssss!" She hissed as his fangs sank deep. She came instantly. Nikolai fed and fed deeply, each suctioning draw sending fire through her pussy and prolonging her orgasm.

Withdrawing his fangs, he licked the wound and watched it seal. He'd fed, but it wasn't enough. With her, it would never be enough. He gripped her hips and pulled her into his thrusts as he picked up the pace. His vision bled red, lit within as passion caused his bloodlust to rise to the surface. He closed his eyes and threw his head back, beating it back into partial submission. He couldn't lose control. Not yet. She wasn't ready.

The position in which he held her caused her breasts to rise out of the water, drawing his attention. He was mesmerized by the way they bounced and bobbed, nipples tight and drawn. He could see the minute tracing of veins just beneath the surface, hear the blood flowing through them. His sheathed fangs ached with the need to release and bite down.

Her claws dug holes in his back as she clutched him to her. The whimpers and moans coming from her throat were driving him out of his mind with lust. Her inner muscles gripped him tight, forcing him to fight to pull out with each withdrawal. Her legs wrapped around him with a strength that would have broken a mortal man.

It was too much. The fragile control he maintained broke. His fangs exploded into his mouth and claws ripped through his fingertips. He latched onto her breast and bit deep; her blood gushed into his mouth. He pumped into her like a madman. No rhythm, no restraint, just the driving force of his lust. He lost all awareness of his surroundings. Dimly, he heard a scream and felt her body stiffen. He fed as the seed burst from his body and coated her vagina before flooding her womb.

Awareness slowly seeped back. His mate lay still in his arms. He retracted his fangs and licked the wound closed before laying his head on her heart. The beat was strong and steady. He shuddered in relief. He hadn't lost control like that since he was a fledgling. He could have killed her. You could never harm your chosen. It's not possible, instinct whispered. Whether it was possible or not, he'd have to be more careful in the future.

He bathed them quickly and exited the tub. Wrapping his sleeping mate in a towel, he carried her and laid her on the bed and lay beside her. She would awaken soon.

* * *

The first thing she smelled was Nikolai. The scent of him brought it all rushing back—the bath, the mind-blowing orgasms. The heat was sated for now, allowing her temporary clarity of mind. Nikolai had fed from her, and she'd allowed it—*begged* for it. He was a vampire. She should be horrified, appalled. She was neither. Instead, she was curious. Curious about how he had found her and why he had chosen her.

It was not normal for a vampire to be attracted to a shifter. They were natural enemies, though they'd given up fighting each other when both species began dying out. There was no future for them, no matter how drawn to him she was or how able he was at turning her body inside out.

Once her heat subsided and the moon waned, she would have to leave and forget this ever happened.

"I'll allow you to leave, but you'll never forget. You are my chosen. We will be together."

Her head jerked in his direction, her eyes wide. "Did you just read my mind? *How* did you read my mind? I'm immune to vampire powers."

"We are linked—blood-bonded."

Shannon pushed away from Nikolai. "I *never* exchanged blood with you." When he only arched an eyebrow at her in response, she grew angry. "I *couldn't* have exchanged blood with you. I would remember. Your mind games don't work on me."

Using his preternatural vampire speed, Nikolai sat up and pushed Shannon back onto the bed. "Look into my eyes," he commanded with a touch of compulsion in his voice.

Shannon did so, unable to resist. As she gazed into them, the memory of their first meeting out on the ridge that her wolf had been suppressing unfolded before her. She watched as Nikolai found her and saw her wolf attack him. She heard him command her to sleep and observed him as he carried her to Alex.

It was *his* memory she was reliving. She had no doubt that it was real, even though her memory of that night was still dim. It all fit. How he knew about her, the dreams, and Alex's refusal to tell her what happened and insistence on her remembering on her own. He didn't want her to know.

While she was putting the pieces together, her body began to respond to the weight of Nikolai's naked body. Her flesh softened beneath his, and her sheath moistened. He groaned when she slid her hands down until she held his flaccid penis in her hand, fondling it until his cock hardened. She wrapped one leg around his hips and lifted toward him, rubbing the tip of his penis against the folds of her sex. Her breath caught as it rubbed against her clit, which was already hard and unfolded from its covering.

She continued to rub against him, prolonging the moment. Finally, when she'd lasted as long as she could stand, she positioned his cock at her opening. Raising her other leg to wrap around his, she pulled down while she thrust up, impaling herself on his cock. He held himself still above her, allowing her to control the depth of his penetration. Shannon rolled her hips, sliding him in and out of her sheath with the strength of her legs.

She kept up a steady rhythm, only faltering when her orgasm began approaching. She tried to fight it, not wanting to come, yet trying to balance right on the edge. Shannon's hands spread out and gripped the sheet beneath her, claws sprouting and ripping into the sheets as she struggled for control. Fangs lengthened as her eyes went wolf, causing blood to well up in her mouth as she bit down on her lower lip. Her legs tightened until they felt like a vise.

She looked down and the sight of his shaft, wet with her juices, sliding in and out of her sheath, sent her over the edge. She pulled him into her and held him there while she shuddered around him. Her neck arched and a howl ripped loose from her chest.

As she relaxed around him, Nikolai took over. The blood on her mouth called to him. He lowered his mouth to hers and licked the blood from her lips while he powered into her. He grabbed her hands and pinned them over her head. His pubic bone smacked forcefully against her own with each thrust, sending shock waves through her clit.

He lowered his head to her neck while her legs once more tightened around his hips, then climbed higher to wrap around his waist, allowing him the freedom to move as he willed. His fangs sliced deep just as an orgasm took him, his sucking causing her to climax. He relaxed for a minute before disentangling himself from her body. Getting up, he walked over to the minifridge concealed in the armoire and brought out two bottles of water. Quickly draining one, he took the other to the bed for Shannon to drink. One look told him she was once more asleep. His little she-wolf was drained. He set the water by the bed where she could see it, went into the bathroom, opened the plug so the water could drain, then removed the tray and put it back where it belonged.

Coming back to the bed, he looked at his mate. One more blood exchange and the binding would be complete. He felt pressed to complete the ritual, instinct demanding he bind her to him as tightly as possible, while his intellect advised caution. He didn't know how her body would react to the third and final blood exchange. It was a guarantee that she would gain power. The last thing he wanted to do at this point was strengthen her beast until they had come to some kind of understanding. He was resigned to waiting until Shannon fully accepted him as her mate before completing the ritual. That day couldn't come soon enough for him.

* * *

Shayla woke with her head pillowed on Rory's back. The last two days and three nights were a blur of sexual ecstasy, but now it was time for her to leave. She had a job to do and commitments to keep. Rory lay as though dead beneath her, barely moving even when she rolled off him and sat up. He had to be exhausted.

Over the seventy-two-hour period, he'd barely slept. What little sleep he had managed had come during the daylight hours when the strength of the sun weakened the moon's hold on his body. Shayla eased off the mattress. No matter how deeply he appeared to be sleeping, he was still a shifter, and she didn't want to chance waking him.

With one last lingering look at him, she crept toward the stairs and made her way silently up them, leaving the doors closed but unlocked behind her. Once she successfully made it to the guest room, she threw her belongings in a bag and dressed quickly but quietly. She desperately wanted a shower, but she couldn't afford to take the risk.

Last night she'd made the mistake of mentioning leaving Refuge, and the man had gone ballistic. He'd shifted into his wolf-man form and taken her from behind. Her hand crept to her neck and settled there in remembrance. He'd bitten her. She'd been unable to avoid it. Of course, at the time avoiding him had been the last thing on her mind. She shivered as the memory brought echoes of sensation alive in her body.

Forcing her mind to the matter at hand, she grabbed her keys and things and left the house, expecting at any moment to hear the roar of an angry wolf behind her. Throwing her belongings into the backseat, she got into the car and quickly drove away. She had a plane to catch. As she'd told Rory, she had a job waiting on her, though she'd been interrupted before she could tell him where. Remembering the possessiveness in his gaze, that might be a good thing. She had no doubt he'd track her down if he could and bring her back, kicking and screaming if need be.

The thought occurred that she might not exactly object to him dragging her back but might instead follow willingly behind him. She shoved it forcefully from her mind. As she'd told Shannon, she didn't do till death do us part commitments, especially not with a shifter.

She'd been thought of as a freak and looked at with fear and trepidation all her life. Being a child prodigy was no easy thing. Thanks to the camouflage of her wild hair, matching outfits, and crazy way of talking, people forgot just how intelligent she was and how inferior it made them feel. She came across as just another computer geek. She could live with that. She could not live with the idea of turning furry once a month and really giving people a reason to be afraid of her.

As she drove through Refuge on her way to the airport, she was surprised at how lifeless and empty it seemed. A lot of the businesses in town had signs in the windows proclaiming CLOSED FOR THE BLUE MOON. If the blue moon had this big of an impact on business, there were far more shifters in the area than she'd previously credited it with.

Her flight wasn't scheduled to leave until seven. She had just enough time to get to the airport and find a place to freshen up. By then, the plane should be boarding. There was no way she was missing this flight. She'd had a close escape, and she wouldn't feel truly safe until the plane was in the air.

* * *

Before he opened his eyes, Rory knew something was wrong. *Shayla!* He couldn't sense Shayla beside him. He opened his eyes. She wasn't lying on the mattress near him. He pushed up with his hands and looked around. The bathroom was empty.

Already fearing the worst but needing to be sure, he looked toward the door leading upstairs. It wasn't locked. Maybe she'd gone upstairs, although he'd told her repeatedly not to do so. Rising from the floor, he went up the stairs. He could sense its emptiness before he even opened the door. He glanced in the room in which she'd stayed. The majority of her things were gone. He could tell she'd packed in a hurry. Knowing what he'd find but needing to look anyway, he walked to the front door and opened it. Her rental car was gone.

He walked back downstairs like a man in a trance, leaving the front door open. Once in the basement, the scent of their mating permeated the room, hitting him like a slap in the face. She'd told him she was leaving, but he hadn't really believed her. He thought he'd have a chance to convince her otherwise, but like a thief, she sneaked away, taking with her something more precious than money.

With a roar that shook the house, he shouted his anger to the sky. He flew into a rage the likes of which he'd never done before. His eyes went wolf and claws sprouted as he let the change take him. Like a man possessed, he ripped and shredded, tearing to pieces everything that could be torn. What he couldn't break, he pummeled and threw until the whole room was destroyed.

When there was no other outlet for his anger, he fell to his knees in the midst of the carnage, threw back his head, and howled his anguish to the sky. His mate was gone, and with her, his unborn child.

Chapter Ten

For the first time in weeks, Shannon woke without the heat plaguing her body. Her mind was clear. She could think, and her first thought was of escape. Not that the time she'd spent with Nikolai hadn't been nice. Actually, it had been *more* than nice, but all good things must come to an end. Rory must be frantic by now, and Shayla. She wanted to know if her friend had made it into the house safely.

She looked at Nikolai lying so peacefully beside her, and her heart lurched. He really was handsome. Remembering the things they'd done brought a flush of embarrassment to her face. He'd far exceeded any dream she'd ever had growing up, back when she used to fantasize about the type of mate she'd one day have before she put away girlish dreams.

Coming up on an elbow, she leaned over him, unable to resist taking one last kiss before leaving. As her lips pressed lightly against his, Nikolai's arms wrapped around her and rolled them until she was on her back, making a place for himself between her legs.

"Going somewhere, my love?"

Shannon heard him clearly in her mind, but her lips were too occupied to answer. She tried mind-speaking with him, not sure if it would work. *"I need to leave, Nikolai."*

"*Soon, but not yet, love.*" His mouth traveled to her breast. "*Stay.*"

"*This won't change anything. I still need to leave. I have people looking for me.*" She arched and pressed her breast more firmly into his mouth.

"They can search for a little while longer."

He pushed into her slowly, allowing her to savor each inch as it filled her sheath.

Thoughts ceased as the sounds of lovemaking filled the air. The slide of skin against skin. Hungry moans and gasps. Heavy breathing. The rocking of the bed as his thrusts became more vigorous. The slapping of flesh on flesh, cumulating in a high, keening moan of completion that drowned out the minuscule sounds of Nikolai moaning while he fed. When Shannon came back to herself, she lay sprawled on top of Nikolai as he slowly stroked her from shoulder to hips.

"When you finish assuring everyone of your safety, come back to me."

"I can't. You know it will never work between us."

Nikolai cupped her head and lifted it up, forcing her to look at him. "What I know is that I will never let you go. You are mine, my chosen. You may leave to get your house in order, but return to me you will." As he spoke, a flame lit deep within his eyes, causing the black to reflect red.

Shannon pushed on his chest and sat up, straddling him, his cock nestled against her moist slit. The red in his eyes deepened until they began to glow. She opened her mouth to argue.

Nikolai cut her off. "If you plan to leave, do so now before I change my mind."

She had the urge to test him, to see if he really thought he could keep her there. The feel of him hardening beneath her changed her mind, caused her to give heed to the cautioning voice telling her pushing him was not a good idea. She had no doubt that he would never hurt her or keep her against her will. The question was, would she want to leave? Already she was wavering, but staying would only delay the inevitable. Their ending had already been preordained.

She rose off him and left the bed. He waved a hand, causing the door to open and reveal the elevator. She walked toward it slowly, forcing herself to keep moving and not look back. Leaving was more difficult than she'd expected. As she waited for the elevator doors to close, she allowed herself one look back. He lay sprawled on the bed in all his naked glory, his cock standing proud and tall, still slick with the juices from her body.

The sight of him caused her sex to tighten. She forced herself to stand there as the doors slowly closed, blocking the sight of him. The elevator rose and deposited her into what could only be a library. It brought to mind old English manors with floor-to-ceiling bookshelves lining three of the four walls. If she had more time, she would explore the titles on the shelves. Many appeared to be first-edition hardbacks.

From the library, she entered into the foyer. To her left was the double-door entrance into the house. Directly ahead was a formal dining room with a table that must seat twenty, at least. To the right, a great room whose wall was nothing but glass doors opened out onto a terrace beyond. She was mighty tempted to go exploring, but she could feel Nikolai's hunger in her mind. If she didn't leave now, who knew when she would get the opportunity.

She stepped out the door and descended the steps until she stood in the courtyard in front of the house. The stone house was massive in the moonlight with an old-world flavor. She shivered as the cool breeze blew over her body, reminding her that she was naked. She shifted into a wolf and made her way home, wondering what surprises waited.

* * *

Rory got a grip and pulled himself together. His wolf might be mourning the loss of its mate, but he had things to do and plans to make. This was not the end. She would be back, of her own volition or by force. Either way, she would return to his side where she belonged.

Now that the mating fever had calmed, he was worried about Shannon. While he hoped her absence meant that she had found a mate, his more pessimistic side was apprehensive. With the combination of the heat and the blue moon, it was entirely possible her wolf had taken the decision out of her hands, leaving her to deal with the fallout.

It had happened before. The wolf sometimes made decisions the human found difficult to live with. Of course, the opposite also occurred. There were occasions that the human part found a mate that the wolf despised. Most of the time, the couple managed to live in harmony, despite the disparity. However, sometimes the beast did all it could to eliminate the mate. In those cases, the best a shifter could hope for was that the mate was stronger than the beast and could subdue it. Otherwise, one might find oneself in the grievous position of having to explain the untimely demise of one's mate.

Rory found clothes that somehow managed to survive the destruction, took a shower, then headed over to Alex's house. He could discover if Alex had heard from Shannon and hopefully get information on Shayla at the same time. While on the way, he thought back to the demolished area formerly known as Shannon's panic room. He was going to have to bring in a crew to clean out the debris and start from scratch.

* * *

Alex lay in the quiet room watching his mate sleep. Kiesha reclined on the very edge of the bed, exhausted. Between her pregnancy, the business she was trying to open, and her new duties as alpha-fem of the Raven pack, he doubted a bomb detonating in this very room would wake her. That belief was quickly proven wrong when the doorbell rang. Its strident tones, immediately followed by heavy pounding, yanked her out of a sound sleep and onto the floor. Alex peered over the edge of the bed. "Are you all right?"

"I will be as soon as you kill whoever is at the door."

Feeling the same way, Alex pulled on a pair of jeans before helping Kiesha back onto the bed. "Stay here. I'll go see who it is."

Whoever it was, they'd better have a damn good reason for bothering him. He was so tired he couldn't see straight. He made his way down the stairs, more by rote than by sight, crossed over to the door, then yanked it open.

Rory pushed past him and strode into the house. "'Bout damn time you came to the door. I've been knocking for over five minutes."

Reminding himself that killing the Sparrowhawks' alpha would cause a war he really didn't have time to deal with, Alex closed the door and followed Rory into the living room. He sprawled onto the couch with his head tilted toward the ceiling, mentally trying to calculate exactly how much sleep he'd had in the last seventy-two hours. Whatever the amount, it wasn't nearly enough. "What can I do for you, Rory?"

"Have you heard any news of Shannon?" Rory paced the living room.

Alex raised his head. "What do you mean 'have I heard any news of Shannon'? She's home, isn't she?"

"If she were, I wouldn't be here bothering you, would I? She never made it back to the house the night she came over here."

Alex shot to his feet. "*Three days!* She's been missing for *three days*, and you're just *now* telling me?"

"I've been a little busy. Shayla came running through the woods with two wolves chasing her. In the ensuing fight, I forgot to ask about Shannon."

"What about later?" Alex was unable to understand. He knew how Rory was about his sister. This just didn't make sense.

Rory gave him a look that spoke volumes. "Shayla's my one. I had to fight for her. You figure it out."

Alex winced in sympathy. The blue moon combined with the aggression of the fight would have brought out every possessive instinct Rory possessed. He wouldn't have been able to function beyond the need to protect and stake his claim. Kiesha was not going to be happy with this development. "Where's Shay?"

"She took off, which is the other reason I'm here. I need to know where she lives. I was hoping you could help me with that."

"She left? You didn't hurt her, did you?" Alex knew it was technically impossible for a male to hurt his mate because instinct required that you saw to her needs before your own, but he had to be sure. He had his own mate's happiness to consider.

"She's fine. We just had a bit of a disagreement. I said she was my mate. She didn't agree."

Alex groaned in commiseration, remembering how it was with Kiesha. "Must run in the family."

"What must run in the family?" The question came from Kiesha, slowly making her way down the stairs.

"Go back to bed, honey. You need your rest."

"I can't sleep. I heard Rory's voice, and I wanted to know how Shayla and Shannon were doing."

Alex cut in before Rory could answer. "Shayla's fine. She left on that business trip she was telling you about. Rory wanted to know how to contact her." He hoped Kiesha would get distracted and forget about Shannon. The last thing he wanted was another argument with his mate. She would blame him for Shannon's predicament, and there would be nothing he could say in defense. Hoping Rory caught the hint, he gazed steadily at Kiesha.

She was just tired enough that the ploy worked. "Why do you need to contact Shay?"

Rory glanced briefly at Alex. "I need some computer work for my business. Your cousin's good. Better than anyone we have around here. I saw the system she set up for you when she installed it on Shannon's computer and wondered if she could create something similar for my business. Unfortunately, she left before I could discuss it with her."

"Oh! Well, I think she left one of her business cards around here somewhere. Or you could just wait until she comes back in town for my wedding."

"Wedding?" Rory echoed. Alex quickly smothered a smile when Rory's eyes gleamed in anticipation. "When is the wedding going to be?"

"About six weeks from now. My whole family's coming in. Shay's actually in it. So, do you want to wait? From what she said, I know she's completely booked. She wouldn't be able to look at your business anytime before then."

"No. Give me her business card. If I wait until the wedding, it may take just that much longer before she becomes available."

"I'll be back in a sec." Kiesha walked toward the kitchen, headed for her office.

Once she was out of hearing range, Rory arched an eyebrow at Alex. "What was that about?"

Alex sighed. "I didn't want you reminding Kiesha I did something stupid and get her angry with me again."

"What did you do?"

"I knew Shayla was going to be leaving so I invited a few of my men to come and meet her, to see if she might be a match. I didn't know Shannon was going to show up as well. Kiesha managed to get them out of here before the males arrived. She was still ripping into me about it when the effects of the blue moon hit us."

Before Rory could comment, Kiesha returned. Thankfully, she didn't notice the look Rory gave him. "Here's her business card. It has her e-mail address on it and her cell phone number."

"Thank you, Kiesha. You don't know how much I appreciate this."

"No problem. Now if you gentlemen will excuse me, I'm going back to bed. I haven't had nearly enough rest." She nodded good-bye to Rory, gave Alex a kiss on the cheek, and trudged her way up the steps.

"I'll bring some food up later." Kiesha waved her hand in acknowledgment.

Alex held up a hand, signaling Rory to wait until he heard the bedroom door close; then he motioned for him to continue.

"It's partly your fault Shannon's missing," Rory said, "although I can't get too upset. If you hadn't done what you did, I probably still wouldn't know that Shayla was my mate."

"What happened that night? They should have had plenty of time to make it back to the house before my men arrived." Alex heard the phone ring and ignored it. Whoever it was could call back later.

"They probably would have if Shannon's truck hadn't broke down. I passed it on my way here. They must have had to get out and make a run for it. Shannon probably ran off in one direction and sent Shayla to the house. It might have worked, if your guys hadn't come chasing after my mate."

"That doesn't make sense. Why would they have chased Shayla when she's human? Especially when Shannon was there and in heat."

"Shayla was also in heat. I didn't realize it until I had shifted."

"What are you going to do now?"

"Prepare for the return of my mate, of course." Rory grinned devilishly at Alex. Alex suddenly felt sorry for Shayla.

* * *

Shannon approached the front of her house cautiously. The front door was open. Rory's and Shayla's vehicles were missing. So was her truck. It must still be on the road. Tomorrow she'd have to go and see if it would crank so she could bring it home. If it didn't start, she hoped it was something easy to fix. It wouldn't be the first time she'd worked on it.

She crept into the house on all fours. If someone was in there, she'd smell them. Rory's scent was powerful, letting her know he'd left recently. Shayla's scent was a bit fainter but still strong. She'd probably been gone a few hours. Shannon stepped lightly, sticking close to the walls and pausing before crossing into open spaces. She couldn't detect anyone else in the house, but it never hurt to be cautious.

She followed Rory's and Shayla's scents to the basement, where they were strongest. She stopped in the second doorway. Shock caused her to shift back to human form. *Oh my God! What the hell happened in here?* The room was destroyed. Totally and completely destroyed, and Rory's scent was all over the wreckage.

She went back upstairs to check Shayla's room, needing to see what condition it was in and hoping it would provide some clue as to what happened. From the looks of things, Shay left in a hurry. Worried, she went into her room and called Kiesha.

"Hello?" Kiesha croaked out the greeting in a groggy voice. Damn Alex for not answering the phone when he knew how tired she was.

"Kee? Hey, it's Shannon. Have you heard from Shayla? Is she all right?"

Kiesha sat up in the bed. “What do you mean? You’re the second person that’s asked about Shay tonight. Is something going on with my cousin I should know about?”

“That’s what I’m trying to find out. When we left your house the other night, my truck broke down, and we got separated. Some of the wolves from the pack caught my scent and were hunting me. I sent her on to the house while I ran off in the other direction. I don’t know what happened after that because I’m just getting home.”

Kiesha waited while Shannon paused to take a deep breath.

“From the looks of things, she only recently left, but she appeared to be in a hurry. She left some of her stuff behind, and I don’t think it was intentional. I wouldn’t be concerned except something must have happened here. My basement’s trashed. It looks like a class-five tornado swept through it.”

Kiesha jumped off the bed and started throwing on clothes. “Stay right there. I’m on the way over. I want to know what the hell is going on around here. Rory is here asking about Shayla, and now that I think on it, he never did answer when I asked about you. I’ve got a feeling that my mate’s involved and doesn’t want me to know. Sit tight. Maybe between the two of us, we can get to the bottom of this.”

She hung up the phone and rushed out of the room, still trying to put on her shoes. The men looked up when the bedroom door banged open. Kiesha got the last shoe on and came running down the stairs, keys in hand.

“Where do you think you’re going?”

"You are in a shitload of trouble, *mate*. That was Shannon on the phone. I'm going to find out what's going on around here and what happened to my cousin. We'll finish this when I get back," she said as she headed for the door.

"That was Shannon?"

"Where is she?" The two men spoke over each other.

Kiesha brushed past them, not responding to their questions. Alex made a grab for her arm, but she surprised him by dodging his grasp with the swiftness of a shifter.

"I'm coming with you," Alex said determinedly.

"No, you're not," Kiesha called over her shoulder. "I want the truth, not just what you've determined I should know." The door slammed behind her, punctuating her words.

Kiesha's SUV roared to life, and they heard her spin out of the driveway.

"Damn, when she finds out what happened the other night, especially about you and Shayla, the shit is going to hit the fan. I've got to get there and do some damage control." Alex did *not* want his mate angry with him again. Once was enough. He slipped out of his jeans and tied them around his neck.

" *What* are you doing?"

"I'll get there faster if I shift, but I'll need something to put on when I change back. I don't think this is the time to explain to Kiesha that nudity doesn't bother shifters."

Shifters spent so much time in the raw that they didn't view it the way humans did. Kiesha was still too new to be comfortable with him being nude in front of another female, even if that female was a shifter as well.

Alex ran out the door, focused on reaching Shannon before Kiesha. She already had a head start. He shifted and took off running through the woods, just barely noting that Rory had shifted and was running beside him, his pants also flapping in the wind.

Shannon placed the phone back on its cradle and stood there. They would be here any moment, and she had no doubt that it would be "they." For where Kiesha went, Alex was sure to follow, and if Rory was there, he'd be close behind.

She needed to shower, to wash Nikolai's scent off her body, but for reasons she didn't want to examine too closely, she was strangely loath to do so. Instead, she went into her room and put on a pair of jeans and one of her mock-turtleneck sweaters. She didn't believe Nikolai left any visible marks on her, but she wasn't taking any chances. She'd barely finished running the brush through her hair when she heard Kiesha pull into the driveway.

Throwing down the brush, she opened the door in time to see Rory and Alex emerge from the woods. Both men were wearing just their pants, which let her know they'd shifted and ran over, probably trying to beat Kiesha here.

Kiesha ran up the stairs to the door, either not seeing or ignoring the men. "Okay. Now what's going on? Are you all right? Where have you been for the last couple of days?"

"I'm fine. I'm more worried about what happened to Shayla. Rory, what happened to my room? It looks like a demolition crew came through and ripped it to pieces." Although Rory was still a good distance away, Shannon didn't raise her voice. She knew he would hear her.

"Never mind about the room," he answered. "Are you all right? Where have you been? I was worried."

"You're alone? You weren't mated?" Alex looked around, puzzled, obviously doubtful that she had made it through her heat without collecting a mate, especially since she was gone for so long.

Rory rushed toward her, his intent gaze checking to see if she was unhurt when he recoiled as though he'd run into an invisible force field.

"*Vampire*!" Rory spat out, looking at Shannon as though she were the devil incarnate.

"What?" Alex looked at Rory like he was crazy. Then the wind shifted and Alex smelled it too, judging by the distasteful expression on his face.

Although part of her withered inside, Shannon stood straight and tall, staring Rory in the eye. While she'd known it could never work between her and Nikolai, she was surprised to realize that a part of her had been hoping that they could find a way. That fragile hope died a sudden and painful death once it was confronted with Rory's reaction to Nikolai's scent. He looked at her like he hated her.

Kiesha looked at the three of them. "Why are you looking at Shannon like that? What's wrong with you two?"

"Where have you been, Shannon?" Alex asked quietly.

"And why do you smell like vampire?" Rory asked in a hard voice.

When Shannon didn't answer, Rory stepped closer. "Did you *mate* with him? If I pull down your collar, will I find his mark on you?" His hand reached out to do just that.

A growl rose up out of Shannon that wasn't her own. It was a warning, a stamp of possession, and a statement of intent. It said, *Keep your hands off, or suffer the consequences.*

"Nikolai, please. Let me handle this."

"He is not allowed to touch you."

"He's my brother."

"I know who he is, and I care not. He will not put his hands on you."

Rory froze when the growl came out of her. "Oh hell. You've gone and mated him, haven't you?" He gave her a look of disgust and walked a couple of feet away as though he could no longer stand to be near her. He kept his back to Shannon as he ran his hand through his hair.

"*Have* you mated him, Shannon? Did you mark him?" Alex asked, watching her closely.

"Mated who?" Kiesha asked.

"No, I haven't marked him, and he's speaking of Nikolai, Kiesha." As she said his name, gentle warmth flooded her being. Nikolai, letting her know she was not alone.

"You and Nikolai?" Kiesha asked, astonishment in her voice.

"He thinks I'm his chosen," Shannon informed them.

"Know, love, I know that you're my chosen."

"What's a chosen?"

Alex answered, "It's the vampire equivalent of a true mate."

Kiesha rubbed her forehead. "Is that possible? I thought you said vampires and shifters don't mix?"

"Hell no. It isn't possible, and damned straight the two don't mix."

Shannon ignored Rory. She watched Alex, waiting to see what he had to say.

"It doesn't matter what he says. You are my chosen. Nothing will change that. Nor does it matter how they feel about it."

"It's rare. *Extremely* rare. So rare that tales of it happening are more legend than fact," Alex said.

Rory spun around in disbelief. "What the hell are you taking about?"

"I've listened to the old ones talk. In times past, before the wars, it occasionally happened. It's rumored that such matings were one of the causes of the wars."

"What wars?" Kiesha asked, intrigued.

"Vampire-Shifter Wars," Shannon answered. "Vampires were our enemies. The two species fought until both were almost extinct. A truce was called, more in an effort to preserve what little of us remained than a true peace."

"Ancient history, love. It has no bearing on us."

"I don't care what may or may not have happened in the past. My sister is *not* mating a bloodsucker," Rory said in disgust. "What kind of children would they have? If they could have any. We're two different species. It won't work. I don't care what went on between you two for the last couple of days. You stay away from him, Shannon. Nothing good can come of it."

Shannon flinched. She hadn't even thought of that. She wanted children someday, or at least, she wanted the option of having them. Being with Nikolai would mean no children—ever. If, by some miracle, he did manage to impregnate her, what kind of child would it be?

Abomination.

The word whispered through her mind, causing her to feel sick to her stomach. Nikolai was strangely quiet, reinforcing her fears.

"Come on, guys. Let's go. It's getting late, and I'm sure Shannon needs some time alone. Rory, you can crash at our place if you don't feel like driving home."

Alex looked at his mate, then at Shannon. "Come on, Rory. Let's go."

"You two go ahead. I'm not going anywhere."

"Rory, please. I need to be alone," Shannon appealed quietly, close to tears.

Rory hesitated, visibly torn. Shannon knew he wanted to stay and make sure that Nikolai didn't come, but it was her house, and she was a grown woman. He couldn't make this decision for her. "Okay, I'll leave. Call me if you need me." He kissed her on the cheek, then walked quickly down the stairs and left.

Kiesha hugged Shannon. "Call if you need to talk." She turned and walked away, grabbing Alex by the hand and pulling him with her as she left.

* * *

Nikolai wasn't perturbed by what he'd overheard. He'd known he would have to fight for Shannon from the moment he made the decision to claim her. Animosity between the two species ran too deep for them to accept her loss without a fight.

It was his chosen who he had to convince. Shannon was strong. If she decided to claim him, she'd let nothing and no one stand in her way. He just needed to convince her that he, and he alone, was who she wanted as her mate.

His mate watched the others leave. No one had noticed the large black hawk seated on the branch of the tree overhanging the driveway. When the vehicle was out of sight, his mate sighed, turned, and went into the house. He could see she was extremely disturbed by the reactions of the others. Knowing she needed some time to herself, he granted her a few hours to adjust to the changes in her life.

Chapter Eleven

Shannon awoke later that evening, naked and covered in red rose petals. It was startling because when she went to bed, she had on an oversize T-shirt. How did he come in without waking her or her wolf?

She propped up on one elbow and looked around. The rose petals trickled off the bed, onto the carpet, and trailed out the bedroom door. Curious, she sat up, disturbing the hundreds of petals blanketing her body. She rose from the bed and followed the trail.

It led out of the room and to the front door, which was cracked open. Hanging on a hook from the door was an emerald green satin nightgown. She reached out a hand to caress the fabric. It was beautiful. She took it down and went back into her room to stand in front of the mirror.

The gown was ultrafeminine and blatantly sensual. She'd never worn anything like it in her life. Halter-style, it had a plunging neckline, and the back dipped so low she knew it was meant to be worn without underwear. She put it on, enjoying its silky feel against her skin, and gazed at her reflection in wonder. A sexy siren with her features stared back at her.

She felt a moment's disquiet.

Shannon knew how to handle herself as a wolf. As an alpha-fem, she knew what males wanted from her, and it all boiled down to the three *Ps*—power, position, and pups. In her world, feminine equated to soft, and soft got you abused or killed.

Nikolai wasn't interested in any of that, which made him an unknown entity. For the first time in her life, she'd met a male who was interested in Shannon, the woman. Frankly, she didn't know how to deal with it or him, but she was too curious to draw back.

Opening the door, the first thing she noticed was the matching ballerina-style slippers. She put them on her feet before following the trail, which continued down the stairs, across the drive, and into the woods.

Once in the woods, the petals switched from red to white. The trail went about twenty feet before slowly tapering off into a small moonlit clearing. In the center was Nikolai. He lay on his side on a quilt, looking luscious. She was so captivated by his appearance it took a while for her to notice the picnic basket sitting beside him.

"Come, love. I've waited hours for you to appear," Nikolai said as he held out a hand to her in invitation.

Shannon crossed slowly to his side and allowed him to pull her to her knees beside him. Nikolai kissed her fingers and then opened her hand to place a kiss on her palm. "You are as beautiful as I knew you would be in that gown."

She self-consciously ran her fingers through her short hair and then wiped her face, remembering that she had sleep creases from her pillow on her cheeks.

"No, love, you are beautiful."

"What is all of this?" Shannon pointed at the basket and then at the wine bucket directly behind it.

"If the way to a man's heart is through his stomach, then surely the path to a woman's heart must be the same." He reached inside and came out with two wineglasses.

"Is that what you're after…my heart?" Shannon watched as he poured them each a glass of white wine.

"For now." Nikolai handed her one of the glasses.

Shannon took a sip. It tasted fruity and was actually quite good. "You said, for now. What about later?"

He gave her a look that she felt right down to her bones. *"Everything, my love. I want everything."*

Shannon tried to look away and couldn't. His gaze pulled her in until she felt like she was falling. Her field of vision tunneled down. All she could see was the black of his eyes. Then Nikolai blinked, and she was free. She sat there for a minute, disoriented.

"Come here."

She looked at him stupidly. "Where? I *am* here." She was kneeling right beside him. What more did he want?

Nikolai didn't bother answering. He reached out and removed the glass from her hand, placing it to the side. Then he grasped her under her arms and lifted her onto his lap. She clutched his shoulders, afraid he would drop her.

"Never. You are too precious to me."

I really wish he would stop reading my mind, she thought.

Intimate laughter flooded her mind in response to her wish. *"Why would I wish to do that when your mind is so intriguing?"*

"It's unnerving, having someone else in your head."

"It's intimate," he countered. "Having someone know your thoughts and sharing yours with them."

"Yes, but I can't read your mind, which gives you an unfair advantage."

"You can if you choose. My mind is always open to you. It is the privilege of all chosen, the ability to read their mate's thoughts."

"You mean you can't do this with everyone?" Shannon looked at him suspiciously.

"No, I am not that powerful. This is a gift given to us because of the blood that we exchanged." He held an appetizer to her mouth. It reminded Shannon of the first time he'd fed her while immersed in his tub.

When she finished chewing, she said, "I've given you blood. I've never taken any of yours, other than that first night when I bit you. That's not enough to be a true exchange."

When he said nothing, she became suspicious. She would know if she'd drunk from him, wouldn't she? Vampires were powerful, but so were shifters. Of course, of the two, vamps had shifters beat, hands down. "We haven't exchanged blood, have we? I would know if we had, wouldn't I?"

Nikolai gazed at her unrepentantly. "We have completed all but the final blood exchange."

Shannon's mind spun with the information. She was one blood exchange away from being a vampire's mate. She opened her mouth automatically in response to the food he placed there. As she ate, she considered the ramifications. "Why did you stop? Why not do all three?"

"For the last one, you must agree." He poured more wine and handed her the glass.

"So, if I don't agree, you'll let it go? You won't do the final exchange?" Shannon gazed at him over the rim of her glass as she sipped the wine.

Nikolai didn't answer. Shannon wasn't sure what his silence meant. She decided not to push, sure she wouldn't like the results. "You aren't eating," she said after a while.

"First you feed, then me."

She felt the blush that suffused her body as she remembered what happened the last time he'd spoken those words to her. Her nipples hardened as her arousal scented the air. She took another sip of wine in an effort to hide her reaction to his words, draining the glass dry.

Nikolai refilled her glass. He fed her until she was unable to eat another bite. Once she was finished, he placed all the items back into the basket and laid it to the side. Then he tumbled her back on the quilt and lay beside her, his leg over hers, holding her in place. Leaning over her, he took his time studying her face. He examined her feature by feature, until she was squirming in embarrassment, uncomfortable with such close attention.

"Do you know how beautiful you are?"

Shannon opened her mouth to protest, and Nikolai planted his finger against it to silence her. “I speak not of outward appeal, though you possess plenty. I speak of inner beauty, of the soul.”

She shook her head silently in disbelief.

“Have the wolves not spoken to you of such as they tried to woo you into their beds?”

She remembered her earlier thoughts. “No,” she responded after a moment of silence. “Wolves on the prowl speak only of strength.” The more cunning ones waited until she was in heat and attempted to use her body against her. None of them had ever tried appealing to the woman in her, as though she were her beast and nothing else. Even Rory tended to speak to her in terms of her wolf.

Nikolai captured her gaze again, distracting her from her depressing thoughts. “I see you.” “*I see you*,” he repeated in her mind, “*and all that you are. I see your very soul, and it is beautiful to me.*”

Shannon’s heart melted. She was appalled at how easily he breached her defenses with pretty words. How starved must she be for compliments that the first man to offer them was building a gateway into her very heart? Unable to cope with his flattery and unable to think of anything else to do, she attempted to redirect his attention.

“Didn’t you say you were going to feed when I was finished? I’m done.”

His gaze narrowed on her. “Are you offering to feed me? Are you asking me to partake freely of your blood?”

There was something about the way he phrased his questions that Shannon found disturbing, but she couldn't think of what it was. Not with his eyes gazing directly into hers. It ruined her ability to think. She nodded her head.

"You must say the words," Nikolai proclaimed.

"Take what you need. I offer it to you freely." The words surged up from somewhere deep inside. At the surge of triumph that blazed across Nikolai's face, Shannon wondered exactly what it was she'd done.

"Since you offered, I can do no more than oblige," Nikolai said huskily, his voice causing shivers to run up and down her spine. His hands slowly glided down her body to her knees. There he gathered her gown until it bunched in his fists, and began to draw it upward, slowly revealing her body beneath.

When it reached her hips, Shannon planted her feet and lifted, assisting him with the removal of her gown. Nikolai dragged it over her breasts and off her body before tossing it casually to the side. "A veritable feast," he proclaimed, allowing his hand to sweep over her bare body. "From where shall I feed? Shall I feed from this spot?" He lifted her wrist and kissed the delicate skin there.

"Or here?" He lightly ran his finger from her earlobe to her neck, causing the hair to rise on her body.

"What about here?" He cupped her breast, molding his hand to its shape before pinching the taut nipple.

Shannon arched into his hand as fire streaked from her nipple to her womb.

"Or shall I feed from here?" His hand glided over her stomach to her mound, bypassing her needy clit, and stroked down to her inner thigh. The skin there was coated with her juices. Shannon was so aroused that the moisture was flowing down her thighs.

Nikolai skimmed his fingertips along the fluid on her leg and followed the stream back to her slit. He rubbed his hand back and forth, coating his fingers liberally before bringing them to his mouth for a taste.

He moaned, and his fangs dropped into place. *"Spread your legs, love, so that I might feast."*

Shannon drew back her knees until she was wide open as Nikolai settled between her thighs. "You don't mind if I play with my food for a while before eating, do you?" he asked wickedly.

"God, no," she burst out as his mouth closed over her clit and began to suck. Within minutes, she was a babbling fool, totally out of her mind with the pleasure he brought to her body. The clearing, with its almost-full moon shining down around them, faded from sight as her focus narrowed down to Nikolai's mouth on the most intimate part of her body.

His fangs scraped her, causing her to buck against him. He clamped a hand over her hips, using his strength to hold her still. His tongue lapped at her as though she were an ice-cream cone and it was a hot summer day. When her vision faded to black and her back arched up off the ground in climax, he turned his head and sank his fangs into her thigh, feeding deeply. Shannon screamed as her orgasm rocketed to another level. He fed until she was a trembling, shuddering mass of nothingness, barely hanging on to consciousness, her body unable to handle any more pleasure. Her heart hammered inside of her chest.

Nikolai licked the puncture wound closed and laid his head on her stomach. “Thank you for your generosity.” His cock was long and hard, and she was ready and willing for him to plow into her softness, but he restrained himself. Apparently this wooing was not about sex. Obviously Nikolai was smart enough to know that while sex had the power to bring her to him, it wouldn’t keep her by his side. He needed to win her heart.

He lounged quietly while she recovered. He held still, barely breathing when she tentatively stroked his head with her hand. When he didn’t protest, the strokes became more confident, and he purred in contentment. She breathed in the night air, her hand buried in his thick hair as she slowly drifted off to sleep.

* * *

The next two weeks went by in a sensuous haze. By day, she worked on the accounts for the stores and caught up the books for Rory’s construction business and the pack. The nights belonged to Nikolai. He romanced her. There was no other term for it.

He took her on moonlit picnics. She lay with her head in his lap while he recited poetry to her. He danced with her beneath the stars. On one memorable occasion, he took her flying. Every night he fed her, making sure her hunger was satisfied before fulfilling his own.

Nikolai did everything except have actual intercourse with her, and it was making her crazy. She wanted to feel his cock in her sheath. Feel him deep inside. She could feel his desire for her. The way he denied himself frustrated her even as it increased her respect and admiration for him. He had a goal in mind and could not be swayed from it, no matter how much she tried. She alternated between sensuous satisfaction and sexual frustration as he satisfied her on every level but one.

She craved him. Craved his body and his presence. She felt complete only when his mind and his body merged with hers. Otherwise, she felt empty and alone. She couldn't imagine being any more connected to him if he were her mate. But then, he couldn't be, because if he were, her wolf would accept him.

As promised, Rory had brought a crew with him to repair the damage he'd done to the basement. He was abnormally quiet, moody even. She thought it was the situation with Nikolai, but after that first night, he never mentioned it. Never questioned her. She was surprised, and a bit suspicious. It wasn't like him not to pry into her business, especially about something like this.

He was like a wolf with a sore paw, or a man who'd lost his woman, but that couldn't be. Rory wouldn't pine over a woman. Besides, the only women he'd been around lately that she knew of were Shayla and herself. He hadn't lost her, and the idea that he might be yearning for Shayla was…well, laughable. The two were more likely to kill each other than mate.

The ringing of the phone interrupted her musings. “Hello?”

“Did you forget our appointment?”

She looked at the clock. “Oh, shit. Alex, I’m sorry. Do you want to reschedule?”

“No. I want you to get in your vehicle and come to my office. I’ll be waiting,” he said shortly and disconnected the call.

Shannon was a little stunned by his manner until she realized that it wasn’t her doctor commanding her presence. It was her alpha. Good thing too. She hated going to his office, and given a choice, she would have simply canceled. However, this thing with her blood was too important for her to play around with.

She shut off the computer and a few minutes later raced down the mountain. She made excellent time and within fifteen minutes walked into his office. When she signed in, the nurse took her straight back to the examining room after taking her blood pressure and weight.

In a surprising twist, Alex was already in the room waiting. She didn’t know whether to be annoyed or alarmed. Usually she had to twiddle her thumbs until the doctor arrived. That he was already there spoke volumes about his concern for her health.

“Hop up on the table, and hold out your arm.” He rolled a tray containing his bloodletting instruments of torture closer to the examination table.

Shannon watched as Alex filled four tubes. If she had to donate blood, she much preferred Nikolai's way of acquiring it than Alex's.

As he untied the band from her arm and pressed a clean cotton ball to her wound, she tried to read Alex's expression. It was a useless attempt. He'd gone into full-blown doctor mode and wouldn't be revealing any of his thoughts until he was good and ready to do so.

"While I run tests on these, get undressed. I want to do a full pelvic exam." He gathered the vials of blood and pushed everything out of his way, his mind obviously focused on his next task.

"Why? Is that really necessary?"

Alex stopped like he'd run into a wall. He turned slowly to look at her, and his power filled the room, making her skin itch. Damn, he was back in alpha mode again. "Because I'm your doctor, and I said so. If that's not reason enough, then do it because your alpha commands you."

Shannon lowered her eyes in submission and nodded her head. *Stupid, stupid, stupid.* You do *not* challenge your alpha, even if he is the mate of your good friend, she chastised herself as he left the room. She felt a gentle nudge on her mind.

"Is all well, my love?"

"Yeah, just dandy."

"You seem troubled. What's wrong?"

"Just angry with myself. I did something stupid."

"*Aaah*!" She felt his smile. "*Call if you need me.*" He caressed her gently and then withdrew his presence from her mind.

Twenty minutes later, Shannon was vividly reminded of why she hated office visits. They made you put on these stupid paper gowns that were never large enough to cover what you wanted covered; then they left you sitting in a room cold enough to raise goose bumps, even with her shifter metabolism.

Another ten minutes went by before Alex waltzed in with the nurse. He was all business as he conducted a full pelvic exam, including a Pap smear. Snapping off his gloves, Alex collected his samples and told Shannon to dress and meet him in his office.

Shannon dressed slowly, wondering what this was all about. She felt fine—wonderful, in fact. Her legs no longer bothered her, and what sleep she did manage was sound.

Alex came into the office and closed the door behind him. He tossed her chart on his desk and sat on its edge rather than in his chair as he had on her last visit. "Level with me. Have you been seeing Nikolai?"

Struggling mightily to keep from squirming, Shannon gave him an honest answer. "Yes."

"Have you been giving him blood?"

"Are you asking as my doctor or my alpha?"

"Both. Now answer the question." Alex's gaze bore into hers.

"Yes," she reluctantly answered, knowing she had to, but feeling it was none of his business.

"How often?"

"Nightly. Is there a purpose to all these questions?"

"Yes. I'm trying to figure out what's different; what changed between this visit and last. Your blood count is within the normal range—the high end of normal, but still normal. If you've been donating blood nightly, your blood count should be low. Since it's not, I'm speculating that your body is producing just enough blood to keep Nikolai fed. The only reason that I can see for this to be happening is if you were his mate and had completed the necessary blood exchanges. Have you ingested his blood?"

Shannon sighed. "Nikolai showed me what happened the night he found me. I attacked him while in wolf form and got a good piece of his arm. I think that's what triggered the changes in my body. According to Nikolai, it was the blood I ingested that allowed him to place me under compulsion."

Alex placed his hand on his thigh and looked down at the floor. "That's entirely possible. Any other times that I need to know about?"

"Not that I can recall, but Nikolai claims that he's completed two of the required blood exchanges."

"Which leaves only one remaining?"

"Yes, according to what I've been told."

"I'll have to run some more tests to be sure, but it's possible that the changes his blood has wrought are irrevocable. For now, Nikolai is the solution to your PV. I don't like it, but I can't see any way around it."

Shannon sat on the edge of her seat, her gaze intense. "What are you saying, Alex? That I should mate with Nikolai?"

"No! Yes. Hell, I don't know what I'm saying. Until I run more tests, this is just speculation. Let's wait and see what the test results have to say before you go making any life-altering decisions. I don't like the idea of you and Nikolai together any more than Rory does. We have too few females as it is. You didn't feel a connection with any of the Raven pack's wolves?"

Even though she knew the answer, Shannon gave the question the careful consideration that it deserved before answering. "Unless there are some I haven't met, the answer is no. I haven't met anyone that I clicked with, nor has my wolf."

"Have you tried, Shannon? Really tried to connect with any of them?"

Halting the growl that wanted to rise, she reminded herself that this was her alpha and she couldn't blow up at him. She took a calming breath before answering. "Alex, I know my duty. It's been drummed into me since I was a child. If I had met anyone who even remotely registered on my radar as a potential mate, I would have pursued it. I'm not being deliberately picky. None of the men from my old pack appealed to me, and I'm having the same problem here. I would be happy, over the moon ecstatic to find a male who appealed to both my wolf and to me as a woman, but I haven't."

"What about Nikolai? How do you feel about him?"

The blush she felt lit up her face was probably answer enough. "If I were human, I'd already be bonded to him. I know I have a responsibility to the pack. Even if I wasn't already aware, Rory's and your reactions brought it home. Besides, it doesn't matter how I feel. My wolf doesn't accept Nikolai." Shannon didn't add anything else, knowing that Alex would understand the implications.

Alex stood up, indicating that the interview was over. "I'll call you when I have the results. See Bernie on the way out. I want to see you back again in eight weeks."

Alex watched Shannon leave. He was deeply disturbed and struggled greatly with his conscience. He'd chosen to remain unmated rather than settle for someone who was simply suitable, even though as alpha he had the responsibility to provide an heir for his pack. He had always considered himself to be open-minded, nonchauvinistic even. He was ashamed to realize that he unconsciously subscribed to the same double standard as the elders. Although he wasn't exerting the pressure on Shannon that Rory had been, he had expected her to find a mate among the males of his pack. It never occurred to him she might do otherwise.

What if Nikolai was correct? What if Shannon really was his chosen? Could he overcome his personal prejudice and do what was best for Shannon? She admitted that none of the men in the Raven and Sparrowhawks packs moved her. That was significant. If any of their males were Shannon's mate, Nikolai's claim wouldn't even be an issue. Shannon would already be mated.

Alex had his own theories about her wolf. Theories he would keep to himself until he got the results back. If they turned out the way he anticipated, he and Rory would be having a long talk.

Chapter Twelve

Shannon escaped Alex's office and headed directly for Hugh's diner, in dire need of comfort food. She went inside and ordered three taco salads—heavy on the meat—to go, three large sweet teas, and three of Mary Elizabeth's dark chocolate brownies with nuts.

It was the peak of the lunch rush, and the place was jumping. Fortunately, Hugh placed a priority on to-go orders so she didn't have to wait long.

"Is this yours?" Hugh indicated the food in the take-out containers in the window.

"Yes."

"Are you headed to the store?"

"Yes," Shannon answered, wondering if he wanted her to deliver a message to Mary Elizabeth.

"Anne, Shannon's food is on the house," Hugh said, surprising her with his generosity.

"Thanks, Hugh," she called out as he rang the bell, indicating an order was ready for pick up. Hugh waved in acknowledgment before disappearing from the window. Shannon grabbed the food and drinks and walked out of the diner.

A few minutes later, she came through the door of the store. Kiesha and Mary Elizabeth must have both been upstairs in their offices because she didn't see them anywhere. "Lunch!" she called out.

"Shannon?"

"I smell food." Their voices floated down the stairs, followed swiftly by their bodies.

"I brought food. Come and get it while it's hot." Shannon cleared off an area on one of the dining table sets on the showroom floor and distributed the food. By the time the other two made it to the table, she was already digging in.

"You sweetheart! I was just wishing that I'd brought lunch. I'm hungry." Mary Elizabeth hummed in appreciation when she saw what was in the container, grabbed her fork, and began eating.

"Smells heavenly. Why didn't you call and tell us you were bringing this? Not that I'm complaining." Kiesha's eyes closed as she took her first bite of the salad. "Mmm, this is so good. How much do I owe you?"

"Nothing. Hugh picked up the tab. And I didn't call because I didn't know I was coming. By the time Alex finished poking and prodding me, I needed comfort food and decided to share. You know the saying. Misery loves company."

"If misery makes you eat like this, feel free to share your misery at any time. I thought I had eaten everything on the menu, but this is new." Mary Elizabeth was hunched over her food like she was afraid someone would take it from her.

"Taco salad was the special of the day. Maybe he's trying something new, seeing if it will sell before adding it to the menu," Shannon speculated.

"The hotel had taco salads on their menu. Hugh loved it. He must have decided to try and recreate it."

"Speaking of hotels, how was your trip? I haven't seen you since you've been back," Shannon said.

Mary Elizabeth turned a brilliant red and buried her face in her hands, food temporarily forgotten. Shannon glanced at Kiesha, one eyebrow raised in inquiry.

"Don't look at me. I asked and got the same reaction. She still hasn't told me what happened."

"You want to know what happened? I'll tell you what happened after I find out why Shannon didn't warn me." The look she shot at Shannon was scorching.

"Warn you about what?" Shannon was completely baffled.

"About how bad the blue moon was going to be! You should have told me what to expect. Kiesha would have if she'd known," Mary Elizabeth wailed.

"Hey, that's not fair. I *did* warn you. I told you about it and the effect it had on shifters. It's not my fault that you didn't believe me and weren't prepared."

"When? When did you tell me about it 'cause I don't remember having that conversation."

"In the diner, when we were sitting at the table. Kiesha, you remember, don't you?"

"Actually, I don't think Mary Elizabeth was at the table when the subject came up. She and Hugh had gone in the back to have their 'little discussion'?"

"See," Mary Elizabeth said. "I *told* you. Not that anything you said would have made a difference. Even if I had known, there was no way to prepare for *that*. My God, I acted like a nymphomaniac. Hugh and I could barely keep our hands off of each other. Was it like that for you too?"

"We didn't get it that bad, according to Alex, because I'm already pregnant. It hit us the hardest at night, when the moon was full. I can't tell you what happened because I honestly don't remember. I seemed to have blacked out. Did you make it to the funeral?"

The blush that had faded came roaring back. Mary Elizabeth lowered her eyes to the table in embarrassment. "My mother was mortified. She still isn't speaking to me. Hugh and I had sex in the parking lot while the casket was being escorted into the church. Apparently someone saw us."

Shannon laughed and quickly turned it into a cough when Mary Elizabeth looked up, her eyes deadly. "Don't you dare laugh. It was horrible, and that wasn't the worst of it." She then proceeded to describe in vivid detail what happened in the elevator as they left for the funeral.

Shannon tried to picture prim and proper Mary Elizabeth caught in such a compromising position. The image came to life in her mind. She glanced at Kiesha and quickly looked away. Both were desperately struggling not to laugh. Shannon snickered first and attempted to hold it in. Kiesha turned her face away from the table and began to giggle under her breath.

Then Shannon got a visual of what the old couple's facial expressions must have been, and that was it. She laughed until tears were flowing down her face and she was holding her sides. Kiesha wasn't in any better shape. Only her grip on the table kept her from falling out of her chair and onto the floor.

"Glad you're finding my humiliation so hilarious, guys," Mary Elizabeth said drily. "It's really not that funny."

"Oh, yes, it is," Shannon disagreed, trying to catch her breath while she wiped the tears from her face.

Mary Elizabeth smiled and then began to laugh as well. Kiesha had laughed so hard that she'd given herself the hiccups. Once they calmed down, they put any further conversation on hold until they could finish eating their rapidly cooling salads. Then Shannon brought out the brownies.

"Oooh, brownies. My favorite. That does it. We're definitely keeping you." Kiesha snatched a brownie out of Shannon's hand and ripped the cellophane wrapping off it.

Shannon held out one to Mary Elizabeth. "No." She shook her head. "That's all right. Ever since we've been back, I can't stand the taste of chocolate."

Kiesha was stunned enough to stop midbite. "Not like chocolate? Are you okay? Do I need to have you examined by Alex?"

Shannon leaned closer to Mary Elizabeth and took a sniff.

Mary Elizabeth shooed Shannon away from her. "Stop it! That's just freaky the way you guys do that."

"Are you going to tell her or shall I?" Shannon nodded her head in Kiesha's direction before arching her eyebrow and pinning Mary Elizabeth with her gaze.

"Tell me what?" Kiesha mumbled around a mouthful of brownie.

"There's nothing to tell. Not yet, anyway. It's too soon to know," Mary Elizabeth said at the same time.

"Too soon to know what?" Kiesha interrupted, trying to wash down her brownie with tea.

"What does Hugh say?" Shannon spoke over her.

"What does Hugh say about *what*?"

"He says what you're thinking, but what does he know?"

Shannon shook her head. "You are one wickedly stubborn female."

"That's it!" Kiesha slammed her hands down on the table. "Tell me what? What is Hugh thinking? Quit speaking in code. Inquiring minds want to know. Somebody better start talking, or I'll…I'll…" She floundered, unable to think of a threat dire enough.

"You'll what?" Shannon asked innocently.

"I don't know," Kiesha admitted ruefully. "I can't think of anything intimidating enough. You two evil heifers are hard to scare."

Mary Elizabeth and Shannon laughed. Kiesha rubbed her stomach. At almost four months, she was finally getting a noticeable bump.

"Mary Elizabeth's pregnant," Shannon announced, "and she's in denial."

Kiesha squealed and high-fived Shannon. "That's wonderful."

"I am not in denial. I just don't believe it," Mary Elizabeth said over Kiesha.

Shannon and Kiesha shared a look. "Denial," they said at the same time with a laugh.

"Y'all are no help. Don't let Hugh hear you. He's just as bad. He keeps insisting that I'm pregnant. Says he can smell it."

"Don't you want children?" Kiesha asked.

Mary Elizabeth took her time answering. "Yes, a whole house full of them, actually. I'm just not certain that now is the time. Hugh and I are still feeling our way. I don't know if we're ready to be parents. A lot of couples break up under the pressure of parenthood."

"Oh, honey. That won't happen to you. Hugh loves you. He's not going anywhere." Kiesha tried to reassure her.

Mary Elizabeth still doesn't have a good understanding of the mate bond, or she wouldn't be this insecure, Shannon thought to herself. Aloud, she said, "Talk to Hugh. Tell him how you feel."

Mary Elizabeth shook her head. "I don't want to upset him."

"You won't upset him. It's his job as your mate to make you feel secure. He can't do that if he doesn't know what's going on in your mind."

"Shannon's right, Mary Elizabeth. Talk to Hugh. I wasn't too sure about the timing of this pregnancy either, but Alex eased a lot of my fears. If you are pregnant, you need to tell

Hugh how you're feeling. His support and love are what you'll need most to get through this. Besides, effective communication is a must for any relationship."

"I'll think about it. Enough about me. I heard you have a hunky vampire chasing after you," Mary Elizabeth said in an obvious bid to redirect the conversation.

"Yes, how is that going? You still seeing him, or did you manage to chase him away?"

Shannon felt herself flush. In that moment, she cursed her fair complexion that showed her reaction vividly.

"Look at the blush," Kiesha crowed. "I'd say that was a yes. She's still seeing him. Good for you. Don't let those dimwits tell you what to do."

"Who's a dimwit?" Mary Elizabeth wanted to know.

"My mate and her brother. They don't want Shannon and Nikolai—that's his name—together."

"Why not?"

"Something about vampires and shifters not mixing. Sounds like a bunch of racial prejudice to me," Kiesha said with a look of distaste on her face.

Mary Elizabeth turned to Shannon with a look of awe on her face. "So, you've got your own Romeo and Juliet-style romance?"

"God, I hope not. Didn't they both die at the end of that story?"

"Yeah, they did. Okay, maybe not the best example," Mary Elizabeth admitted. "But you've got your own star-crossed lovers thing going on."

"To be honest, I don't know what I have. The man's totally wrong for me, except he fascinates me."

"Why is he wrong for you?" Kiesha demanded.

"Because he's a vampire."

"That's bull, and you know it. Are the two species incompatible? No, can't be or Nikolai wouldn't think you're his chosen," Kiesha said firmly, answering her own question.

"What's a chosen?" Mary Elizabeth asked.

"The vampire equivalent of true mates."

"How can I be his chosen? That's what I don't understand. Shouldn't his chosen be another vampire or even a human? Whoever heard of a shifter and a vamp? That doesn't make sense. Besides, if I were his chosen, wouldn't my wolf accept him?"

"That's not exactly true, Shannon. Remember, Alex said he'd heard of vampire-shifter matings in the past. Besides, whoever said love had to make sense?"

"Shannon, do you want to be with Nikolai?" Mary Elizabeth asked softly. "Do you love him?"

"It doesn't matter what I want. Nor does it matter how I feel. I have a responsibility to the pack and to my species as a whole to find a shifter I can tolerate and mate with him."

Kiesha shook her head. "Tolerate? Do you *hear* yourself? Why should you have to settle for less than love? Screw the pack. Screw your species. If they haven't died out by now, you mating with Nikolai won't make a bit of difference. This is your life we're talking about. You have to do what's best for you."

"Because you weren't born a shifter, Kiesha, you don't understand. You saw what the reaction was when Rory and Alex knew that I had been with Nikolai. Rory's my brother, and Alex is my alpha. Imagine how the rest of the pack will react. I would be ostracized." Shannon shook her head. There was no way her friends would be able to understand. Shifters were raised with a pack mentality. Every decision was made with careful consideration of how it affected the pack as a whole because everything you did affected the pack.

Mary Elizabeth laid her hand on Shannon's forearm, which was resting on the table. "What if Rory and Alex accepted Nikolai as your mate? Would you be with him then? That is, assuming you want to be."

"If Alex accepted Nikolai and my mating, then the rest of his pack would have to follow his lead. Rory will never accept it. I could live with that. I love my brother, but I wouldn't let his opinion of Nikolai keep me from him. The biggest problem is my wolf. She hates Nikolai, and as long as she does, a mating between us won't work. I would never be able to relax with him, always have to be on guard so that my wolf didn't surface with him."

"I think Nikolai can handle your wolf. He seems to be the type that can handle anything. You never answered Mary Elizabeth's question. Do you *want* Nikolai? Forget about all the reasons why you shouldn't. Be honest with yourself, at least. If none of these obstacles were in the way, would you take Nikolai as your mate?" Kiesha's gaze drilled into Shannon's, daring her to admit the truth.

She was silent for a moment, allowing herself to imagine the possibility. "Yes," she said quietly. "Yes, I would."

"If you want him, then go after him," Mary Elizabeth advised, squeezing her arm encouragingly before pulling back. "Don't let anything stand in your way. Forget about everything and everyone and just follow your heart."

"Don't worry about Alex. I'll handle him. He'll handle the rest of the pack. You won't be ostracized."

"What about the problem with my wolf?" Shannon worried aloud.

"Talk to Rory," Mary Elizabeth suggested. "Tell him how you feel. If he sees how much you want Nikolai, he won't stand in your way. Give him a little time to adjust to the idea. He may have the solution to your wolf issue."

Shannon looked at the two women who'd become good friends over the last couple of months. She could see from the expression on their faces that they really wanted what was best for her. "I'll think about it. I promise."

They were all quiet, each with their own thoughts, when Shannon asked, "So, what happened with the will? Are you megarich now?"

"I don't know. The executor read the will and is sending out copies to all of the heirs, which is a good thing. I was too busy trying to keep my hands off of Hugh to hear much of what he was saying. I do know that we were given thirty days to contest if we didn't agree with any of the provisions listed."

"You think anyone is going to contest it?"

"Who knows? I'm not even sure why Charles wrote me into his will to begin with, although the man was crazy so maybe no other explanation is needed."

"Think of all the good you could do with that money," Kiesha continued.

"That's what I said. Hugh still doesn't like the idea of my receiving anything from Charles. '*It's a man's responsibility to provide for his mate*,'" Mary Elizabeth said, mocking Hugh's deep voice.

"Hey, don't knock it. A lot of men want the women to do the providing while they sit on their sorry butts," Kiesha offered while Shannon nodded her head in agreement.

"I'm *not* knocking it. I'm glad he feels the way that he does. I don't particularly *want* Charles's money, but since he gave it to me, I'm going to use it."

"Hear, hear," Shannon said as she raised her cup of sweet tea in salute. Kiesha raised hers as well, looking at Mary Elizabeth expectantly. When Mary Elizabeth lifted hers, they touched cups together in a toast.

* * *

Alex viewed the test results in his hands. He'd run them twice to be sure. There was no doubt. He picked up the phone and dialed Rory's number.

"McFelan Construction."

"We need to talk."

"Same place as last time?"

"Yes."

"Be there in an hour."

Alex flipped his cell phone closed and slid it back in his pocket. Then he went and cleared his schedule for the rest of the afternoon. An hour later, he was at Lover's Lookout, pacing beside his SUV as he awaited Rory's arrival.

Rory pulled up five minutes later in his company truck. "Sorry I'm late. Got detained at the last minute. I presume this concerns Shannon?" he asked as he got out of the truck.

"It does. Here, read this." He thrust the papers at Rory.

"What's this?" Rory's eyes were scanning the paperwork.

"It's Shannon's lab test results."

Rory looked at him sharply before returning his gaze to the document. "What does this mean?"

"I compared the results of this test to the one I took a few weeks ago. Shannon's changing. Her DNA is changing," Alex clarified.

"Changing how?" Rory pinned Alex with a look that demanded the truth.

"Becoming more. Something other. She's not vampire, but neither is she simply shifter. Her cells are still mutating, from what I can see."

Rory crushed the papers in his hand. "It's that damned bloodsucker. He did this to her. I'll *kill* him."

Alex held out a hand in warning. "Before you go running off and getting yourself killed, you need to consider a few things." Rory visibly bristled at the implication that he couldn't defeat Nikolai. Alex ignored him and continued. "Shannon's life may depend on her mating with Nikolai."

"The hell you say."

"Remember the blood condition I told you Shannon has?" Alex waited until Rory gave a terse nod. "It was triggered not by Nikolai, but by Shannon."

"You're blaming *Shannon* for this mess?"

"Rory, I'm not blaming anyone. I'm just telling you that Nikolai is not the villain you're trying to make him out to be. He is the one who found Shannon out on the ridge and brought her to me. Apparently, Shannon attacked and bit him, ingesting his blood when he got too close, not knowing he was there to help. That's what caused the initial transition and allowed Nikolai to bond with Shannon."

"What are you saying? I was there that night. It was a shifter who found Shannon, one of yours. I would have attacked anyone else who came near her that night."

"Nikolai wanted you to think he was a shifter. He must have masked his scent. He's powerful enough to do so."

"If what you're saying is true, then this whole mess is my fault. If I hadn't chased Shannon out there, she would never have met Nikolai."

"It's nobody's fault. I believe Nikolai is right. Shannon is his chosen. This would have happened no matter what any of us did. She is his chosen mate, the one the Creator intended for him to have. Her body is changing. She's producing the blood Nikolai needs to sustain him. His feeding from her is actually helping her stay healthy."

"Is there any way to reverse this? Some way to break his hold over her? There has to be some way around this, Alex." It was evident to Alex that Rory just did not want his sister mated to a vamp.

Alex shook his head. "I don't believe so. They've already completed two of the exchanges. There's only one remaining. That's not the only—nor the most important—consideration. Shannon's spent all of her life in your pack and never found a mate. We both assumed she would find one in the Raven pack. She's met every one of the unmated wolves, and none of them appealed to her on any level. The only man to have captured her interest is Nikolai."

Alex was silent, allowing his words and their implications to sink in. He watched as Rory struggled to take in what he was saying.

"*A bloody vamp*? Do you know what you're asking me to accept?" His accent was so strong, Alex had to listen carefully to understand what he was saying.

"You know he'll take good care of her. He can do no less. She's his chosen, his mate. Blood of his blood. She's safe with him."

"I know, but…it's just a lot to take in. A bloody vamp in the family," Rory muttered to himself as he paced. Finally, he stopped and turned to Alex. "Have you told Shannon the results?"

"No, I wanted to speak with you first."

"Don't tell her." Alex opened his mouth to object. Rory cut him off. "At least, not yet. Shannon needs to make up her own mind about the bloodsucker. If she decides she wants him, nothing we say or do will stop her from mating with him. It has to be her decision, with no outside influences."

"What if she decides that she doesn't want him?"

"I really don't see that happening. Do you?"

"No. She wants him. I don't know if she wants him bad enough to go after him after all we've said to her, but I know she wants him."

"Then we'll wait and see what happens. If she really is Nikolai's chosen, she'll go to him soon. If not, I'm sure Nikolai will come for her. It's what I would do, given the opportunity."

"It's what we all would do. Nothing stands in the way of a male claiming his mate, including a reluctant mate."

* * *

Another week passed before Shannon reached the point of no return. She craved Nikolai with an almost-painful intensity. She desired all of him, and not just his body. She wanted to go to sleep curled up in his arms and to be there when he took his first true breath of the day. She needed more than the stolen moments they spent together. More than the precious hours spent nightly in his arms.

She had to "come out of the closet," as it were, and boldly proclaim to all who would listen that Nikolai was her mate. Her chosen. The man she desired above all others. She would like to spend the rest of eternity with him, and if the Creator was feeling benevolent, she wanted her belly to swell with his seed and to present him with a child.

There was only one thing standing in the way. Her wolf had to accept Nikolai. If not as its mate, then at the very least it had to recognize Nikolai's dominance over it. Shannon needed help. She needed answers. So she turned to the one person she'd always run to when she was in trouble. She went to Rory.

She was waiting on the porch when he came home from work. She set the swing in motion and lifted her face to the breeze as he got out of the truck and came toward her.

"Why didn't you wait in the house? You have a key. How long have you been sitting out here?"

"Not long. It's a nice day so it was no hardship. Besides, I no longer live here. I couldn't just walk in, even if I do still have a key."

Rory sat down beside her on the swing. "Shannon, this will always be your home, no matter where you live."

"Do you mean that? Really?" She brought her foot up on the swing and turned to look at him, resting her chin on her knee.

"Little bit, you're my baby sister, and I love you. Never, ever doubt that. And never doubt the things that I would do to see you safe and happy." He ruffled her hair.

Shannon slid closer to him and laid her head on his shoulder, the way she used to when she was younger. Rory dropped his arm around her, held her close, and started the swing to swaying. They sat quietly in the gathering twilight, enjoying the weather and each other.

"I love him, Rory." Shannon spoke softly.

"I know." Rory's answer was equally low, as though he was reluctant to disturb the peaceful atmosphere.

"I want to mate with him, but my wolf…it wants nothing to do with Nikolai. It's the only thing standing in my way."

"What about me?"

"You're my brother and your opinion means a lot to me, but I love Nikolai. He completes me. I hope that you can accept him. Even if you can't, I still want him. I'd still go to him."

"And the pack? What if they ostracize you? Are you willing to risk losing the support of the pack to have Nikolai as your mate?"

Shannon took a deep, shuddering breath. "Yes, even if it means separation from the pack. I want Nikolai as my mate."

She felt it when Rory released the breath he was holding and squeezed her close in a one-armed hug. "Now I know that you really love him, and it's not just the sex."

Shannon lifted her chin until she could see Rory's face. He looked down and met her gaze. "Did you really believe that sex was all there was between us?"

"There was always the possibility. He is your first lover. You wouldn't be the first to confuse love with sexual pleasure."

"And now that you know that it's love?"

"I'll help you claim your mate."

"Just like that? No argument?"

Rory cupped her face with his free hand and bent to rub his nose against hers. The action brought tears to her eyes. He hadn't given her a "nosey" since she came out of elementary school. "I want you to be happy. If this vamp makes you happy, then I'm okay with it. I know what it's like to love someone and not be with them." A haunted look entered his eyes before he blinked it away. "As far as your wolf goes, you need to treat Nikolai like he's a shifter."

"What do you mean?"

"Fight him. Make him prove his dominance over you."

"Fight him," she echoed, not certain she'd heard right.

"Shannon, if Nikolai were a shifter and tried to claim you, what would you do?"

"Make him prove he was strong enough to keep me," she said without any hesitation.

"By…"

A light went off in her head. She abruptly sat up, jarring the swing to a halt. "Making him fight me. That's it! It's so simple, it's brilliant. You're a genius. Why didn't I think of it?"

"Because you're not me. That's why." His voice was extremely smug.

Shannon threw her arms around him and hugged him tight. "Thank you. Thank you so very much."

"You're welcome," Rory said as he held her close.

"You're the best big brother in the world," Shannon said as she kissed his cheek. Keeping her arms around him, she drew back a little until she could see his face. "She'll come back, Rory. You'll see. Don't lose faith. She's running from herself, not you."

"You know?"

"I didn't at first. It didn't seem possible, given your reaction to each other. Then I realized that your bickering was to hide the attraction you were feeling. Am I right?"

Rory nodded. "You know I didn't want a mate and pups."

"And now you have one, and not just any mate—a true mate. The Creator has smiled on you."

"You're sure that it's a smile? It feels more like I'm the butt of a joke."

"Don't feel that way, Rory. Shayla's perfect for you. She'll be back. You'll see, and all will be well. The Creator is never wrong." She hugged him again and then stood up. "I've got to go talk with Nikolai."

"Tell the bloodsucker I said hello, and that if he doesn't treat you right, my pack and I will play a little game of 'hunt the vampire.'"

"*Rory.*"

"What?" he asked innocently. "Doesn't he suck blood?"

Shannon just shook her head and walked to where her truck was parked. As she climbed inside, Rory called out, "Maybe the bloodsucker can talk you into buying a new truck."

Her laughter rang out as she backed out of the driveway. With one last wave, she drove off down the street.

Rory watched her leave with a heavy heart. Shannon had always been more like his daughter than his younger sister. Now he was no longer going to be the most important man in her life. She'd have someone else to turn to. Someone else to run to when she was in trouble. It was hard letting her go, but he knew he had to do it. His little bit had a mate of her own now, but she'd always love her big brother. He consoled himself with that thought.

Chapter Thirteen

As Shannon drove back toward Refuge, she reached deep inside herself to the place in her psyche where she was linked with Nikolai and did something she'd never done before. She called out to him.

"Nikolai."

She felt his surprise and then his pleasure a second before the warmth of his presence engulfed her. So strong was his presence that she felt goose bumps rise on her body and she had to force herself to concentrate on her driving, lest she kill herself and all this be for naught.

"Yes, my love. To what do I owe this pleasure? Whatever you want, it is yours for the asking."

"Brave words to give to any woman. What if I want something you don't want to give?"

"For the joy you give to me by reaching out to me heart to heart, in the manner of chosen mates, anything I have is yours for the giving."

"I need to see you, as soon as possible. I have something to tell you. And don't read my mind and spoil my surprise. Wait until you see me and let me tell you face-to-face."

"Where are you now?"

"I'm on my way back to Refuge. I should be there in another half an hour."

"*Meet me in the clearing.*" He sent her a mental image so she'd know which one.

"I know the place. See you soon."

Though he stayed silent, she was aware that Nikolai remained linked with her. She couldn't wait to be with him. For a second she worried, wondering if she was doing the right thing. Then she pushed her worries aside. This was the only way. It had to be done. If she didn't have faith in Nikolai's ability to dominate and be stronger than her wolf, then she didn't need to be with him. If he couldn't dominate her wolf, then he wasn't worthy of being her mate.

When she got to the house, she got out of the truck and stripped. This close to the full moon, it was always dicey calling on her wolf, but she did it anyway. She shifted and ran to the clearing where Nikolai was already waiting.

When she saw him, she shifted back into her human form and ran into his arms. Shannon ground her mouth against his and thrust her tongue into his mouth, the intensity of her passion causing her to lose all sense of self. She rubbed herself against his erection and tried to climb his body. "*Make love to me*," she commanded, unwilling to separate her mouth from his, even to speak.

Nikolai grabbed her by her hips and lifted her body so that she could wrap her legs around his waist. Suddenly, they were skin to skin as his clothes disappeared, and his erection prodded her opening.

"*Please*," she whimpered, trying to impale herself on his shaft.

She held on to him tightly as he sank to his knees, cupped her hips in his hands, and pulled down as he thrust up, embedding himself deeply. He immediately began a driving rhythm, shafting her deeply with each thrust. Shannon kissed her way down to his throat and then bit him hard, causing him to cry out and his fangs to explode in his mouth.

"*Bite me*," she demanded and then fell back, trusting him to catch her.

Nikolai caught her by the waist and lowered her back to the ground, still thrusting deep, his gaze focused on her quivering breasts. Shannon brought her hands up and cupped them in an offering to him. "*Bite me*," she begged, "*please bite me*."

Nikolai's eyes blazed red just before he surged forward and locked his mouth around her nipple. His fangs sliced into her body, and he began to draw deeply, sucking her blood and her nipple at the same time. The pace of his thrusts increased until he was jackhammering into her and her body convulsed around him, the dual pleasure of his cock and his feeding too much for her to bear.

He withdrew his fangs and licked the wound closed as his body shook in the unmistakable sign of orgasm. When the last tremor left his body, he slumped on top of her.

Shannon smiled as she held him, his size restricting her ability to breathe properly, but she didn't care. She was too euphoric at being able to reduce her big, strong vampire to this quivering mass of weakness.

"*I heard that*," he said and rolled so that Shannon lay on his chest and he on the hard ground.

Shannon giggled, something only he had the power to make her do. "If you don't like what you hear, stay out of my head."

"Never. *Your* vampire, hmm? Does this mean what I think it does?" Nikolai asked as he stroked her back.

Shannon pushed up off his chest and straddled his body. Reaching her hand between her legs, she opened the folds of her sex and settled on top of Nikolai's semierect cock. As the moisture from her sheath lubricated his shaft, she slid back and forth, tilting her pelvis at the end of each glide so that the head of his penis rubbed against her clit. "Yes, my vampire. I've decided to claim you, but there's something you have to do first."

"What might that be?" Nikolai asked through gritted teeth.

Shannon reached down and grabbed hold of his rapidly hardening penis, lifted it, and impaled herself, almost within the same motion. Slowly, she began to ride him. Lost in the pleasure of his body, she took her time answering.

"Shannon?"

"Yes, love?" She lowered her head to his chest and began to nibble delicately at his nipple. Her action caused her hips to rise until only the tip of his penis remained embedded inside. She moaned and dug her nails into his side as this position caused his cock to rub against the G-spot located on the front wall of her vagina.

Nikolai reached up and dug his fingers into her hips, trying to force her to take more of him. "Answer the question. What do you need me to do?"

Shannon called on her power and allowed her fangs to grow. “Fight me,” she responded, right before she sank her fangs into his chest, marking him as her mate.

Nikolai hissed his pleasure as his fangs dropped into place. His hips arched up off the ground, and he began pumping violently into her sheath. Shannon withdrew her canines from his chest, locked her knees against his sides, and held on for the ride. Her back arched sharply, and she howled as her release roared through her.

Nikolai flipped her onto her back and lifted her legs until her ankles were on his shoulders. Pushing forward until her knees were level with her chest, he hammered her as he locked his teeth into her shoulder in the manner of a shifter male, marking his mate. The bite caused Shannon to cry out as another release roared through her body. Her vagina clamped down on his cock, milking it of its seed.

When Nikolai could think again, he remembered what she had said. “What do you mean ‘fight you’?”

When he didn’t get a response, he lifted his body off hers and looked down into her face. Shannon lay there, barely conscious, a goofy smile on her face. Nikolai couldn’t help but smile at the knowledge that he’d literally fucked his mate silly. Still, he didn’t have time to wait for her to snap out of it.

He rose to his knees, straddled her body, and lifted her shoulders off the ground. He shook her slightly as he demanded, “Come on, love. Tell me what you meant. If you don’t tell me, I’ll look and see for myself.”

"S'okay," she slurred, "need a nap." Her head lolled back as her eyes closed.

Knowing she was in no condition to answer, he searched her memories for the information. When he found what he needed, Nikolai lay Shannon back down and sank back on his knees. He thought about what he'd learned. In order for Shannon's wolf to accept him, he was going to have to subdue it and mate with it. He wasn't too keen on the idea of mating in wolf form, but if that was what his mate needed to accept him as her chosen, he'd do what he must.

He allowed Shannon to sleep for an hour while he prepared himself for what he needed to do. When he was ready, he woke her. "It's time, love. Allow your wolf out to play."

Shannon searched his face and must have found whatever it was she was looking for. She kissed him lightly on the lips before motioning him away from her. Glancing at him one last time, she turned her gaze to the moon, which was almost full. He felt her reach deep inside and unlock the cage in which her beast resided, giving it complete control.

She shifted in a dizzying rush. Nikolai could find no trace of his mate. She'd buried herself deep within the red she-wolf. Nikolai shifted into the form of the large black wolf he'd assumed on prior occasions.

He knew the minute the she-wolf had spotted him. It snarled deep in its throat and assumed the attack position. Nikolai mirrored the she-wolf, growling in a command for it to submit and recognize him as dominant. The she-wolf bared its teeth in reply and launched itself at him.

Nikolai leaped out of the way and turned quickly to face it. To gain respect, he had to defeat her as a wolf and not use any of his vampire powers against her. It put him in a difficult position. The she-wolf would try to kill him; however, he could not forget that the wolf was his mate, whom he was sworn to protect. It went against his instincts to harm Shannon, no matter what form she was in.

The she-wolf was aggressive, attacking over and over again, determined to remove this threat from its life. Nikolai assumed a defensive position, blocking each attack while waiting for the she-wolf to tire itself out. Finally, he spotted what he was looking for, an opening in its defenses.

The next time the she-wolf charged him, he waited until the last minute to dodge. Moving so fast that he was a blur, he had the she-wolf pinned with his teeth locked on its throat before it knew what was happening. The she-wolf struggled in his grasp. Nikolai growled and tightened his grip on its throat. It hesitated for a moment, before finally admitting defeat. It whimpered in submission and arched its neck more fully into Nikolai's mouth.

Knowing only half the battle had been won, Nikolai released the she-wolf and nudged it to its feet. Circling around behind it, he nipped at its hindquarters until it presented itself for mounting. Swallowing his distaste in the act, he allowed his wolf's penis to drop from its sheath and mounted the she-wolf, penetrating her until she accepted him as her mate.

As soon as he recognized that the battle had been won, he thrust his power deep inside the she-wolf until he located the spot where his mate rested. "*Shift*," he commanded.

As she flowed seamlessly from wolf to human, Nikolai shifted with her, never losing contact. When Shannon was back to herself, he pressed down on her shoulders until her breasts touch the ground, arching her hips higher in the air. With his knees, he spread her legs wider apart, increasing the depth of his thrusts as he covered her with his body.

Shannon rocked back into his body, tightening her sheath around him and riding his cock. Nikolai brought his wrist to his mouth and tore into the skin with his fangs, then brought his wrist to Shannon's mouth. Linking his mind with hers, he compelled her to drink, though it was no longer necessary. As she fed from his wrist, he locked his fangs into her neck and fed deeply, completing the third exchange.

When they'd both consumed enough blood, he released his fangs from her shoulder and commanded her to release his wrist, which he then licked until the wound was sealed. Bracing her shoulders with his arms, Nikolai hunched over Shannon and plunged into her, driving them both to release. As soon as their orgasms had passed, Nikolai commanded Shannon into a deep sleep.

* * *

When Shannon awoke, she was once more in Nikolai's bed.

"Ours now."

She stretched and wrapped her arms around his neck, drawing him down for a kiss. "*Is it done*?"

"*Yes*," he answered as he covered her body with his own.

Shannon took mental inventory. "*I don't feel any different.*"

"*What did you expect?*" Nikolai smiled as he arched his eyebrow.

"I don't know. Something. Anything. This just feels so normal."

"*Let's see if I can help you with that.*" He sheathed his hardness inside of her softness and gently made love to her, drawing the pleasure out for a long time.

When it was over, Shannon lay resting on his chest. *"I still don't feel any different inside."*

Nikolai laughed deeply, bouncing her on his body so that she had to grab ahold of him to keep from falling off. *"You've already done all the changing you're going to do. Your body will continue to feed mine, and my blood will increase your life span so that as long as I live, you live."*

Shannon reached down and tickled his sides, causing Nikolai to buck beneath her. "You couldn't have told me this before? You knew I was worried."

He smiled smugly as he rolled her beneath him and pinned her arms above her head. "And still you came to me, not knowing what would happen." In his voice was all of the pride and love that he felt for her, his chosen.

"How could I do any less? I love you."

"*Indeed*," he agreed as he began to love on her again. "*Now about those children you wanted…*"

* * *

A lone male wolf stood on a ridge, high above the valley. Throwing back its muzzle, it howled, the mournful sound echoing off the rocks, before slowly fading away. The massive red wolf settled down on its haunches until its muzzle rested on its outstretched paws, a single tear drifting from the corner of one eye.

Zena Wynn

I love to read. I love books that can take me out of my ordinary life into an extraordinary reality. I don't just read. I become. To me, a really well written book is like a mini-vacation, without all of the hassle. My greatest hope is that after reading one of my stories, you'll feel the same.

The mother of three (four, if you count Lady, our family dog) and grandmother of two, when not busy with family or church, I can most likely be found in front of the computer writing or escaping into a book.

TITLES AVAILABLE In Print from Loose Id®

A GUARDIAN'S DESIRE

Mya

ALPHA

Treva Harte

ALTERED HEART

Kate Steele

HOWL

Jet Mykles, Raine Weaver, and Jeigh Lynn

LAST HOPE

Moira Rogers

LEASHED: MORE THAN A BARGAIN

Jet Mykles

MANACLED IN MONACO

Jianne Carlo

THE BLACKER THE BERRY

Lena Matthews

TRY A LITTLE TENDERNESS

Roslyn Hardy Holcomb

WILD WISHES

Stephanie Burke, Lena Matthews, and Eve Vaughn

Publisher's Note: The print titles listed above were previously released in e-book format by Loose Id®.

Non-Fiction by *ANGELA KNIGHT*

PASSIONATE INK: A GUIDE TO WRITING EROTIC ROMANCE

Breinigsville, PA USA
17 November 2009

227743BV00002B/14/P

9 781607 374060